## Praise for 43 Light Street from Romantic Times BOOKclub

### FACE TO FACE

"Harlequin's first lady of suspense... a marvelous storyteller, Ms. York cleverly develops an intricately plotted romance to challenge our imaginations and warm our hearts."

### PRINCE OF TIME

"Get ready for the time of your life.... Breathtaking excitement and exotic romance...in the most thrilling 43 Light Street adventure yet!"

### TILL DEATH US DO PART

"Readers will delight in every page."

### TANGLED VOWS

"A bravura performance by one of the best writers ever of quality romantic suspense."

### MIDNIGHT KISS

"A sizzling, seductive tale of dark mystery and brooding passion."

### WHAT CHILD IS THIS?

"Chilling suspense and snowballing excitement from a master of ̶

D1132568

# REBECCA YORK

*USA TODAY* bestselling author Ruth Glick published her one hundredth book, *Crimson Moon,* a Berkley Sensation, in January 2005. Her latest 43 Light Street book is *The Secret Night,* published in April 2006. In October she launches the Harlequin Intrigue continuity series SECURITY BREACH with *Chain Reaction.*

Ruth's many honors include two RITA® Award finalist books. She has two Career Achievement Awards from *Romantic Times BOOKclub* for Series Romantic Suspense and Series Romantic Mystery. *Nowhere Man* was the *Romantic Times BOOKclub* Best Intrigue of 1998 and is one of their "all-time favorite 400 romances." Ruth's *Killing Moon* and *Witching Moon* both won the New Jersey Romance Writers Golden Leaf Award for Paranormal.

Michael Dirda of *Washington Post Book World* says, "Her books...deliver what they promise—excitement, mystery, romance."

Since 1997 she has been writing on her own as Rebecca York. Between 1990 and 1997 she wrote the Light Street series with Eileen Buckholtz. You can contact Ruth at rglick@capaccess.org or visit her Web site at www.rebeccayork.com.

# 43 LIGHT STREET

# REBECCA YORK
*For Your Eyes Only*

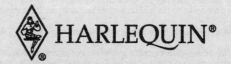

## HARLEQUIN®

TORONTO • NEW YORK • LONDON
AMSTERDAM • PARIS • SYDNEY • HAMBURG
STOCKHOLM • ATHENS • TOKYO • MILAN • MADRID
PRAGUE • WARSAW • BUDAPEST • AUCKLAND

ISBN-13: 978-0-373-36066-6
ISBN-10:    0-373-36066-5

FOR YOUR EYES ONLY

Copyright © 1997 by Ruth Glick and Eileen Buckholtz

This edition published by arrangement with Harlequin Books S.A.

® and TM are trademarks of the publisher. Trademarks indicated with
® are registered in the United States Patent and Trademark Office, the
Canadian Trade Marks Office and in other countries.

www.eHarlequin.com

Printed in U.S.A.

# CAST OF CHARACTERS

*Jenny Larkin*—She felt responsible for her friend's murder, and vowed to find the killer, even if it put her own life in danger.

*Detective Ben Brisco*—He wanted to keep Jenny safe, but needed her help to catch a psychopath.

*Arnold Heizer*—Women with secrets were his obsession.

*Duke Wakefield*—He wanted to make his ex-wife pay.

*Marianne Blaisdell*—The date she'd made online was a deadly mistake.

*L. J. Smith*—He scored his hits on the banking industry with an elite guerrilla warfare unit that pillaged and ran.

*Jessie James*—He was a man of many disguises, who liked women—dead.

*Erin Stone*—She didn't want to see her friend get hurt.

*Denton Kane*—He wanted Brisco out of the picture.

# *Prologue*

He felt the excitement in his blood. In his bones. In his fingertips where they lightly caressed the computer keyboard as he waited for the modem to make the connection.

Got ya!

Today was the day. He knew it with the instinct of an avid hunter who has finally run his quarry to ground.

With barely controlled excitement, he typed in the bogus membership number and password he'd acquired. Marianne was already online, waiting for the man she thought of as Oliver.

He'd given the pseudonym a good deal of thought. It came from his broad reading background. This time the book was that piece of romantic claptrap, *Love Story,* about a young husband named Oliver. He was devoted, sensitive, sweet and understanding. Nobody named Oliver could be a murderer.

Marianne responded to his log-on with an immediate greeting.

"Hi," he typed. "I've been counting the hours until I could get back to you."

"It's been a long day."

He picked up on the hint immediately. Women liked it when you commiserated. "Bad day at work?"

"Uh-huh."

He had to sit through a five-minute recitation of how her boss had given her a report to complete that shouldn't have been her job. But he was ready with the right sympathetic responses.

"Poor baby. Why don't you unwind with me over dinner?" he typed.

There was a short pause before she responded. "I'm not so sure that's a good idea."

"Why?"

"We've never met."

He came back with a reassuring answer. "We're not going to meet until you break down and let me into your life."

"I know."

"We've been friends for two months now." A long time to wait for gratification. "You've told me so much about yourself. And I think you know me pretty well."

"As well as you can know someone over a computer network," she hedged.

"I'd like to take the next step."

"What if—I mean—what if you're disappointed?"

So that was it. She wasn't worried about *him*. She was worried about what he'd think about *her* when they finally met. Sweet anticipation swelled in his chest. He was glad he was typing instead of speaking, because he knew he couldn't keep his voice steady. "I know I'm not going to be disappointed," he soothed. "I already know you so well. Your sense of humor. Your intelligence." He stopped there because he didn't want to lay it on too thick.

"Oliver, there's something I haven't told you. Something that might make a difference."

"We've come so far. You can trust me with the rest," he coaxed.

She answered quickly, getting it over with. "I have a vision problem. I'm not blind. But I do need to wear very thick glasses. And I use a special computer that reads to me."

A feeling of power gathered in his body like warm, sweet honey. This was it. The knowledge that made the relationship work for him. She had told him her secret. "Do you seriously think that would make any difference to me?"

"I was afraid it would."

He pretended to be hurt. "Marianne, I thought you trusted me."

"I do. And I feel so relieved."

"Meet me tonight. There's this little bar and restaurant in Fells Point that I bet you'll love. We'll start with drinks—then dinner. And the band is wonderful. It's a good place to unwind."

"All right."

He gave her the address, and they chatted for a few more minutes. When he disconnected, he sat rubbing his hands together, squeezing them harder and harder—anticipating the feel of his fingers digging into the smooth skin of her throat.

# Chapter One

The timer on the exercise bike beeped, signaling the end of her forty-minute workout. Jenny Larkin swiped back a strand of honey-brown hair that had plastered itself to her forehead and slowed her pace, giving herself a couple of minutes to cool down. As her long legs continued to pedal in time to a Beatles oldie, she laced her hands behind her neck and stretched. She felt wonderful, exhilarated by the energy boost.

Converting this spare bedroom into an exercise room had been one of her better ideas. It was one of the first steps in her plan to arrange her life exactly the way she wanted it. Like moving back to this great old house where she'd lived with Gran when she was a kid. Some of her friends had argued that it was dangerous for someone like her to live alone on an isolated old farm. She'd be better off selling the property and using the money to buy a nice, convenient condo. But she didn't need more money. She needed freedom and autonomy. And this old farmhouse was the perfect retreat— a place where she could kick back and relax without trying to live up to anyone's expectations.

Before she started on the weight machine, she turned off the tape deck and switched to a talk-radio station. The newscaster was reciting yesterday's basketball scores as she straddled the bench and began to do lat pulls. The next news item made her fingers freeze around the rubber grips at the ends of the handlebars.

"To repeat our top story, the body of a woman in her mid-thirties was found early this morning behind a vacant row house in West Baltimore. She had been strangled. Police are withholding her identity pending notification of next of kin."

The perspiration clinging to Jenny's skin turned icy. She listened for more information, but there was nothing else—nothing specific to indicate it might be Marianne Blaisdell.

"It's not her," Jenny whispered. "It can't be her."

Yet she kept remembering the way her friend had sounded last night when she'd called from a bar. She'd been much too giddy and reckless, bursting with the news that she was finally getting together with her computer pen pal. Bars weren't Marianne's scene. Neither were blind dates.

"This guy—how much do you know about him?" Jenny had asked gently.

"He's sweet and sensitive."

"That could be an act."

"Why are you suddenly so cynical? You're the one who encouraged me to meet new people."

Jenny sighed. "I know. But it sounds like you've made a snap decision. At least promise me that you won't go anywhere with him. Not in his car or anything."

"You're being ridiculous," her friend said sharply before hanging up.

There had been nothing more Jenny could do last night.

Now, unclenching her hands, she ordered herself not to panic. She'd gotten used to taking life as it came, not making unwarranted assumptions. Still, her movements were jerky as she climbed off the bench. She was so off her stride that she bumped into the wall phone in the corner of the room before she realized she'd reached it.

"Klutz," she muttered under her breath as she rubbed the sore spot on her upper arm. Taking a deep breath to steady herself, she punched in Marianne's number. When nobody picked up on the first two rings, her chest tightened and she slid her back down the wall until she was sitting with her shoulders pressed against the cool plaster and her damp legs sticking to the exercise mat. Three rings... four...six. With each passing second, it became harder to breathe. And the clogged feeling in her chest only increased when the answering machine kicked in.

She waited through the familiar upbeat greeting before leaving a message. "This is Jenny. I'm still at home, but call me at work in case you're in the shower or something." She might have added that she wanted to hear how her friend's date had gone. But she couldn't force out more than her office number.

For a long time after hanging up, Jenny sat huddled on the exercise mat, replaying last night's conversation in her head. Finally, with a sigh, she roused herself. She couldn't sit here forever, her van pool would be waiting.

This time when she crossed the room and made her way down the hall, she was careful to pay attention to her surroundings—the familiar worn floorboards under her feet that curved gently down in the middle, the banister that marked the top of the stairs. In the bathroom, she shucked off her damp clothes and stepped into the shower. The hot spray pounding against her body made her feel better so that by the time she began to blow-dry her hair, she'd almost convinced herself there would be a message from Marianne waiting at work.

HE CRUISED DOWN Marianne Blaisdell's street, studying the working-class neighborhood with its rows of wood-framed boxes wedged onto small lots. Many houses needed a paint job, and some yards were cluttered with junked cars and overgrown weeds. Turning the corner, he drove a few blocks closer to the avenue, as if he might be going to the little coffee shop on the corner. Instead, after parking the car, he headed in the other direction. He was still wearing the uniform from last night, a meter reader, complete with one of those hand-held computers. Pulling his cap low on his head, he snaked his way through the network of alleys to reach her house.

After pulling on a pair of surgical gloves, he slipped a key into the back door lock. He looked around the tiny kitchen with its old appliances, chipped tile floor and beige walls. Somehow, he'd pictured her living in a more upscale setting. For a second, another dilapidated kitchen scene swam in his vision: Meema bending over him with that angry look in her eyes and a thin leather belt in her hands. He didn't need to be reminded of that. Not here, not now, when he had work to do. But he couldn't stop the rush of remembered pain. Seven years old. His first fight. Blood dripping from his nose and one eye swelling painfully shut where Willy Dumbrauski had slugged him. He'd come running home, hoping for comfort. Instead, he'd gotten ten lashings for "acting like a little punk." It hadn't been his fault. But Meema wouldn't listen. She'd always hated him. He'd learned to hate her back. And hate the terrible secret she forced him to keep. He despised women with secrets. But he'd found a way to get even with women like that. Like Marianne.

With the iron will he'd learned to exercise as a little kid, he forced the memory to the back of his mind and concentrated on the present. Hate was replaced by a flow of warmth. A little thrill zinged up his spine as he thought about being in Marianne's house after what they'd shared.

Her PC was in the corner of one of the bedrooms. This baby wasn't some economy model. It was a custom processor with a set of peripherals that would make any hacker salivate. What the heck was he dealing with?

He felt around the side and flipped the On switch. With a beep, the machine booted and then ran some program that took over the system and locked up the keyboard. No matter what he typed, nothing happened. God, he hated it when things didn't work.

He found a thick manual tucked beside the machine, but instead of words it was filled with a series of little dots. Braille, he figured, since she'd told him she was going blind. The dots began to dance in his vision. Red anger boiled up inside him, and he slammed his fist against the computer. The pain in his knuckles helped ground him—helped calm his emotions so he could think this through logically.

Finally it came to him. The system must be triggered by a remote control. The attachments. The key was in the attachments.

Some sort of virtual reality device. Maybe voice activated. He'd seen prototypes at the COMDEX show in Las Vegas last year. They'd been featured with high-tech video games. But the same technology might be used to aid a person with a visual impairment. Someone like Marianne.

After finding the infrared remote signal that unlocked the keyboard, he reached for the helmet with the built-in microphone sitting on the desk. He couldn't quite get it on, but he could pull it over his face enough to use it. Rapidly he ran through the file system, looking for the messages that might link him to Marianne.

He glanced at his watch. He'd been here half an hour. The police had already found the body, thanks to an old lady with insomnia who'd been peeking through her dirty curtains. He'd seen her jump back when he looked up and scanned the windows across from the vacant house. He'd considered going after her, but he knew she could call 911 before he got there. And there was no way she could identify him. Not in this uniform—with his cap pulled down over his face. Even the car was okay. He'd stolen it for the occasion. But he had to assume the police would be here soon. Quickly, he tried to delete the World Connect files, but the system wanted voice verification.

With a trick he'd learned during his freelance hacker days, he managed to overwrite the directory. Hopefully, he'd done enough damage to destroy access to the file system.

After turning off the computer, he grabbed the reference manual, and made for the back door. The book wouldn't do him a damn bit of good. He couldn't read braille. But neither could the police, if they didn't have it.

BEN BRISCO'S HAND closed around the coffee mug on the back of his desk. The hand was like his shoulders, wide and rock-solid. He wasn't a tall man. But he was well-muscled and fit, and charged with a kind of waiting tension that could translate thought into instant action. The body went with a square face that reinforced the tough-guy image. Brenna, his ex-wife, had told him his best features were his high cheek-bones and his chocolate-brown eyes. He suspected that to some women, the eyes gave away an involuntary sensitivity he'd rather keep hidden.

Standing and stretching, he headed for the coffeepot in the corner of the squad room located on the sixth floor of police headquarters. He had a talent for crime solving. But lately he'd been wondering if it was time to get out of homicide, out of police work entirely, like his friend Mike Lancer, who was doing fine as a P.I. Or he could get into one of the low-key units—Larceny or Fraud, where he wouldn't find himself matching wits with the young drug dealers and gang members who regularly snuffed out each other's young lives. When you put one in the joint, another popped up to take his place.

Yet there were still cases that had the power to bring out his protective instincts. Like when a child got caught in the crossfire. Or the murder he could hear Pete Diangelo and Lieutenant Morgan discussing. The body of a young woman had been discovered around 2:00 a.m. in West Baltimore. The killer had worked her over for a while before he'd strangled her. Another crazy on the loose.

Diangelo, who'd caught the early shift, was already into the nitty-gritty of the investigation. He was telling the lieutenant that he'd stopped at the victim's house around eight-thirty that morning. He'd been through her effects and hadn't found an address book. Maybe she kept it in her computer, but he hadn't figured out a way to access it. So far he had a "stone-who-done-it." A murder without a clue.

Ben didn't envy Diangelo. His friend was looking at long days of chipping away at details and interviewing everybody in sight until he got a lead, which probably wouldn't get him anywhere.

After downing several swallows of the hot coffee, he returned to the stack of reports on his desk. He'd given up cigarettes five years ago, but he wasn't going to add caffeine to his private list of controlled substances.

As he came within earshot of the two men, he heard Diangelo rattle off a list of names. One of them—Jenny Larkin—made him stop dead in his tracks.

Lieutenant Morgan glanced inquiringly in his direction. "Something I can do for you?"

"Sounds like my kind of case," Ben heard himself saying. His kind of case? Nobody wanted this kind of case.

Morgan waited.

"I, uh, think I could give you some help," Ben said. "Remember that computer course I took last year? There was a unit on non-standard equipment."

Diangelo looked relieved. "Be my guest."

"Okay with you, Lieu?" Ben asked.

"Sure. Pete's the only one who's been assigned. Everyone else was out on a case when the call came in," the squad leader answered.

Morgan headed back to his office, and Ben pointed toward the sheet of paper Diangelo was holding. "Did I hear you've got a list of people who called the victim's answering machine in the past twenty-four hours?"

"Yeah." Diangelo handed over the printout.

Ben scanned the transcripts of the phone messages and the names. Stars indicated that Phil Tracy, Larry Lipcott, and Cameron Randolph had left their full names and numbers. Jenny had left a work number, although her message had sounded personal. The other woman caller was someone named Sue. Both women's last names had come from phone-company records.

"You interview anybody yet?" Ben asked.

"Give me a break. It's only ten."

"I could leave the computer for this afternoon and help you out with these. Maybe the perp was stupid enough to give his name and number."

Diangelo laughed. "Sure."

"Why don't I take the women? And you interview the men."

"Hey—"

"The women are probably her friends. You want the job of telling them she's dead?"

Diangelo reconsidered. "Okay."

"It sounds as if there are some ritualized aspects to the M.O.," Ben said. "But I don't remember hearing about anything similar."

"One of us better put in a query to the FBI database," Pete suggested. "Whoever gets back first can check with the feds."

Ben nodded, figuring he was going to get the job. Back at

his desk, he reached in the top drawer for a piece of hard candy. This month it was cinnamon, last month it had been peppermint. After copying down the phone information on the women, he used the office cross-reference to find the addresses. Then he grabbed his jacket and headed toward the garage. Not until he was in his car did he allow himself to think about his motives for getting assigned to the case.

Well, not motives exactly. More like a reflex action when he'd heard Jenny Larkin's name. If anyone had known him well enough to ask the right questions, he would have said emphatically that he'd gotten over Jenny Larkin years ago. If "gotten over" was the right term. But it seemed he hadn't forgotten.

How long had it been since he'd seen her? Twelve years. A lifetime ago—back when she'd been a senior at Howard High School and he'd been a junior. The age difference had put her out of his reach. Not to mention that he hadn't been the big-man-on-campus type she'd dated. On top of that, he'd been new to the county the year before. So he was willing to bet she couldn't even remember his name.

He'd lost track of her, hadn't even known whether she was still living in the Baltimore area. He glanced at the work address—43 Light Street. He wondered what kind of job she held. And then he wondered why he was getting into such deep speculation with so little information. This Jenny Larkin might not even be her.

Probably the woman wouldn't be able to tell him much, anyway. He'd interview her once, type up the report for the case file, and that would be the end of it. As he approached her building, he pulled another cinnamon candy from his pocket and tossed the wrapper on the floor of the passenger side. Then, realizing his pocket was stuffed with wrappers, he emptied them onto the floor with the other one.

He managed to keep his mind in neutral gear as he studied

the directory in the lobby. The woman he was looking for was at Birth Data, Incorporated, an organization he'd learned about when he'd had a murder suspect with amnesia. They put adoptees in touch with their birth parents. Jenny's title was computer analyst. Interesting, he thought, considering what had happened to her.

By the time he stepped off the elevator on the third floor, he felt like the tongue-tied kid he'd been twelve years ago. But he strode down the hall like he owned the place and barreled into the office waiting room.

A receptionist looked up with a startled expression as he made a quick inspection of the premises. His eyes lit on a young woman working at a computer terminal. From the back, she looked a lot like the Jenny Larkin he remembered. Long, honey-brown hair. Slender waist. Narrow shoulders.

The receptionist near the door finally found her tongue. "May I help you?" she asked.

He snapped his attention back to the desk in front of him and flashed his detective's shield. "Ben Brisco. Baltimore City police. I need to talk to one of your employees, a Jenny Larkin, about an investigation I'm working on."

The woman at the computer must have been tuned in on the conversation. At the mention of her name she turned in Ben's direction.

A welter of conflicting emotions surged through him as he stared into the face he hadn't seen since his carefree high-school days. It was his Jenny Larkin, all right.

## *Chapter Two*

No mistake. She had the same delicate features, the same creamy, unlined skin and honey-brown hair, the same crystal-blue eyes. No, not precisely the same eyes.

It looked as if she was staring straight at him through the open doorway, and he went very still as if he were a burglar suddenly caught in the glare of a spotlight. He stifled the impulse to make sure his short, dark hair was neatly combed and his tie was straight. Then he realized that while her face was turned toward the outer office, she was waiting for an auditory cue to zero in on his exact location. Like everyone else in school, he'd known she'd been blinded in a car accident. Obviously she hadn't miraculously gotten her vision back.

It flashed through his mind that he might come right out and say that he'd gone to Howard High with her. Lay it all out on the table right at the beginning. But he discarded that plan as soon as it surfaced. After the accident she'd withdrawn from everyone and everything she'd known. He had no reason to believe she'd changed her mind about her former school-mates. Besides, raking up the past might interfere with the present investigation. At least, that was how he justified his decision.

"Miss Larkin?"

"Yes." She stood up and reached for a long white cane he

hadn't noticed because his attention was so tightly focused on her. It was propped against the wall beside her desk. He watched her swing the cane to the left as she took a step with her right foot, then to the right as her left foot moved, making sure there were no obstacles in the way as she came toward him. Her progress was surprisingly rapid, and her assessment of his location very accurate. She stopped about four feet from him, waiting.

He cleared his throat, wondering if she'd recognize his voice now that they were standing close enough that he could smell the lilac scent of her perfume.

"You…you say you're a police officer," she said hesitantly. "And you want to talk to me?"

He was accustomed to reading people. She was pretty uptight below her controlled exterior, as if she had something to hide.

"Yes. A police detective, actually. I'm afraid I have some bad news about your friend, Marianne Blaisdell."

Her face drained of color. "Oh, God. Is she dead?"

He noted the intensity of the reaction. "Do you mind my asking how you came to that conclusion?"

She sucked in a deep breath and let it out in a rush. "Ever since I heard that news story about the dead woman on the radio, I've been worried that it was Marianne. I left a message on her answering machine this morning, but she hasn't called me back. Is she the woman they found at that vacant house?" she asked.

"Yes. I'm sorry."

Her hand fluttered beside her and came to rest against the wall. As soon as she connected with something solid, she slumped sideways, and he stifled the impulse to pull her against his shoulder and hold her steady while she absorbed the shock.

"I—I was worried… but it's hard to believe…." A gasp stole away the rest of her words.

"I'm sorry for your loss." The official expression of sympathy. He'd uttered it countless times, but today it sounded particularly cold and stilted.

"Why were you worried about Miss Blaisdell this morning?" he pressed.

She pushed herself erect, struggling with a turmoil of sharp, twisting emotions that played across her face. "Uh—do—do you mind if I sit down?"

"That's fine."

Her steps were leaden as she turned and headed back into her office.

He followed slowly, watching her drop into her desk chair as if her legs would no longer support her weight.

"Can I get you something? A drink of water?" he asked.

"No. I'll be okay."

Taking the visitor's chair, he studied her with a sense of freedom that was tinged with guilt. Usually the only time he had the opportunity to observe someone so blatantly was through a two-way mirror in an interrogation cubicle. Despite the shock—or partly because of it—she looked astonishingly young and fresh. She wore her straight hair in an unadorned style that brushed her shoulders, and she was dressed simply in an aqua shirt and a khaki skirt. The colors were good on her. He wondered who'd helped her pick the outfit.

She was the one who broke the silence, although her voice was still a little breathless. "I'm a friend of Marianne's. But how did you know to contact me specifically?"

He stopped making unprofessional personal assessments and flipped open his notebook. "We're interviewing everyone who left a recent message on Miss Blaisdell's answering machine. You sounded worried. Why were you concerned about her?"

Jenny gestured with her hand as if searching for words. "I know it doesn't sound so alarming when I try to explain. She had a date last night—with a man she'd been talking to on a computer network. She hadn't met him in person before, but she kept telling me how nice he was."

"You didn't agree?"

"Well, I never talked with him myself, so I couldn't make any personal judgments. But I warned her to be careful about…intimate contact. Oh, God… I must sound like a guest on one of those dreadful talk shows or something." Jenny took a deep breath and started over. "She was acting so out of character. And I'd just read an article about computer networks—about how people can project any personality they want when they're not meeting face-to-face."

"Read?" he asked.

"In braille," she shot back. "A lot of magazines and journals have braille translations."

He cleared his throat. Stupid mistake. "Let's set aside the computer contact for a moment. Did she have any enemies? Anyone who might want to hurt her?"

"Her ex-husband."

Ben's pen hovered above the notebook page. "Name?"

"Duke Wakefield. Marianne took back her maiden name when she got divorced. In the back of my mind I was sort of wondering if *he* might have been the guy she was talking to on the computer. I mean, I wouldn't put it past him to play that kind of dirty trick on her. The only problem with that theory is I doubt he could afford a computer. Or know how to use it," she added in a lower voice.

"You think he would take her life?"

"Well, I'm not sure I would go that far."

"But the divorce wasn't amicable?"

Jenny's features narrowed. "He was the one who dumped her—when she started losing her sight. Then he was angry that the court awarded her such a generous settlement."

Ben took down the information. She sounded pretty

positive the husband was a jerk. But being a jerk didn't make him a murderer.

"He's still in Baltimore?"

"As far as I know." Jenny stroked her fingers along the edge of the chair arm. "Marianne hated being alone after Duke left her. I know she felt self-conscious about her vision—and Duke's rejection. I was encouraging her to get out and meet people and suggested she try the computer. Probably it's my fault that she was on the network in the first place. Now look what happened." The last part came out on a choked gulp.

"She made her own decisions. You said you tried to talk her out of the meeting, and she didn't listen."

Jenny appeared to be staring down at her hands, which were now clasped tightly in her lap. "Yes, but I'm the one who pushed her to try something new. Then she threw herself into it with a—a kind of giddy enthusiasm. I should have… I don't know…" she trailed off helplessly.

A swell of protectiveness surged through him. "Don't blame yourself," he said softly. He wanted her to know that he understood what she felt. She couldn't see his face, so he laid his hand softly on her shoulder, molding his fingers around the feminine curve.

Probably it was too intimate a gesture, given that he was a police detective come to interview her about a case. But when she raised her face toward him, he saw that her eyes were bright with moisture—and full of pain and regret.

"It sounds like the computer chats filled a need she had," he murmured.

"And someone took advantage of that." There was an edge of anger in her voice. "I want you to catch whoever it was."

"We'll do our best." He wished he could promise he'd close the case. Instead, he gave her shoulder a quick squeeze, then awkwardly removed his hand. "Did she tell you the name of her new friend?"

She sat up straighter. "Oliver—although I know that doesn't mean anything."

"It's a lead we can follow. Perhaps he contacted other women. Do you know which computer service she was using?"

"She had trial memberships on several."

"Did she call you from home last night?"

"No. I think she was at the place where they were meeting." He leaned forward. "Where was that?"

She shrugged apologetically. "A bar or restaurant. I wish I'd made her give me the name."

He tried not to let his disappointment show in his voice. "I'll leave my card so you can contact me if you think of anything else that could be pertinent."

"It'll be better if I write it myself." She gave a good imitation of having pulled herself together as she turned toward her desk and picked up two hinged plates, one with die-cut patterns of dots. After inserting paper between the two plates, she began to press rapidly across the sets of dots with a stylus.

Strangely, she worked from right to left. He'd imagined writing braille would be slow and cumbersome but she wrote with the same speed as someone using a pen.

"Okay, I've got your name. What's your phone number?" she asked.

He gave it to her and added that she could talk to Pete Diangelo if he wasn't in the office. She took down the information, all business as she completed the note, folded the paper with the reverse side out, and stuck it into one of the vertical holders along the side of her desk. "Leave the card, too, in case someone else needs it."

"Sure." Ben was about to stand up, when the secretary poked her head in the door.

"Jenny, I hate to interrupt, but didn't you say you had to be somewhere at eleven-thirty?"

"Is it that late already?" Her fingers went to the watch on her left wrist, and she opened the cover. As she checked the time, her expression clouded. "My ride should have been here by now."

"Where are you going?" Ben asked.

"I'm meeting with a student who's considering getting a degree in computer science. She's interviewing me at the National Federation of the Blind."

For the second time in as many hours, Ben spoke before his brain had time to catch up with his mouth. "I could give you a lift."

"Oh, I wouldn't want to put you to any trouble."

"No trouble at all."

She'd given him an out, but he hadn't take it. And he refused to ask himself why.

THE DOWNTOWN Baltimore sports bar was noisy with a lunchtime crowd. Accountants, lawyers, investment bankers and office staffers laughed and argued good-naturedly as they ate crabcakes and downed imported beer. Despite the congenial atmosphere, the man known to his few friends and numerous enemies as L. J. Smith was all business as he studied the blunt features of Joe Cornelius, the new client from Chicago. He didn't like face-to-face meetings, or telephone calls either. E-mail was more his style. But a lot of money was on the line today and more business to follow, if all went well. So he'd made an exception.

L.J. liked to compare himself to Bill Gates. They were both computer geeks who'd left college before graduating and both were visionaries of a sort. But while Gates arm-wrestled with IBM and Netscape in public, Smith scored his hits on the banking and credit industry with an elite guerrilla-warfare unit that pillaged and ran.

Cornelius glanced up and down the aisle to make sure no

one at the other tables was paying attention. "You've got my order?"

"High-roller gold cards, twenty-to-fifty-thousand limits." L.J. pulled out a leather case from his coat pocket and pushed it across the scarred wood table.

"There were no problems with the I.D.s?"

"You'll find everything exactly as ordered. Eight men, four women. Assorted verification documents. Of course, the 48-hour turnaround and the photo IDs are going to cost an additional twenty-five grand."

"That's highway robbery!"

Smith laughed. "We're the only shop that's figured out how to duplicate that new tamper-proof hologram. Besides, you still get a clean fifteen thousand on even the low-limit jobs and a thirty-day-minimum window for use. Out of state, of course."

Cornelius pulled out a pocket magnifier glass and went over the sets of cards and identities with the expertise of a jeweler appraising a diamond. "They'll pass. Where are the rest?"

"When you've paid in full."

For several long seconds, Cornelius looked as if he would walk. Instead, he shoved his briefcase across the table.

L.J. snapped it open and verified the cash inside. "It appears that everything is in order. We'll expect the additional fee within twenty-four hours, and you'll get the rest of the order. You know how to reach us."

"ARE YOU PARKED in the garage across the alley?" Jenny asked Detective Brisco as she heard him scrape back his chair.

He laughed. "Police muscle. I'm in the no-parking zone in front of the building."

"I guess you must have known I'd be in a hurry," she

answered, trying to match his light tone, trying not to think about why they'd met. She hadn't liked falling apart in front of him. Or anybody else, for that matter. Later, when she was alone, she'd grieve for her friend. Now her mission was to convince a blind girl named Barbara Taft that she could go after any career she thought she could handle. Slipping the strap of her purse over her shoulder, she led the way out of the office.

If she'd been better acquainted with Detective Brisco and they were in unfamiliar surroundings, she might have taken his arm and let him lead her. But she knew the way to the elevator as well as she knew the layout of her kitchen at home. Swinging her cane to make sure there were no obstacles in the way, she managed to stay several steps ahead of the detective as they walked toward the elevator.

She wondered why she was letting him give her a ride rather than simply calling a cab. She'd used the excuse that she didn't want to keep Barbara waiting, yet she knew that wasn't the only reason she was still in Ben Brisco's company. He interested her. Or maybe she wanted the satisfaction of figuring him out.

She already knew a fair amount about him. He was a muscular man. Not too tall, judging from where she heard his voice. Not heavy for his height. Agile. She could tell both those things from the way he walked. And his hands were large and warm and a little callused. The last silent observation was accompanied by the ghost of a shiver that made her wonder why she was responding so strongly to this stranger. Probably because his bad news had thrown her so off balance, she told herself. And he cared. She'd felt that in the touch of his hand on her shoulder, and in his voice.

The elevator came, and they stepped inside, each claiming an opposite wall. Neither of them spoke, and the silence was no more satisfactory than anything else that had passed between them. She found herself speculating about what he was thinking. She'd picked up that he was nervous about interviewing her. The little changes in his voice, the subtle alterations in the way he drew in his breath, told her almost as much as seeing his facial expression.

An involuntary shiver traveled up her spine.

"What's wrong?" he asked without missing a beat.

So he'd been staring at her, she guessed, feeling her skin flush.

Fighting the impulse to turn away, she kept her face toward him. "I was wondering about Marianne. Is there something…something bad about…" It was harder to say than she'd expected. "The way she was killed?"

"Murder is always bad." There was no mistaking the edge in his voice.

The door glided opened. She stepped out into the lobby but didn't go any farther. "But there's something you'd rather not tell me?"

"How'd you pick up on that?"

"You're uncomfortable. Either it's me—or the murder."

He made a noncommittal noise, and she chose to assume it was nothing personal.

"What about Marianne?"

"I'd rather not go into detail."

"What you mean is that I'd rather not hear."

"That, too."

They stood facing each other for a moment. When he didn't volunteer anything else, she turned toward the street entrance.

He came after her, forging ahead. She heard the heavy lobby door swing open. Outside, she took several breaths of the crisp spring air. A little breeze was blowing, and under other circumstances she would have enjoyed the feel of it ruffling her hair.

"It's like this," he said. "When we're investigating a crime, there are usually details we withhold from the public. If someone comes forward with information or confesses, we use those details to determine the veracity of the information."

"Oh. I didn't think about that." Probably it wasn't the whole story, but she wanted to accept the explanation.

He crossed the sidewalk. A car door opened.

"Right here," he said, his hand on her shoulder again.

She slipped inside and stowed her cane between the seat and the door. Then she reached down to see what her feet were touching and came up with a handful of cellophane wrappers. Mostly they seemed to be from cinnamon balls, judging from the distinctive spicy smell. But there was a sprinkling of lemon and peppermint mixed in.

"Sorry," Brisco muttered after he slipped behind the wheel. "I would have cleaned up, but I wasn't expecting company." He sounded like a little boy who'd been caught with his earthworm collection spread across the dining-room table. The image was so telling that she couldn't hold back a little laugh.

"I think I've discovered your secret vice," she murmured.

"That's true." He touched her again. This time his large hand closed around hers. It was strong, capable. The gesture was very intimate in the close confines of the car. She wanted to ask how he'd gotten the calluses across the pads of his fingers. Instead she pressed her lips together. She wasn't acting like herself. She didn't know what was going to come out of her mouth next.

Long seconds passed before he took the papers from her. One fluttered to her lap, but thankfully he didn't try to retrieve it. While he stuffed the wrappers into the ashtray or something, she toyed with the one in her lap. She liked the texture of the cellophane. But she wouldn't kid herself. Playing with the wrapper was a way to cope with tension—to focus on a small physical activity rather than the overwhelming man in the seat next to her. She didn't know him well enough to figure out what was happening between them, or perhaps she was too out of practice with the opposite sex.

"So can you direct me to the federation?" he asked, the strained quality back in his voice. It was reassuring to know she wasn't the only one reacting.

It was a bad idea to encourage him, she told herself, so she kept her answer businesslike as she slowly slid the candy paper between her fingers. "It's on Johnson. I, uh, haven't had to find it on my own."

"That's okay."

She heard the distinctive crinkle of a large map. "Square three-H," he muttered.

The car started. He spun the wheel sharply and pulled out into traffic. A radio crackled, and she heard a dispatcher ordering nearby units to the scene of a traffic accident on Eutaw Street.

He didn't hit her with any personal questions. Was he curious about her background? she wondered. A lot of people wanted to know if she'd been blind from birth. In fact, they asked all kinds of probing stuff, as if her blindness gave them a license to be impolite. But he was either incurious or well-mannered.

Despite her earlier resolve, she found she was the one who wanted to keep the conversation going. "You have other interviews?" she asked.

"Yes. The other detective I mentioned—Pete Diangelo—and I are splitting them up. I'll try to get a line on the ex-husband."

He made a left turn, then a right. "We're across from the building, beside a park. I can make a U-turn and put you right in front of the entrance."

"No. This is fine. Thank you for going out of your way."

"No problem."

Maybe she'd been mistaken. Maybe he wasn't as interested in her as she'd thought. She should be relieved. Instead, she was disappointed.

After locating her cane, she felt for the door handle.

"Push the latch to the right," Brisco told her.

She followed directions and the car door opened. "Well, thanks again for the lift." Automatically she listened for the sound of approaching cars before stepping off the curb and starting for the other side.

THERE WAS NO REASON to hang around. But instead of pulling away from the curb, Ben sat, watching Jenny, enjoying the glint of sunlight on her hair and the way her hips moved as she walked at a quick pace. She was lithe and graceful, and were it not for the cane you wouldn't know she couldn't see.

He'd known damn well he was making her nervous in the car before he'd told himself to cool it. But not as nervous as she would have been if she'd realized what he was thinking. Probably he shouldn't have touched her again. But he'd wanted an excuse to find out if her hand felt as feminine as her shoulder. Only he hadn't been staring at her hand. He'd been admiring the gentle swell of her breasts. Not too large, but oh so tempting beneath the clinging fabric of her blouse—with the outline of her nipples slightly raised so that he could see them.

He'd reacted to that. Oh yeah, he'd reacted, all right.

"Very professional, Brisco," he muttered.

By an effort of will, he'd torn his gaze away. There was no future in getting turned on by Jenny Larkin, because he couldn't have her. And it was no fair taking advantage of the fact that she couldn't see. Still, it was going to take a nuclear explosion to get her out of his mind.

The crackle of a call over the radio reminded him that he couldn't stay here obsessing about her. He was about to pull away from the curb when he saw a blue pickup swing around the corner and come barreling down the blacktop.

A curse that was part surprise and part panic erupted from his lips when he realized the truck was heading straight for Jenny.

# Chapter Three

Ben's reaction was swift and primal. He was out of the car and running before he realized his fingers had jerked the door handle.

"Jenny—watch out!" he shouted as he closed the distance between them. Too far. Too damn far.

It was all happening much too fast. Yet he felt as if he were viewing the scene in slow motion. Jenny standing stock still in the middle of the narrow street. The truck making straight toward her.

At the warning shout, she half turned, her face registering alarm and confusion. He knew with a sick feeling that the only thing he'd accomplished was to make sure she was no longer a moving target for the juggernaut coming toward her.

Like a desperate sprinter surging toward the finish line, he leaped across the last five feet that separated him from Jenny. With stiff fingers, he grabbed her shoulders and yanked her back. She screamed as his hands closed around her, screamed again as the vehicle whizzed by, the side mirror missing his arm by a hair. The tail wind buffeted them so strongly that he was almost knocked off his feet. Swaying, he managed to keep them both from falling as well.

When he had the presence of mind to look up, the truck

was halfway down the block and picking up speed. There was no way he could make out the license number as it receded into the distance. He saw the right rear taillight was shattered, but all he saw of the driver was a dark head through the back window. He couldn't even tell if it was male or female.

Jenny had his sportcoat in a death grip. Her other hand still clutched her cane.

With a strangled exclamation, he folded her close, cradling her slender body protectively against his. She was trembling. And he wasn't all that steady on his feet, either.

His vision was a shimmery blur. Closing his eyes, he rested his face against the top of her head, unconsciously moving his cheek against her soft hair. Another few seconds and that truck would have— He didn't allow himself to complete the terrible image.

Her hand opened and closed around a fistful of his jacket. "Wh-what happened?" she asked in a hoarse gasp.

His own voice came out low and strained—a strange, grating sound. "A truck was heading straight for you."

"I thought…I was sure…there was no…no…traffic," she quavered, raising her head and looking as if she was trying to figure out how she'd messed up.

"You were right about the street being clear," he rasped. "It wasn't your fault."

It was the most natural thing in the world to pull her back into his embrace and envelop her protectively with his body. Her arms crept around his back, and they stood quietly holding each other. Her body felt fragile, fine-boned, pliant. With a little sigh, she leaned into him. Her posture was totally trusting, like a woman giving herself to the man she loves for the first time.

For several heartbeats Ben managed to shut out the reason he had taken her into his arms. He was nothing more than a man, glad that he had a very desirable woman in his embrace.

His lips skimmed the side of her silky hair and he breathed in the delicate scent of citrus.

Perhaps she was just as befuddled as he, because she murmured something that didn't sound as if it were born out of panic, something that danced along his nerve endings like a caress. Wanting more, his hands moved up and down her back as he gathered her closer. His lips drifted toward hers. They were parted, inviting, the warmth of her breath heralding the touch of flesh to flesh. Seconds before the contact, a horn honked in back of him, and reality came surging back. He remembered they were still standing in the middle of a city street and that a truck had come within inches of hitting her.

It was an effort not to curse the impatient man glaring at them through the windshield of a sporty green coupe. Hadn't the fool seen that they'd almost gotten blown away by a reckless driver? Ben settled for shooting the guy a scathing look.

"We'd better get out of the street," he muttered as he drew Jenny out of the traffic lane and back toward his car. She came without protest, a dazed expression on her face. Finally they were standing in front of his vehicle.

"It's okay. You're safe."

She drew in a ragged breath. "It was so close—I could feel the wind whipping us around—and smell the exhaust like a poison cloud."

"The damn thing materialized out of nowhere. It was heading straight toward you," he barked.

Bewilderment was etched across her features. "Why?"

"I don't know. Maybe it was some nut who likes to go after people who can't see him."

He felt a shudder wrack her body as the nasty implications sank in. She could be as careful as a fire-eating woman in a carnival sideshow, and it wouldn't protect her from a deliberate attack.

Wishing he'd kept the speculation to himself, he led her around the side of the car. "Come on."

By the time he eased into the driver's seat, she was sitting very still, shoulders hunched.

He started to touch her arm, but thought better of it. "Are you okay?"

"Just shaken up. Thanks to you." She straightened and raised her face toward him. "Tell me again. What happened?"

"A truck came around the corner like he was heading for a three-alarm fire. But there was no way he could have missed seeing you. Unless he was blind."

She gave a sharp laugh, and he felt his face heat.

"I mean—"

"It's just an expression. I know what you meant."

"Yeah."

"Blind people don't usually drive trucks. Even in this neighborhood."

This time he was the one who laughed.

She waited for a moment before speaking. "When you dashed into the street and grabbed me—you could have gotten killed," she said in a low voice. "I—" She swallowed hard. "Thank you."

"I'd offer you a drink but all I have is cinnamon candy."

"Actually, that sounds a lot more enticing."

He reached in his pocket for a candy for each of them.

"I'm too finicky a housekeeper to throw the wrapper on the floor," she said as she handed it to him.

He was conscious of the brush of his fingertips against hers. He wanted to ask what she'd been feeling when he'd held her, but he knew he had no business asking that kind of question. They were still strangers. Or rather, he was stuck pretending that they were.

He watched her lips as she sucked the candy as if the sweetness could wipe away the earlier horror. "I haven't had these since I was a kid," she said. "Now I may have to get a bag of them."

"Don't tell the department I have an addiction."

She grinned. "Does this mean I have something on you?"

"Only if you're unscrupulous."

"Can I get arrested for that?"

"It's not in the statute books," he countered. He liked the way she smiled and seemed to relax. But he knew he had to question her about what had happened. "We need to talk about that truck."

He cursed silently as her posture stiffened. "The way that driver was heading for you, it's hard to believe it was an accident. Is there someone who has a grudge against you?"

She looked startled. "Of course not. At least I don't think so."

"Nothing like this has happened to you before?"

"Well, not like that." She sighed. "When you first start traveling on your own with a cane, your judgment isn't all that good. A couple of times I stepped off the curb when a car was turning. But the driver always hit the brakes. He didn't try to run me down."

"When was that?"

"A long time ago. I was in my teens." She paused before going on quickly, and he saw her fists bunch in her lap. "I was blinded in an automobile accident. So I had to play catch-up to learn the skills most blind kids are taught in elementary school. I was at a rehab center in Colorado for six months before I went to college."

"Oh." He answered her recitation with a noncommittal syllable. She'd given him the perfect opportunity to say he already knew about the accident that had blinded her. But the deadened tone of her voice stopped him cold.

He started the engine.

She looked startled. "Where are we going?"

"Across the street." He made a slow U-turn and brought them directly in front of the ramp leading to the building's entrance.

"We're right at the front door," he told her.

She nodded gravely, then switched the subject. "Did you get a look at the driver of the truck?"

"No. I'm sorry. If I had to give any kind of detailed testimony, I'd make a lousy witness." He cleared his throat. "I was focused on you, not him. By the time I looked up, all I saw was the back of his head."

"But you think it was a man."

"No. I was only making an assumption. You don't usually see a woman driving a pickup."

"Yes." She raised her eyes to his, and it was hard not to believe with utter conviction that she was focusing on him.

After a moment she said, "Thank you again for what you did."

"Sure," he answered, as if he threw himself into the path of speeding trucks every day.

She snapped open the glass of her watch and ran her fingertips lightly over the face. "It's late. I've really got to run."

Again she opened the car door and stepped out. Only this time she didn't have to cross the street. All she had to do was walk a few steps along the sidewalk and climb the ramp to the building entrance. At the top, she turned and gave him a cocky little wave. He waved back before he realized that, of course, she couldn't see him. Then she was gone.

IT WOULD LOOK pretty stupid if she'd been waving to empty air, Jenny thought as she stepped into the paneled lobby. But she'd known Brisco was still there because she hadn't heard the car pull away. And if he were there, he would have been watching her.

She wasn't relying on some extraordinary sixth sense that

had miraculously taken over for her lack of vision. That was the kind of romanticized claptrap blind people had to fight all the time. But she had plenty of reasons to believe that Ben Brisco would have been watching her with unnerving intensity.

For starters, he was a cop. He would have been watching to make sure nothing else happened to her.

She drew in a shaky breath and let it out slowly. Only Ben's quick thinking—and his bravery—had saved her. She hadn't been exaggerating when she'd said he'd risked his life to snatch her out of the truck's path. The only thing she'd been able to do afterward was cling to him. She'd had the right to be afraid. But not dependent, ineffective, clinging. All the things she'd vowed she wasn't going to be. Perhaps the worst part was that while she'd been in Detective Brisco's arms, she'd been content to stay there as long as he wanted to hold her. Her only consolation was that she probably wouldn't be seeing him again. So she wouldn't have another chance to make a fool of herself.

"Jenny, what's wrong?"

She recognized the voice of Shelly Lipman, one of the federation's lawyers. On any other day Jenny would not have felt at a disadvantage with the sighted woman. Today she was upset that Shelly had reacted to her facial expression when she hadn't even known she was being observed.

"I'm fine," she answered automatically.

"You look upset."

She shrugged and prepared to deny the obvious. One of her rules was not to complain about the little things that made her day difficult—or to let people know when she was hurting. But in this instance she thought better of the prevarication. The truck was hardly a little thing. What if someone really was out on the streets trying to run down the blind—or people in wheelchairs, for that matter? If she kept quiet and somebody got hurt, she'd feel terrible.

"I had a narrow brush with a speeding truck," Jenny allowed.

"Oh, my...are you all right?" Shelly asked.

"Just a little bit shaken up. A good Samaritan got me out of the street in time." She decided not to explain that he was a policeman in the middle of a murder investigation. "He, uh, said the truck looked like it was deliberately trying to mow me down. You don't know of anyone else who's had problems like that, do you?"

"My gosh, no."

"Well, I don't want to alarm anyone, but if we hear about any other incidents near the building, maybe we'd better put a warning in the newsletter."

Shelly wanted more details but Jenny adroitly sidestepped her questions. "I've got an appointment." And with that she entered the waiting elevator.

AT LEAST THERE was no one around to hear him cursing, Ben thought as he stared at the blank monitor. It stared blandly back—except for a blinking cursor. So much for his bravura offer to help Diangelo with the Blaisdell woman's computer.

In the past hour and a half all he'd done was turn on the machine and get a C prompt. He couldn't even find a reference manual though there was some kind of bizarre helmet on the desk.

At the rear of the processor he found a metal tag with a serial number. Another plate identified the processor as a Beta test model being developed by Randolph Electronics. He called the number listed there, but the message said the technician in charge of the project was out sick. Emergency questions would be answered if the caller left a name and number. Ben complied, giving his pager, station house and home numbers and ending by stating that his business was urgent.

Then he went out to interview the other woman on the list

he'd split with Diangelo. Like Jenny, Sue was horrified to learn about the murder, but had no information for him. Apparently Jenny was the only friend to whom Ms. Blaisdell had confided her computer-dating intentions.

Was Jenny dating anyone? he wondered as he walked away from yet another row house in Duke Wakefield's neighborhood where nobody appeared to be at home. The question brought him up short, and he stopped beside a scraggly sycamore tree. Pulling off a strip of the loose bark, he crumpled it in his hand the way he'd done when he was a kid. Before this morning he hadn't consciously thought about Jenny in years. Now she was becoming an obsession. A strange twist of fate had once again thrown her into his path. As a policeman, he'd developed a healthy respect for fate. Take the case he'd investigated six months ago, when a gunman had been shooting in a crowded mall. An old man had been killed by a random bullet. The father of three standing next to him had been untouched. It had nothing to do with whether either one of them was good or bad, rich or poor, old or young. Or whether one of them deserved to live and one to die. It was simply a random toss of the dice. And good luck for the young father.

Another toss had landed Jenny back in his life. Could you call that good luck? All he knew was that he didn't want to let her slip away from him again—whether he deserved her or not, he added silently. But he'd have to come up with a good excuse if he wanted to interview her again. And then what? For one thing, homicide detectives didn't end up getting socially involved with friends of murder victims. For another, he was pretty sure that Jenny wouldn't welcome any kind of relationship with him when she found out about their past association.

He dropped the last bit of sycamore bark on the pavement and brushed off his hand. He was heading back to his car when his beeper sounded. From the number displayed, he knew it was the Randolph technician finally returning his call. He looked at his watch. Four in the afternoon. The guy had certainly taken his sweet time. Maybe he could shake him up a bit.

On his portable phone, he called back.

"Richardson speaking," a man answered. He sounded as if he were in pain.

"This is Detective Ben Brisco of the Baltimore City Homicide Division. Official business."

"Homicide?" Richardson wheezed. "What's this about?"

"A woman using one of your experimental computers, Marianne Blaisdell, has been murdered. I need to access her data files."

"Jeez. Marianne? I just talked to her last week. What happened?"

Ben gave the same brief account of the murder he'd been repeating all day then got down to business. "Can you show me how to use her computer?"

Richardson sighed. "Listen, I'd like to help you out, but I'm home in bed with a stomach flu that, believe me, you don't want to get."

"Can we do it over the phone?"

"No way," Richardson answered. "All the commands are nonstandard."

"I got far enough to figure that out."

Richardson gave a little snort. "You need a skilled operator to show you the ropes."

"Isn't there anyone else who can help me out?"

"The company president designed the equipment. But he's in California at a conference."

"Great."

The technician hesitated. "Uh…we do have several other users who are completely familiar with the system. Ordinarily, information about testers is confidential, but if it's a murder investigation…"

"It is."

"Your best bet is a woman named Jenny Larkin."

Ben blinked. "Who?" he said, although he was pretty sure he'd heard the name correctly.

"Jenny Larkin. She's a computer programmer at Birth Data, Inc. She was one of our first testers. She picked up the nuances of the system faster than anyone else, and she's given us several suggestions that have improved the machine's performance. She's using a test model just like Ms. Blaisdell's."

"Thanks."

Ben hung up, bemused at the strange turn of events. Fate was playing with him again. But if he told himself he wasn't glad, he'd be lying.

# Chapter Four

The secretary was out when Ben came back to the Birth Data office, so there was no one to announce him. Quietly, he walked halfway across the waiting room and stood watching Jenny work. Apparently she was adding a column of numbers, which the machine called out for her in a stilted, mechanical voice.

He'd been secretly hoping that he'd somehow exaggerated this woman's hold over him. He knew the instant he saw her that he was every bit as captivated as he'd been when he'd first come here. He liked her crystal-blue eyes and creamy skin; he liked the way her hair framed her face, and her slender but enticing curves. However, his attraction had as much to do with the conflicting mix of inner qualities that went with the appealing exterior. One moment she was the most self-possessed woman he'd ever met. The next, she was as wary as a doe sniffing the wind for predators before she stepped from her hiding place.

Fighting a rush of tangled emotions, he cleared his throat to let her know he was there. "I hope the interview was a success."

Jenny's head jerked in his direction. "Brisco?"

"Sorry if I startled you," he apologized. "The receptionist is away from her desk, so I just barged in." As he spoke, he tried to read her expression. It was more guarded than this morning. When she drew in a deep breath, the doe image came back to him. She was sniffing the wind before venturing out into the meadow.

But why not? He hadn't exactly brought her good news when he'd come here this morning, and her day hadn't gotten any better while she was with him.

He moved toward her, watching her note his progress across the small office. As he drew to a stop in front of the desk, she swallowed.

He shifted his weight from one foot to the other. "After I left you, I went to Ms. Blaisdell's and spent two hours trying to figure out how to use her computer. Then I called the technician at Randolph Electronics. A guy named Richardson."

"Terry Richardson," Jenny supplied. "He's not just a technician. He and Cameron Randolph designed the system specifically to meet the needs of blind users."

"Well, unfortunately he's got a stomach flu, so he couldn't run a demo for me." Ben moved so that he could take a look at the computer sitting on a table beside her desk. "Damn."

She tipped her head inquiringly to the side. "What's wrong?"

"Richardson told me you know more about the system than he does. But this isn't the same model."

"No. This is the machine Birth Data purchased when I came to work here. The one I'm testing for Randolph Electronics is at my house."

"So could you show me how to use it?" He tried to make the question sound casual.

She hesitated for several moments, pushing a rubber band across her desk blotter with her finger.

"I wouldn't bother you, but I haven't come up with any other leads."

"All right."

"Tonight, if possible," he pressed.

Her face wrinkled. "My van pool usually picks me up at five-thirty."

"I'll be glad to give you a ride home."

"It's out in Howard County—Elkridge," she answered, as if it were somewhere west of the Cumberland Gap.

"That's okay. We could have some dinner first," he said, knowing the line had been in the back of his mind for hours.

She kept her face lowered. "That isn't necessary."

"I'd like to."

"Why?"

He had more invested in the invitation than he wanted to admit. Yet he hadn't expected her to question his motives. "Does a guy need a reason to take a pretty woman to dinner?"

Her fingers twisted the rubber band into a tight circle. "You and I don't exactly have a social relationship."

"So I'll put it on my expense account if that'll make you feel better."

She caught him off guard with a low chuckle. "I guess in that case, I can't refuse."

He was surprised by his feeling of relief. "Good."

She checked the time. "I'd better cancel my ride before it's too late to reach them."

He waited while she made the call, her fingers moving over the keypad as rapidly as if she were able to see the numbers. The conversation was short. After hanging up, she opened the bottom drawer of her desk and took out her purse.

"I should tell my boss I'm leaving a few minutes early."

He moved to the door, where he could watch her walk rapidly down the hall to an office in the back. He saw her talking to an attractive, dark-haired woman who looked up and gave him a quick inspection. He nodded stiffly.

After the brief exchange, Jenny continued down the hall, probably to the ladies' room. Ben turned away to look at her office, noting the large volumes with braille labels lined up on the shelves beside the window and the way every piece of paper on the desk was neatly filed. No wonder she'd been put off by the candy wrappers on the floor of his car. He'd never seen an office so neat—but how else could she keep track of things? Footsteps made him turn quickly. To his surprise, he found Jenny's boss standing in the doorway. Up close, she looked too young to be the head honcho, yet she projected a maturity beyond her years.

She stepped into the office, studying him with more than casual interest. "I'm Erin Stone, director of Birth Data."

"Ben Brisco. Baltimore City police."

The woman pitched her voice low. "Jenny told me about your coming to see her this morning. She was quite upset about her friend's death."

Ben matched her low tone. "I'm sorry I was the one to break the bad news."

"We all think a lot of Jenny here," Erin continued.

"Yes, well, she seems like a remarkable woman."

"I wouldn't want anything to happen to her."

His thoughts flashed to the truck. "Neither would I."

As they stared at each other, Ben wondered why the director of Birth Data had come down the hall to give him a personal warning. She couldn't possibly have this kind of conversation with every male who came to see Jenny Larkin. So she'd singled him out. Could she read something in his eyes? Or was she going on Jenny's reactions? Before he could ask her a direct question, he heard Jenny in the doorway.

"Erin? Did you need something?"

"No. I was saying hello to Detective Brisco."

"Oh."

"Well, I have a few things to finish up before I go home," Erin said before departing.

Ben noted Jenny had combed her hair and put on fresh lipstick. For him? Or simply because she was eating out?

"Where do you want to go?" he asked as they headed toward the elevator.

"You pick. I don't have dinner downtown very often."

"Why not?" he asked, before belatedly deciding that was none of his business.

"I like to get home early."

"I won't keep you out too late. Do you like Italian?"

"Yes."

"What about Guido's, in Little Italy? It's off the beaten track, but the food is great."

"Sounds fine."

He smiled and wished the gesture wasn't lost on her, so he added "Good" in what he hoped was a warm tone. Maybe too warm, judging by the way her hand fluttered slightly.

Jenny waited until the elevator door had closed behind them before asking, "What did Erin want?"

He shrugged automatically, then realized it wouldn't get him very far. If he was going to spend much time with her, he'd have to learn a whole new set of responses. "I don't know."

"She let me talk about Marianne this morning. It helped."

"Good."

The elevator stopped on the second floor, and a woman got on. Jenny stopped talking, and he gathered she saved personal conversations until she could be sure who was listening. She didn't speak again until they were sitting inside his car.

After fastening her seat belt, she sighed. "Erin didn't need to tell you how to act with me."

"She didn't," he answered automatically, yet he wasn't sure it was true.

"Only because I came back when I did."

She cocked her head toward him. "I think sometimes people assume I'm more—fragile—than I really am. I'm tougher than you think."

"I'll keep that in mind," he said gruffly.

For the rest of the ride she sat with her hands folded in her lap, and as he pulled into a parking space down the block from the restaurant, Ben wondered if dinner was a mistake. Once inside, he was even more unsure. He remembered the place as small and cozy. Now he saw it as small and cramped. The aisles were narrow, and Jenny moved slowly as she followed the woman from the front podium to a table against the wall. When she pulled out her chair, she bumped into one at the table behind her.

"Maybe I should have picked another place," he murmured.

"No. I'm fine," she assured him, seating herself and propping her cane out of the way.

The waitress hesitated as she approached the little table, then set two menus between the cutlery. Moments later, a busboy filled their water glasses. When the attendant's footsteps had departed, Jenny tapped the menu. "I bet this isn't in braille."

"You're right. I'll read it to you."

"Thanks."

Opening his own menu, he leaned forward across the small table to read to her. The leading edge of the large folder struck Jenny's glass, knocking it off the table.

His exasperated expletive was punctuated by Jenny's leap backward as some of the water splashed on her.

"Sorry! As you may have guessed, I knocked over your glass. Let me—"

Before he could finish, the waitress came scurrying back, a stack of napkins in her hand. Kneeling, she began to blot at the wet patch on the carpet. "It's perfectly all right," she murmured to Jenny. "Nothing to worry about." But her annoyed expression didn't match her soothing words.

"I was the one who spilled the water," Ben informed her.

She gave him a doubtful nod and went back to her task.

"There you are, hon. Good as new," she said to Jenny when she'd finished blotting the rug. "So don't you worry about it."

"I said I was the one who spilled the water," Ben insisted sharply.

"Uh-huh," the woman agreed with a decided lack of sincerity before departing.

"She didn't believe you, did she?" Jenny asked.

"I don't think so." Ben tried to control his anger.

Jenny surprised him with a tiny giggle that turned into a genuine laugh. He surprised himself by joining her.

"Your face lights up when you laugh," he said.

"And your laugh has a nice timbre. Full. Rich."

"Nobody ever told me that before."

"I'm an expert," she allowed. "But if somebody across the room spills his soup, she'll probably assume I did it."

"You're taking it extremely well."

"I try not to let nonsense like that bother me—especially at the end of a long day."

*Very long,* he thought. Yet Jenny had made him forget about the frustrations. "I suppose you get a lot of similar garbage." It was a personal question, but she seemed to be opening up with him. And he wanted more.

"It comes with the territory. You were probably a uniformed police officer. I'll bet people made assumptions when you walked into a restaurant in your blue uniform."

"Yeah, that either I was getting a free meal, or I'd come to arrest somebody."

"So, did you walk around with a chip on your shoulder?"

"No. But I knew I wasn't going to be in a uniform forever." As soon as he'd said it, he wished he hadn't.

She was silent for several moments. "And I'm serving a life sentence."

"I wasn't thinking."

"It's okay. It means you're comfortable enough with me not to censor your comments."

*Sometimes,* he thought.

She felt around the table, checking the position of the cutlery, plates and glasses. Her hand came back to the fork, and he watched her stroke the cool metal, running her fingers over the raised design as if touching it gave her pleasure. "My life has…changed because I'm blind."

"Yeah."

"It doesn't make as much difference as you think," she said, her fingers still caressing the fork handle. He couldn't take his eyes off those fingers, imagining them caressing his skin with the same delicate care.

He cleared his throat. "It would to most people."

"Well, mainly it's inconvenient. Some things take me a little longer—like weeding my garden, because I have to do it by touch. And there are other things I can't do by myself. Like read a menu. But that's not a tragedy. Unless *you* can't read. Then we'd both be in trouble."

This time he was the one who laughed. Lord, Jenny Larkin was something else.

Her fingers went back to the cutlery, playing with the spoon, tracing the shape of the bowl, then the handle—and back again. Probably she used touch to calm her nerves. Did they need calming now? Did she know that practically every gesture was a turn-on to the man across the table? That would make her nervous, all right. Like in the car when she'd played with one of the candy papers, he remembered. He'd watched her fingers then and he watched now, drinking his fill of her with secret pleasure.

She broke the silence. "Since you've been here before, just

tell me what's good, and we won't have to worry about spilling any more water."

"Suppose my taste is different from yours?"

"I hope I've got a veto. I won't let you order me squid with octopus-ink pasta."

"Not a chance."

He scanned the selections, then leaned back and stretched out his legs under the table. His foot hit hers, and she jumped. He cleared his throat and moved back a little. "I like the grilled veal chop or any of the pasta."

"Do they have stuffed shells?"

"Yes."

He signaled for the waitress—letting Jenny give her own order and selecting the veal chop for himself.

"What about a glass of wine?" she suggested when the waitress asked if they wanted anything else. "No—you're probably on duty,"

"Technically, I'm off for the evening. So—"

"Then I'd like a glass of Chianti."

"Excellent idea." Ben ordered the same.

The wine came a few minutes later, and they sat sipping and talking. Jenny probably didn't drink much, he decided, because her face was a little flushed, and a small smile played around her lips. He liked the effect.

"So, what are you thinking?" he murmured.

She took another sip of wine. "It's strange, but I feel as if I've known you for a long time. I've felt that way all along, actually."

Suddenly he went from relaxed to alert. "What do you mean?" he asked carefully. Had she finally remembered where they'd met before?

Her next words took the edge off his anxiety. "Maybe that you're easy to talk to. Or that I'm having a good time."

"So am I."

She turned her wineglass in her hand. "I guess I forgot for a minute why we're having dinner."

"I think I wanted to forget," he confessed.

"Oh?"

"My life has been kind of regimented lately. Not quite all work and no play, but close."

"Want to tell me about it?"

"I'll end up talking about my divorce and I'd rather relax and enjoy the evening."

"Until we go over to Marianne's."

"Yeah."

He knew the dose of reality had been deliberate on her part. A way to shatter the closeness enfolding them. He should thank her. Instead, he couldn't help feeling a bit resentful. After their food arrived, they concentrated on the meal. Then Jenny declined both coffee and dessert.

When he started to pay the bill, she pulled out her wallet. "Let me get my share."

"Remember, I told you I can put it on my expense account."

"You're sure?"

"I'm not in the habit of lying," he shot back before he realized what he'd said.

"I didn't mean it that way."

"I'm sorry." He knew he was overreacting because of the omission in his introduction that morning. For a split second he considered telling her they really had met before, a long time ago when she could still see. But then he pictured her getting angry and flouncing out of the restaurant. And he really did need her help with the Randolph computer. So he kept his mouth shut for the time being. Later, he'd set things straight.

JENNY COULD FEEL the silence hanging heavy around her and told herself to relax as she stood just inside the living-room doorway of Marianne's house.

She heard Brisco snap on the light and walk into the living room. He walked forward on the balls of his feet—with a springy step that would normally have sounded pleasing. When she didn't follow, he said, "I guess it makes you feel uncomfortable to be here."

"Yes," she answered, wondering if he could read the stress on her face. Marianne was dead. She would never talk with her, laugh with her again. Coming here brought that home as nothing else had. Sucking in a deep breath, she caught the unpleasant edge of a new odor hanging in the air. Cigarette smoke.

She sniffed the acrid scent more sharply. "Someone's been in the house. Someone besides Marianne," she added, her voice rising as she spoke her friend's name.

"I was here earlier." His hand gently cupped her shoulder.

She knew he meant the gesture to be calming. Although she wanted to lean against him, she kept her body rigid.

"Somebody who smokes," she clarified.

"It was Diangelo—the guy who's working the case with me."

"When was he here?"

"This morning."

"This morning," she repeated slowly, wondering if her nose was really that sensitive.

"Why don't you show me how to use the computer?" he asked.

"Okay," she answered automatically. The house felt like a trap. And she'd walked into it. But maybe it wasn't simply because her friend had been murdered. She was nervous about being alone with Ben Brisco, because she was attracted to him. Because they'd gotten too chummy in the restaurant too quickly. What was it about him that made her respond in such unfamiliar ways? She wasn't sure how deeply she wanted to examine the emotions all twisted up inside her as she made her way to the bedroom where Marianne had a combination guest room and home office.

She was so unsure of herself—of what had begun happening at dinner. The feeling of intimacy had been disturbing, so she'd deliberately shattered it—and spent the rest of the meal feeling disappointed. Now she wanted to dazzle Brisco with her ability to unlock the secrets of the computer Randolph was developing.

She could hear him right behind her as she sat down in the desk chair and booted up the machine. Feeling over the surface of the desk, she located the headset and put it on. Luckily it fit her pretty well, since she and Marianne were close to the same size.

"What's that?" Brisco asked.

"Part of the controls."

"No wonder I had problems," he muttered, his voice only inches away from her ear. She wished he wouldn't stand so close, while at the same time she knew she'd be disappointed if he backed off.

He moved behind her, leaning over her shoulder, still near enough that she could sense his body heat and feel his breath on the side of her face. Was he trying to see what she was doing—or did he find the proximity as stimulating as she did?

She pressed her lips together to keep from asking him what he looked like. She wanted to find out if he was anything like the picture she'd formed in her mind as they'd sat across the table at dinner. He was intense. That went with dark hair. And dark eyes. He had a firm chin line. A lower lip fuller than the upper... It took an act of will to stop herself from contemplating his lips.

She made a small sound.

"Jenny?"

"The machine's slow," she muttered, wondering if he believed her.

While she waited for it to finish booting, she silently waxed philosophical. She'd told him blindness was a nuisance. That was true. But sometimes it was frustrating, even maddening, that things sighted people took for granted were beyond her reach.

She had friends who'd been blind from birth. They didn't wonder what things looked like because they'd always functioned by relying on their other senses. She'd been sighted until she was eighteen, and it was different for her. Sometimes it was an advantage, because if she had a visual description of something, she could see it in her mind. But you couldn't go around asking people to describe themselves.

The machine beeped twice, signaling that it was ready to receive commands, and she snapped to the task at hand—dazzling Brisco. No, make that helping him find the person who had killed her friend.

When she spoke into the microphone, the machine began to give her a list of directories.

It took a moment to get the machine to recognize her voice. After that, it was like using the equipment she had at home. With a turn of her head, she put the voice output in fast mode so she could cover the territory more quickly.

Behind her, Brisco gave a frustrated sigh. "Can you put information on the screen so I can see it?" he asked.

"Sorry." Deftly, she provided a visual display.

"Thanks. This is like being a visitor on the bridge of the Starship Enterprise."

"No. Voyager," she quipped. "Captain Janeway at your service."

It was a good beginning, but things didn't go so smoothly after that. Although she was able to get a list of directories, when she tried to access the files, the machine drew a blank. Frustrated, she tried again.

"What's wrong?" Brisco asked.

"Something odd. I'm not finding her files. Let me try

something else." She went to another section of the disk. "Here's the list of phone numbers for her modem. So you can see which online service she's using."

"World Connect," Brisco said. "Can you bring it up?"

"Probably not without her password. But I'll try." She attempted to make the connection, but the computer wouldn't put through the call.

"Just a minute." She heard Brisco pick up the phone receiver. "The line's dead."

"It is?" She took off the headset, and laid it on the desk. "Was it working this afternoon?"

"I didn't check. I assumed—"

Jenny reached to grab his arm. "Shh—" she hissed.

"What?" Brisco whispered.

"I heard something. Maybe a floorboard squeaking…in Marianne's bedroom."

"Sit tight." He took several steps toward the door. Then he was making his way quietly down the hall. Jenny waited with mounting tension, listening intently. It was hard to simply sit and do nothing. The silence lengthened. Then she heard a muffled noise that could have been a blow. It was followed by a grunt and the sound of something hitting the floor. Something about the size and weight of a man's body.

God, someone was in the house, all right. And either Brisco had decked him, or it was the other way around.

She gripped the arms of the chair, straining all her senses for more information.

Moments later footsteps returned along the hall. The hair on the back of her neck bristled. It wasn't Brisco. Not unless he'd totally changed the way he walked.

# Chapter Five

Could she be mistaken?

"Brisco?" she called out. In the next second, she was sorry she hadn't kept her mouth shut.

Time seemed to slow as she waited for an answer to her question. No one replied. In the ominous silence, she shrank down in her chair, wishing she could disappear entirely. She pictured herself crouching behind a mass of clothes in the closet. But she wasn't even sure where to find the closet. Heavy footsteps thumped closer, faster. It sounded like a man walking on his heels rather than the balls of his feet. Either that or a pretty hefty woman. Someone who had surprised Brisco and—

Her heart gave a painful lurch. She couldn't sit here waiting for the same thing to happen to her. Spinning the chair toward the desk, she reached for the phone to call 911, before she remembered Brisco had told her the line was dead.

She was on her own. Fear swelled inside her, closing her throat, threatening to cut off all rational thought. Yet she knew in some tiny corner of her mind that she couldn't fall apart. She had to save herself—and Brisco—if he was badly hurt and needed medical attention.

The footsteps drummed in her brain. How long did she have?

Sliding open the middle desk drawer, she scrabbled for some sort of weapon. The best she could do was a long screwdriver. With a quick, furtive motion, she concealed it in the folds of her skirt.

The footsteps stopped. In the doorway, she judged. Someone was standing there looking at her, breathing hard, deliberately blocking her escape. Hoping her face showed no emotion, she turned toward the presence in the doorway. "Who's there?" she asked, trying to keep her voice steady. It was high and reedy.

No one answered, and never before had her blindness brought such numbing terror.

She could hear the man who was watching her shifting from one foot to the other. And she could smell him—acrid sweat and cigarette smoke. Somehow her numb mind continued to function, continued to draw conclusions. She'd smelled him the minute they'd stepped in the front door— because it wasn't a leftover odor. He'd been here all along. He'd come to the house for something and he'd finally gotten tired of waiting for them to leave. Either he'd messed up and made a noise. Or he'd done it deliberately—to lure Brisco down the hall and attack him.

She sat very still, mouth so dry she couldn't swallow. He was studying her, probably pleased she was cowering in her chair. She could feel his gaze moving over her flesh. It was like hundreds of insects crawling across her skin.

She wanted to scream because he could see her and she couldn't see him. Or maybe her blindness was actually an advantage, she told herself. Maybe the terror would be worse if she knew what he looked like.

When the wait became unbearable, she asked another question. "What do you want?"

Only the sound of his rapid breathing—and the blood pounding in her ears—broke the silence. Perhaps when he'd come down the hall, he hadn't known she was blind. He must know it now, must be making plans accordingly.

"What have you done to Detective Brisco?"

Silence. Thick smothering silence that almost drove her to the brink of madness.

Then, suddenly, he moved like a predator making his strike. The footsteps advanced toward her, confident, rapid. With them came the sweat and the cigarette smoke.

A rough hand clamped onto her arm, pulling her out of the chair. She had no time to think about finesse or a plan of attack. No time to do more than wield the screwdriver and pray that she hit something. She felt the blade tear through fabric and then flesh as she heard a cry of surprise and pain.

The assailant fell back. "Bitch!" he spat out.

Jenny followed the sound and sprang at him, landing on his body, and scoring a second hit on what felt like his face.

This time he screamed, and she felt a surge of satisfaction.

She swung again, but he threw her roughly off. She hit the wall, gasping for breath, and he scrambled away from her. Before she had time to fill her lungs with air, he was running. Sagging against the wall, panting, she clutched the screwdriver in a death grip.

Every muscle tense, she listened to the sound of footsteps retreating down the hall. When the front door opened, cautious relief flooded through her. Had she really driven him away?

Tears spilled from her eyes and slid down her cheeks. She waited, expecting that he'd change his mind and come back—twice as angry and twice as determined. But as the seconds ticked by, the likelihood of another attack grew fainter. He'd probably thought she'd be an easy mark, and she'd startled him with her show of force. Pushing herself up, she ran a shaky hand through her hair, then wiped away her tears.

Still clutching the screwdriver in one fist, she made her shaky way back to the desk and found the slender cane she'd propped against the wall. As she headed in the direction of Marianne's room, the familiar rhythm of swinging the cane in front of her brought back a measure of calm.

"Brisco?" she called as she hurried down the hall.

No answer.

"Brisco?" she tried again as she stepped through the doorway and moved slowly into the room.

She gasped as she encountered something bulky in the middle of the floor. Sinking to her knees, she reached out and touched Brisco's shoulder. He didn't move, didn't answer as she continued to call his name.

"Brisco, say something," she begged. "Talk to me."

When he didn't respond, she felt for his chest and pressed her palm flat. At the steady beat of his heart, she let out the breath she hadn't known she'd been holding.

Telling him over and over that he was going to be all right, she ran her hands carefully over his body. She could detect no injury to his arms or chest or neck. His skin felt warm but not hot, his chest rose and fell as he breathed, and his heartbeat remained steady. With fingers that shook slightly, she touched his face. She'd wanted to know what he looked like, she thought almost hysterically, as she traced her fingers over his high cheekbones, jutting nose, and full lips, but not like this. Not with him lying unconscious on the floor.

Trying to stay calm, she skimmed his closed eyelids, brushing his long lashes, then found his short, almost blunt cut hair. On the back of his head she discovered a lump as large as a hen's egg. It was sticky. Now that she'd found the wound, she smelled the blood.

"Brisco?" she tried again.

He didn't move or speak.

Every protective instinct urged her to stay and keep watch

over him; yet in this case, she knew instinct was dead wrong. She had to get help.

Finding her cane again, she stood and checked her watch, then she hurried down the hall again. It was only a short distance from Marianne's front door to the uneven brick walk of the neighbor on the immediate right, yet it felt like miles. An elderly woman lived there, Jenny remembered. A Mrs. Clayborn.

She tripped on a loose brick and had to slow her steps as she proceeded up the walk. Finally, she made it to the front porch.

"Who's there?" a quavery voice asked in response to the third chime of the doorbell.

"Mrs. Clayborn? It's Jenny Larkin. I'm a friend of Marianne's. We met a few months ago."

"Marianne was murdered. Didn't you hear about that?"

"I know about Marianne. Please, I need your help," she repeated.

"I don't remember you. Go away."

"I'm the blind woman!" Jenny cried out in frustration.

"Oh yes. I remember now. Such a pity when you're so pretty."

Jenny ground her teeth. Pity was the last thing she wanted from anyone, yet she kept her cool. Speaking rapidly and persuasively, she got Mrs. Clayborn to pull aside the curtains and look out while she explained about the attack. Finally the door swung open, and the old lady showed her where to find the phone. As she dialed 911, she could feel Mrs. Clayborn fluttering nervously about.

Quickly she gave the address and a brief description of what had happened. "Hurry," she begged before hanging up.

"I'm sorry I wouldn't let you in. But with the murder and all…" her hostess apologized.

"I understand," Jenny flung over her shoulder before turning her attention to the rough walkway.

When she gained the sidewalk, she felt her watch. Eleven minutes. Anything could have happened. But at least she'd summoned help.

As soon as she stepped back into Marianne's living room, she heard Brisco groan. When she rushed to the spot where she thought she'd left him, he was gone. Panic seized her. She swept her arm across the floor in a wide arc and finally collided with his shoulder.

"Watch out! My damn head hurts." The unexpected words startled her.

"I'm sorry. I didn't mean to hurt you."

This time she touched him softly, gently. His body quivered, but he didn't protest. He was sitting against the wall, his knees pulled against his chest. And he was breathing hard, as if moving a few feet from where he'd lain had been a tremendous effort.

"How do you feel?" she asked, knowing that it must not be good. Should she keep him talking? It had been years since she'd had a first-aid course, and she struggled to recall what had been said about head injury.

"Dammit, Brenna, how many times have I told you not to leave your exercise equipment all over the floor," he grated.

"What?"

"Your damn equipment."

Apparently he didn't know what had happened or even who she was. "Brisco, It's okay. It's Jenny," she murmured as she soothed her hand across his shoulder.

He cursed and grabbed her wrist hard. "Take your paws off me."

She tried to jerk away, but he held her with painful strength.

"Brenna? What are you doing here?" he asked as if she hadn't spoken.

"Jenny. It's Jenny," she repeated her name.

He flung her hand down and kept talking. "Are you trying to kill me? Or just make me mad enough to leave?"

His grating voice made her flinch, but she didn't move away. He was confused. He thought this was a different place and she was someone else. He was angry. And as much as she hated to admit it, he was also dangerous.

The safest thing would be to back off, yet she couldn't retreat. Probably Brenna was his ex-wife. Or maybe he'd lived with somebody. It seemed she wasn't his favorite person.

After taking a deep breath, she spoke soothingly. "Brisco...Ben. It's not Brenna. It's Jenny. Remember, we came here to work on Marianne's computer?" She said it several times, hoping for a response. "You couldn't use it, so you asked me to help you. We had dinner first."

There was only silence, except for the sound of air wheezing in and out of his lungs.

Then, "Jenny?"

"Yes," she said on a sigh. They were making progress.

Was it all right to touch him now, or would that set him off again, she wondered. It was taking a chance, but gingerly she touched his arm. This time he didn't flinch or push her away.

Encouraged, she inched a little closer. "It's Jenny Larkin," she repeated, pressing her hand over his.

"Wh-what happened?" he asked.

"We were working with the computer. We heard something, and you went to investigate. Then I heard a scuffle." She hesitated for a moment, then skipped her own encounter with the intruder. Probably it would upset him, and she wanted to keep him calm. "When I got here, you were on the floor unconscious."

He swore.

"He hit you on the head with something. I'm sorry you were alone when you came to, but I'd gone to get help."

"I'm…fine!" he growled, his shaky voice and uneven breathing belying the assurance.

"You're going to be okay. I called an ambulance."

"You didn't need to do that."

"You're not thinking straight. Your head is bleeding." God, he probably had a concussion. Or worse. When he tried to stand up, she pressed down on his shoulder. "Stay put."

He ignored her. Acting instinctively, she scooted a little closer, wrapped her arms around him, and held him tight. That did the trick, because he stopped resisting her. She felt him sigh as he settled back against the wall.

"You need to stay quiet," she whispered.

"I know what I need," he growled. To her surprise, he gathered her closer.

"Brisco?"

At that moment, everything altered. His hold on her changed as his head tipped and his lips touched hers.

There was no hesitation on his part. His lips settled, took fuller possession. She should pull back, she told herself. She was the one who claimed to be thinking straight. Yet she was powerless to draw away from this man who had stirred up a maelstrom of emotions within her. In the short time they'd spent together, he'd affected her so powerfully that there was no comparison to any other experience in her life.

She wanted—

No, that wasn't important. *He* needed. She knew by the way his lips moved urgently over hers, by the way his hands were pressed to her back and the way his body strained toward hers. And she let herself be wrapped in that need.

Then his lips parted, and the intoxicating taste of him drove any remnants of thought from her mind. It didn't matter why he'd taken her in his arms. She was here, and this was where she wanted to be.

As if they had a will of their own, her hands slid up his

back and across his shoulders. If she couldn't see him, she was tuned to him in every other way. The feel of his skin against her cheek—rough where his beard had grown during the day, soft along the line of his hair. The smell of him—not simply the faint remnants of after-shave lotion, but the indefinable scent that was his alone. The touch of his strong hands—tender and gentle as they moved over her back and shoulders.

She marveled at the current that seemed to flow between them, starting at the contact point of their mouths and radiating throughout her body.

Her hands moved restlessly over his face, his shoulders, his arms, touching skin, then well-honed muscles under annoying layers of fabric.

"Yes," he murmured, his voice low and husky.

She craved more, but there was no need to tell him. As if obeying an unspoken plea, he deepened the melding of his mouth with hers. She hadn't dared contemplate how much she wanted this. It felt so completely right. So good. As natural as breathing, yet as exciting as skydiving.

He turned her body toward his, to fit more firmly against him. She felt enveloped, cocooned, lost to sensation that rapidly built beyond her imagining.

"Ben," she whispered, hardly able to cope with the emotions surging through her. They were too new, too abandoned.

"Lord, Jenny," he murmured, "you don't know how much I've wanted—"

His hands cupped her breasts. It wasn't a subtle caress. His fingers kneaded, stroked, then found her hardened nipples. She gave a small sigh that might have started as a protest but ended in pleasure.

Somewhere deep in her brain, she knew she had to stop him. The blow to his head had stripped away his normal inhibitions, but she still had control. However, control was a subtle illusion. Heat shot through her body. Her strangled moan was answered by a rumble in his chest as he coaxed a stronger response from her, and then stronger still.

His mouth came back to hers, urgent, insistent.

She made little sounds in her throat as his tongue stroked the insides of her lips, then delved farther like a hummingbird gathering nectar.

She was melting in his arms.

Then, somewhere outside the little world that included only the two of them, a noise intruded. A loud wailing noise. A siren.

As abruptly as the frantic encounter had begun, it came to a halt.

Brisco lifted his head.

"The ambulance," she gasped as she pushed herself a few inches away from him and leaned against the wall, her heart pounding, her body hot and shaky. Moments later, two sets of feet thumped into the room. As someone set down a heavy case or box, she pulled her knees against her chest and hugged them tight, lowering her head so that her face was hidden. She might look strange, but it was better than feeling so terribly exposed.

"We have a report of a head injury," a voice announced.

"Him," she somehow managed, pointing toward Brisco.

"You okay, lady?"

"Yes." She heard the speaker kneel beside Brisco.

"How'd you get hit?" the questioner repeated.

Brisco cleared his throat. "I'm police detective Ben Brisco," he said without answering the question.

In a strange, detached way Jenny marveled at his ability to sound so coherent when her own mind was still reeling. One moment they'd been intimately entwined in each other's arms, the next Brisco was giving his name and rank like a trained soldier.

"How'd you get hit?"

"An assailant was hiding in the house," he snapped.

"He didn't harm you, miss?" another man asked Jenny.

"No." She dared to raise her head a fraction. "Who are you?"

"Paramedics. I'm Casey."

"Tenley," another voice chimed in.

Casey sounded as if he was speaking over his shoulder. Tenley was the one beside Brisco. In the spot where she'd been. She could hear Casey getting out equipment. Then metal clanked against metal and clothing rustled, and she assumed they were checking Brisco over. Rising, she realized she didn't have a clue where she'd left her cane. Rather than scrabble around on the floor for it or interrupt the medical examination, she decided to get gracefully out of the way and sit in the overstuffed chair she remembered in the corner. But she bumped against the end of the bed on her way, and in her haste to stop calling attention to herself, she didn't discover the pile of newspapers on the chair cushion until she'd sat on them. Red-faced, she got up again so she could deposit them on the floor. So much for grace and charm.

There was a moment of silence before anyone spoke. "I, uh, guess you didn't see what happened, did you, miss?" the one named Tenley said.

"No." Brilliant deduction. He'd seen her flounder around the room, all right. They were busy, she guessed, because they didn't address her again. "How is he?" she finally asked.

"Blood pressure's a little low. Heart rate is stable. But the head injury is going to need some stitches and tests. We're taking him to Mount Olive."

"Hell," Brisco muttered.

More footsteps came into the room, quick and purposeful. "Ben," a deep voice said. "What hit you?"

"Pete. What are you doing here?"

"I heard the call coming over the radio and recognized the address. I'm Detective Diangelo," he added for the benefit of the others in the room. "Brisco's partner."

Jenny flushed as she imagined that he could somehow figure out what had been going on.

There was a hurried conversation between Brisco and Diangelo. Mostly, it was pitched too low for her to hear, but she gathered Brisco was filling in the newcomer. She didn't catch much besides her name and "blind" and "computer."

It took all her willpower to keep from interrupting. If there was anything she hated, it was people talking around her as if she wasn't there. But in this case, perhaps it was justified. Diangelo needed to know the facts.

Wheels squeaked on the floor. Then Jenny heard sounds she couldn't identify. Not knowing what was going on became intolerable. "Someone tell me what's happening," she demanded.

"They're putting Ben on a stretcher and taking him to the hospital," Diangelo said. "He's going quietly," he added in a firm voice, and Jenny suspected he might be advising the patient.

"Ben," she called out, her voice rising and thinning.

He didn't answer. No one did. And she knew she was alone in the room.

"Ben," she whispered again, wrapping her arms around her shoulders. She wanted to go with him, to stay with him until she was sure he was going to be all right. But she knew he wouldn't welcome her fluttering about, especially in front of his colleague.

The sound of the stretcher wheels faded into the distance, and she was left with a hollow feeling that started in her chest and spread throughout her body. Brisco could have been seriously hurt. But that hadn't stopped her from kissing him. Not just kissing him. They'd been doing a lot more than that.

Things she wouldn't dream of doing with a man she'd just met. But she had.

Her thoughts came to an abrupt halt as footsteps retraced a path down the hall. Someone walked rapidly toward the far side of the room and she heard fabric rustle.

"What are you doing?" she asked.

"There's a foot-long plaster statue on the floor," Detective Diangelo answered. "The head's broken off. I think it's the weapon."

Her fingers dug into the arms of the chair as she imagined a hand slamming the sculpture into Brisco's head hard enough to break the plaster. "How did he look?" she asked.

"Look?" He sounded surprised by the question.

"Did Brisco seem like he was going to be all right?"

"Uh, I guess he looked pale. In pain. Angry."

"But you think he's going to be okay?" she persisted.

"Yeah," he answered, and she knew he was just saying it to keep her calm.

She struggled to pull herself together.

"So Brisco contacted you this morning?" he asked in a businesslike voice. "You're a friend of the victim. Jenny Larkin?"

"Yes. Detective Brisco asked me to help him with Marianne's computer after he found out I'd been trained on the same model. It's specially equipped for the blind and visually impaired." God, she sounded like a Randolph Electronics training film or something. "I got into the system, but I had trouble retrieving her files. Something wasn't working correctly," she explained in the same stilted voice.

"We'll leave the computer for later. Brisco didn't fill me in on how he got hit. I don't suppose there's anything you can tell me?"

She didn't bother to set him straight about her capabilities. Besides, in this case he was right—even if it was for the wrong reasons. "We were down the hall in another room.

There was a noise, and he went to investigate. I heard him grunt and fall to the floor. I mean, I assume that's what happened. The next thing I knew, the—the assailant was, uh, coming at me."

"At you? Brisco didn't mention anything about that."

"He doesn't know. By that time, he was out cold."

"You're okay?"

"Yes. I—I stabbed…the assailant…with a screwdriver I found in the desk drawer. Then he ran away."

"What?" the detective asked, his voice taking on a note of incredulity. "He went after a hundred-and-seventy-five-pound man, but he ran away from you?"

"I think I hit him in the face. Maybe the eye. I guess he wasn't expecting much from a blind woman. *You* weren't."

Diangelo made a low sound. After a few moments, he said, "I'm sorry. "

"That's all right," she replied, knowing she didn't sound sincere. But the day had been too emotionally and physically draining for her to put energy into pretense. "You're right if you're assuming that I can't give you much of a description. I don't have a clue about his hair color, eyes, complexion. That sort of thing. But I do know that he smokes. He hadn't bathed in a couple of days. He's probably about medium height. He's muscular and walks heavily—on his heels, I think, instead of on the balls of his feet."

"Did he say anything?"

"Not until after I stabbed him. He screamed and called me a bitch. His voice was high, probably distorted by pain. He stood in the doorway studying me for a long time—" She shuddered, as she remembered the way his gaze had made her feel like insects were crawling over her skin. "At least that's what I assume."

He continued to interrogate her, and she added as many details as she could. But the returns began to diminish rapidly.

"Any questions?" he finally asked.

She sat very still. "Was he the man who killed Marianne?" she finally whispered.

"It's likely. But there's no way to be sure until we have more information."

She felt goose bumps rise on her skin, and rubbed her arms. He'd watched her, then he'd pounced on her. Had he started that way with Marianne?

"I'll give you a ride home," Diangelo said.

"Thanks," she replied wearily. "Do you happen to see my cane anywhere on the floor?"

"Right here."

She heard him pick it up and held out her hand. It was a relief to wrap her fingers around the familiar handle, as if she'd finally become grounded, safe.

The cane was a symbol. Not only of security. But of what she'd been through over the past twelve years and what she'd made of her life. She'd tried to be prepared for every eventuality. The trouble was, there was no way she could have been prepared for all the things that had happened today.

IT WAS LIKE having a license to make money, L. J. Smith thought as he leaned back in his comfortable chair and gazed through the one-way glass window of his private office at his busy little staff manning their workstations. Only no government agency had issued the license. In fact, the government didn't even know about his sweet little operation, which meant he made his money tax-free, using the most sophisticated computer information retrieval and graphics setup available. Most had been bought on the open market for the dummy corporation he'd set up to make it look as if he was a legitimate businessman. But when he needed a piece of cutting-edge equipment that wasn't yet for sale, he hired out the contract to an "acquisitions expert"—not to put too fine a point on the definition.

The secure line on his desk rang, and he picked it up. "Smith speaking."

"I have a request for a set of Sprangerbank cards," the voice said.

Smith tried to hold down his irritation. "I can handle the order—but not until next week. We're swamped."

"I need them sooner."

"I can get what you need faster if you go with Great Tortuga," Smith suggested. "They handle the same clientele."

"My client is set on Spranger."

"Then I can't do it right now."

The call concluded quickly. Smith sighed as he hung up. He hadn't exactly been telling the truth. His inability to fill the order had nothing to do with the present volume of business. Unfortunately, Spranger's was one of the systems protected by an encryption system he couldn't crack. But he'd have it nailed when he got the prototype of a super-high-performance, virtual-reality workstation being developed by Randolph Electronics. When he got his hands on that baby, he'd have access to the records not just of Spranger, but a couple of other choice houses as well.

The Randolph prototype wasn't exactly essential to his operation. There were still plenty of institutions he could raid. But he liked to stay out in front of the pack. For one thing, it kept his staff happy. They were all first-rate hackers who got as much pleasure from breaking into classified databases as they did from the fat fees and bonuses they earned on his payroll. He understood them, because he'd been one himself—cracking networks for fun instead of doing his boring homework when he was in high school.

He smiled. His hacking-for-fun days had ended abruptly when he'd gotten the bright idea of seeing how far he could get with the authorization number off a stolen credit card. A lucrative career had been born. Only he didn't do the work himself anymore. He left that to his staff.

Minimizing his risks, he made sure none of his illegal transactions could be traced back to the East Baltimore warehouse that looked like a dump on the outside and a prestigious banking house on the inside. He was totally secure. And he'd be happy as a pig in manure if the man he'd hired to scoop up the Randolph prototype would just phone to say he'd gotten the goods.

# Chapter Six

Tides of powerful emotion surged through Jenny until she felt battered by first one overwhelming force and then another. She tried to cope with the aftereffects of being assaulted, but the sweet memories of making love with Brisco interrupted. Either one was enough to swamp her; together they threatened to tear her apart.

She went back to the whirlwind of activity that had claimed her since six that morning. She'd cleaned the house and weeded the garden. Now there was nothing left to do but fill all the bird feeders.

Drawing in a long draft of the warm spring air, she listened to the wildlife around her as she worked. A little breeze rustled the leaves of the trees. In the dogwood above her head she could hear a cardinal scolding her, its characteristic metallic call ringing through the woods. Finally, she was starting to feel a little better.

"Okay, guys, enjoy yourselves," she murmured as she headed back toward the ground-level deck she'd had built at the side of the house. It was one of the few exterior improvements she'd made to the old house where she'd lived with her grandmother after her parents had died. When she'd moved back, she'd set up paths with borders of rocks and garden ties to make it easier for her to get around. The last few steps before the deck were paved with wooden boards secured to the ground with metal rods, so she could tell when she needed to take a step up.

With a little sigh, she settled into one of the Adirondack chairs and sat as still as she could, breathing in the scent of daffodils and narcissus in a nearby bed. If she didn't move, the birds would come to feed while she was still outside. Although she couldn't see them, she remembered what many of them looked like. The bright blue jays, the red male cardinals and the brownish females, and the dear little warblers with the brown and white stripes on the sides of their faces. Now she marked them by their characteristic sounds.

After several minutes, a woodpecker began to drum on a tree trunk several hundred yards away. Then delicate flutters of wings announced that the smaller birds were returning to the feeder.

She'd made her home into a place where she felt totally secure—with everything she needed or wanted. She should be completely at ease. Yet the deep peace she sought was light years beyond her grasp.

She'd called Erin that morning to say that she might be late for work, but her friend had persuaded her to take the day off. She was trying to make the most of it.

The bucolic scene around her faded into the background as she stroked her finger across her lips, remembering what it had been like to kiss Brisco. She'd been caught in a spiral of sensation—yet it never should have happened.

He'd said he needed her, but whom had he needed? When she'd come back into the room, he'd thought she was somebody named Brenna. Perhaps he hadn't even known whom he was kissing, whose breasts he was touching. She made a strangled sound in her throat. Could it have meant the same thing to him as it had to her?

And what had it meant when he'd held her in his arms after

the truck had almost run her down? Or when he'd talked so openly with her at dinner? She shook her head slowly, wishing she had enough experience to know.

At seven-thirty she'd called Mount Olive hospital. All they'd told her about Brisco was that he was being discharged in the morning. So they'd kept him overnight, probably for observation. Surely he was all right, or they wouldn't have sent him home.

Her heart squeezed. He hadn't called. He wasn't going to call. And it was for the best, because it was a bad idea to get all wound up with thoughts of Ben Brisco. What was wrong with her? She'd stayed detached from most other men—even the ones she'd dated. None of them had touched the tender core of her. She hid her vulnerabilities too well behind her chipper exterior. No one else had made her yearn for all the things she'd convinced herself she couldn't have and didn't even want.

Then Brisco had come storming into her life, swept all her certainty away, and replaced it with a treacherous longing. Tension pounded through her like the thrumming of a snare drum. She closed her eyes and tried to submerge herself once more in the warmth of the sun and the smell of the flowers. The struggle lasted for less than five minutes before the crunch of tires on the gravel drive made her sit up sharply.

No one should be coming here at eleven-thirty on a Wednesday morning. Maybe Brisco was stopping by to tell her how he was doing. Then a more sinister thought made her cringe. What if it was the man who'd attacked her last night? He'd gotten a good look at her. Suppose he'd found out who she was and was coming here to finish what he'd started?

She knew she was being paranoid. Still, she couldn't turn off the wild sense of alarm.

A car door slammed and footsteps approached. Someone walking briskly and purposefully. Not the killer's walk, she told herself.

Fingers gripping the edge of the chair, she waited for what seemed like an eternity, but was probably only a few seconds. "Jenny, it's me," a cheerful voice called out.

She should feel relieved that it was Erin. Part of her did, yet she knew her face was stiff with tension as she followed the progress of her friend along the gravel path.

"What are you doing here?" she asked more sharply than she'd intended.

"I brought lunch," Erin answered easily. "You haven't eaten yet, I hope?"

"No." Jenny picked up a cluster of pine needles that had fallen on the arm of the chair and began to break them into pieces.

"I thought you could use some company."

"I'm fine." She made an effort to compose her face.

"I brought some of those thick corned-beef sandwiches from Lombard Street. And nice sour-dill pickles and black-cherry soda."

One of her all-time favorite lunches. Erin had gone to a lot a trouble for her. "You shouldn't have."

"Sure I should. You deserve a treat. Want to eat out here?"

"Yes."

"I've got paper plates and napkins. You don't have to do a thing." As she spoke, she crossed to the patio table and began unpacking the supplies.

They didn't speak again until they had taken several bites of their lunches.

"This is wonderful," Jenny said.

"But woman can not live by corned beef alone. Do you need anything else? Groceries?"

"No. Hester Anderson took me to the store a couple of days ago."

"Good." There was another long silence. Then Erin asked, "Are you really okay?"

Jenny strove to sound unruffled. "More or less. I'm still kind of shaken up."

"Getting mugged will do that. Remember, I know from experience."

"He didn't hurt me," she said quickly.

"But you're looking over your shoulder, so to speak."

"Yes," she admitted in a low voice.

"Did Brisco call to say he was okay?" Erin suddenly changed the subject.

"Why should he?" she shot back.

"Because if he has half a brain in his head, and he does, he knows you're worried."

"Erin, I just met him yesterday. He doesn't have to check in with me. He was interviewing me because Marianne was killed. It was just business. He and I don't have any kind of relationship," she finished, having enumerated all the reasons why she shouldn't feel the way she did.

"He didn't have to come back and take you to dinner."

"He needed help with the computer."

"Sure. But I saw you with him. I saw the way he looked at you. It was open, unguarded, because he knew you couldn't see him."

The air seemed to vibrate around Jenny as she leaned forward. "Open—unguarded—and what else?" she asked softly.

"He wanted to get to know you a whole lot better. And I saw the way you looked at him—although that's probably not the right word."

Jenny flushed.

"Your expression matched his."

"I'm probably not going to see him again," she murmured.

"Why not?"

"When he finds out he was decked by a man I fought off with a screwdriver, he's not going to be happy."

"That's his first reaction," Erin retorted. "Give him time to think about it."

"You're making too much out of it. Erin, we hardly know each other."

"Jenny, I've seen you with lots of people. Men. You tend to stay detached. You weren't detached with Ben Brisco. And neither was he. He'll be back because he can't stay away from you. If he's not man enough to act on his desires, then he's not worth it, anyway."

"So you believe in love at first…sight," Jenny whispered.

"If that's what's meant to be."

Jenny clenched her hand so hard around the soda can that the aluminum made a buckling noise. Setting the can down, she tightly linked her fingers in her lap. She rarely discussed her personal life with anyone, but Erin was forcing things out into the open, and she found it almost impossible not to voice her fears. "Erin, I'm scared."

"I know you are, honey. Because you didn't figure on a guy like Ben Brisco walking in the door."

In a rush of words, she went on as if her friend hadn't spoken. "Suddenly, I have no control—over the things that are happening around me or my feelings."

Erin reached across the table and covered her hand. "But you have the strength to deal with it."

"I—don't know." Ben Brisco was a challenge she'd never expected.

"Don't cut yourself off from him because you're frightened of getting close."

"Assuming I have the choice," Jenny murmured.

WITH THE KEY he'd obtained from the super, Ben opened the door to Duke Wakefield's tiny apartment. The moment he stepped across the threshold he was assaulted by the stench of old garbage. It was only one sign that the occupant had apparently left in haste. Around the apartment were strewn the contents of drawers, and closets.

Ben poked through the pile of trash in the corner, picked up an almost-empty bag of cheese popcorn crawling with ants and threw it down again with a grimace. Deciding to cut his losses, he backed out of the room. His head was throbbing, and he knew he should be home in bed instead of working the Blaisdell case. But after the fiasco of the night before, he needed to redeem himself and the only way he could do that was by catching the killer. However, it didn't look as if that was going to happen here.

In his car, he sat with his eyes closed and head thrown back against the headrest. Immediately, he was ambushed by a picture of Jenny's face floating behind his closed lids—the way she'd looked, panicked and upset, when they'd carried him out on a stretcher last night. He'd been too angry with himself to say anything when she frantically called his name.

Lord, he hated the mess he'd made of things. Ten hours after he'd met her, he was caressing her breasts and kissing her like a starving man invited to a feast. Only he hadn't exactly had an invitation. Never mind that he'd gotten hit on the head and lost all his normal inhibitions. He gave a little snort. Yeah, so what? He'd still known what he was doing. Taking advantage of the situation. Even now when he thought about it, he felt a mixture of chagrin and arousal that was as maddening as it was disconcerting.

When he'd gotten out of the hospital, he'd thought about calling her to tell her he was all okay. She had the right to expect it. But he'd been ashamed to face her.

Not only because he'd practically made love to her, but because there was no excuse for screwing up and letting the bastard conk him over the head. Probably it was the guy who'd murdered Blaisdell. He could have killed Jenny, too, he thought with a shudder. Except that Pete had told him she'd fought him off with a screwdriver, for God's sake. He should be grateful the guy had run away, but he couldn't stop thinking that Jenny had done a hell of a lot better job of protecting herself than he had. And he was the one who had put her in danger in the first place.

For all those reasons, it would be better for both of them if he stayed away from her. Still, it was impossible to get her out of his mind as he started the car and drove back to headquarters.

HE STOOD LOOKING at his closet, thumbing through his considerable wardrobe deciding what to wear. Not the fancy outfits he liked when he went out to his favorite bars, or the meter-reader's uniform that had come in so handy the other night. Something more subdued for his computer-bulletin-board and chat-room activities. Maybe a khaki shirt and pants for his new persona. A few days ago he'd been Oliver from *Love Story* but now he'd selected a new character to play— Lieutenant Frederick Henry, from Hemingway's *Farewell to Arms*. An American volunteer in the World War I Italian army, Henry gets shot in the leg and meets an accommodating English nurse in the hospital. He knocks her up, and they run off together to the Swiss Alps or somewhere like that and have a glorious winter together, until she goes into labor. She dies having the baby; the kid dies, too, and poor Frederick Henry is left with nothing. Perfect.

Humming to himself, he slipped on the khaki shirt and admired his image in the mirror. He was a good-looking guy— tall and muscular, and he could get the better of any woman. Wrap his hands around her neck and squeeze the life out of her—if that was his pleasure. He wasn't a sniveling little kid anymore, at the mercy of a woman who hated his guts for something he hadn't even done.

He whispered his real name: "Arnold Heizer." It was on

his birth certificate. Yet he'd been forced to play a role all his life—even when he'd been a baby in diapers back in Oklahoma City. Now he was his own man, and he could pick any role, any name he wanted.

As he buttoned the khaki shirt, he felt a jolt of anticipation. Of course, it wasn't necessary to dress up tonight. His new lady friend wouldn't care what he looked like until they actually met. But wearing the right outfit helped him to get into the part he'd chosen—and find the right woman. She had to be worried about her appeal, naive, ready to take a chance on a stranger. But most of all, she had to have a secret that was poisoning her soul. Like the big secret Meema and Mom had made him keep.

Only now that he was his own man, he'd figured out a way to ease the pain of his childhood and make himself whole again. He'd been lucky with Marianne. That second-story man he'd met at work had told him about her and her computer. And he'd nosed around the Internet services and found her on World Connect. It had been easy to break into the system and make some modifications that let him identify users by their names and addresses. So he was going to stick with it for a while, find himself a good woman, and settle down to a relationship. It wouldn't last more than a few weeks. He couldn't sustain it for longer than that. The pressure to complete the act built up too fast. Which was getting to be a problem, because he couldn't date too many women in Baltimore or the police would catch on and he'd have to leave the great job he had here and look for work in another part of the country.

But meanwhile, he was all set to go hunting in his favorite cyber-preserve.

EARLY THURSDAY evening Jenny pulled her chair in front of her home computer screen and with a few deft commands booted the software she'd ordered from the 800 telephone number a couple of days ago.

It was from World Connect, the on-line service Marianne had been using. For a nominal installation fee of twenty dollars, payable by credit card over the telephone, the company had been glad to download a version of their software for the visually impaired directly into her computer via modem.

She assured herself she was just curious about the venues where members could meet. Maybe if she explored a little bit, she could find out where Marianne had been hanging out.

Brisco would tell her to leave the investigation to the homicide division, but Brisco hadn't bothered to get in touch with her over the past few days. And Brisco wasn't feeling guilty that he'd steered Jenny's friend into an activity that had gotten her killed. Brisco probably didn't feel guilty about anything.

Banishing him from her mind, she accessed the list of chat rooms and bulletin boards. There were hundreds. Systematically, she thought about her friend's interests. Marianne had loved to read and she was interested in genealogy. And low-fat recipes, because she was always worried about her weight.

Taking the plunge, Jenny navigated to the cooking section and found a sizable group of people interested in diet recipes. When she started to enter their chat room, she quickly discovered she'd have to give her name and ID to participate.

No way. *Not yet,* she thought with a little shiver. She already felt like a kid who'd snuck into the adult section of the library. She wasn't ready to let anyone know she was there.

Investigating further, she found that on the bulletin boards she could remain anonymous as long as she only read messages and didn't reply. So she began paging through the posts, looking for names. It took only a few minutes to find a message from Marianne asking about good-tasting low-fat salad dressings. Several people had answered, including three men. It all sounded so friendly and normal, Jenny thought, as she deftly used her braille slate and stylus to take down their names and ID numbers. When she finished, she ran her hand over the raised dots that symbolized the letters. She could give the names to Brisco as possible suspects. But then what? Probably they were simply overweight junk-food addicts who would be horrified to find out that Marianne had been killed.

For several minutes she sat there, figuratively staring into space. She should probably give this up, she thought. But she was too wired to quit.

Switching to the literature-discussion group, she paged through the recent posts. The comments of a man named Oliver caught her attention. He was arguing rather eloquently that contemporary writers took themselves much too seriously—for the kind of product they turned out. Marianne had backed him up. From their comments it seemed they knew each other pretty well. Jenny jotted down his name and ID number.

The next day Oliver had changed the subject and launched into a discourse about literary characters with secrets. Then he made a generalization from literature to life. Secrets were poison to the soul, and you ought to get them out in the open before they ate away at you, he said.

Jenny wanted to challenge that observation. Everybody had things they felt compelled to hide. Why should you feel obligated to discuss your innermost thoughts? But she reminded herself that jumping in without knowing more about these people was risky.

She was about to switch to another topic when the doorbell rang, and she jumped in her seat.

"Jenny? Are you home?" a voice called from the front porch.

A little frisson went through her as she realized who it was.

## Chapter Seven

"Ben Brisco."

The way she said his name was like a warm flush of pleasure. She must be glad to see him, he decided as he stood on the porch in the twilight. The light came on, and he strained to see her through the translucent curtain in the door panel. He could make out her long hair and the suggestion of her features. What he wanted to see was her expression. Did it confirm the lilt in her voice? Or was he making that up? he wondered, pressing his sweaty palm against his thigh.

His heartbeat accelerated as the lock turned and the door swung open. He'd given himself a lecture on why it would be smart to stay away from her. But here he was with a bona fide excuse to be on her front porch—and his stomach tied in knots.

Taking a step forward, he drank in the details of her. The light was still too dim to make out her expression, but he could see she was wearing a pair of faded jeans and a T-shirt with a Far Side cartoon. It showed two Japanese-style monsters demolishing New York City. One was saying to the other, "Hey, Konga, fancy meeting you around here." Konga's head stuck out slightly where the fabric covered her right breast, and he felt a jolt of awareness as he remembered cupping that soft, warm weight in his hand. Thank the Lord she couldn't see his hot face, he thought.

"Brisco?"

"I like your shirt," he managed.

"Thanks," she murmured. "A friend picked it out."

"Can I come in?" he asked. "Or are you upset that you haven't heard from me?" He hadn't intended to say that. The words had simply zinged from his mind to his lips the way so many things did when he was with her.

"Yes," she replied softly as she stepped aside to let him in. He assumed she was answering yes to both, but he wasn't going to make things worse by asking.

Closing and locking the door gave him something to do. Then he had to turn and face her.

"Are you all right?" she asked.

"Yes."

He watched her swallow.

"I was worried about you."

"I'm sorry," he said. Another line he hadn't exactly planned. But as he said it, it sounded right. "I've been pretty busy. One of the guys on our squad is sick, so the rest of us have been putting in overtime on a drive-by drug-dealer shooting."

"Aren't you working on Marianne's case?"

"I am. But there are over three hundred murders a year in the city and only fifteen homicide detectives." At her nod, he continued, "Look, could we sit down? I've brought your friend's answering machine."

Her hands fluttered in front of her. "Oh."

"I don't want to put you out."

"Don't be silly."

*Meaningless dialogue,* he thought. They were avoiding the key issues. But that was probably for the best.

She turned quickly and led the way to the living room. After switching on a couple of lamps for him, she sat in an overstuffed chair next to the couch. He stopped in the doorway and looked around. He'd pictured her house without any particular visual interest, but she'd fooled him again. The living room was decorated with flair, in warm cinnamon and peach with gray-blue accents. The cinnamon color of the walls picked up one of the colors in the slipcover of the couch. The furnishings were traditional, comfortable. But a number of accent pieces like the Mexican bird on the mantel appeared to have been selected for their whimsy. The whole effect brought a little smile to his lips. He'd wanted to place Jenny in her environment, now he could do it whenever he liked.

"I'm plugging in the answering machine over by the window," he told her. "The cord's a bit of a hazard."

"I'll stay away from that side of the room," she answered stiffly. Apparently she'd thought better of the spontaneously friendly greeting. Maybe because she was remembering the way he'd practically made love to her on the floor of her friend's bedroom. That should make her nervous, all right.

Neither one of them had said a word about that. He wasn't capable of mentioning it, so he continued setting up the machine on the end table, then looked across at Jenny. She was sitting as if the chair back were full of cactus thorns, and he knew it wouldn't work to keep avoiding the subject of the other night. He had to say something. At least about the attack. "When we went to work on the computer, I was supposed to be protecting you," he said abruptly. "And I screwed up. I feel pretty bad about that."

"You didn't know someone was in the house."

He ran a hand through his hair. This wasn't going the way he expected. "You suspected he was there. I should have paid attention to what you were saying."

She didn't reply, and he didn't like the silence. Imagining what she was thinking, he plowed ahead before she could get the drop on him. "A good cop doesn't make assumptions that could get an innocent bystander killed."

"You feel guilty?"

He sidestepped the direct question and gave her more of his personal philosophy. "A good cop doesn't get hit over the head by a guy hiding in the dark."

"We were there for over an hour. He had a long time to prepare for the attack."

"You fought him off with a screwdriver!" he practically shouted, finally getting the worst part out in the open.

"You wish I hadn't?"

"I wish—" He caught the intensity on her face, and a caldron of seething emotions bubbled up inside him. He reached toward her, then let his hand drop back. He missed her only by inches because she was leaning forward, an urgent expression on her face.

"So after the attack, when you kissed me, did you know it was me? Or did you think it was the woman named Brenna?" she asked in a strangled voice.

He swore. "I mentioned Brenna?"

"Yes."

"I...don't remember that."

"Was it me you were kissing?" she insisted.

"Yes," he answered tightly. He owed her that much honesty.

A sigh dragged out of her. Her features relaxed and her face registered relief, and a kind of peace.

He wanted to leap off the couch and take her in his arms and hang on to her—body and soul. Yet he'd spent days telling himself that making any kind of declaration was the wrong thing to do. So he fell back on the arguments that he'd been using on himself. "It shouldn't have happened. It wasn't appropriate. I was out of line."

She sat very still, her hands folded in her lap. "You had a head injury. You weren't responsible."

"Yeah," he agreed quickly.

"So you don't have to blame yourself. And we don't have to worry about it anymore," she said softly.

In the middle of letting out a sigh, his feeling of relief evaporated. She was setting his mind to rest, giving him an easy out. Which must mean she was as anxious as he was to get past the kiss and down to business. Or was she sparing her own feelings?

"I presume you've brought something important on Marianne's answering machine," she said a bit too brightly as she settled into her chair.

He tried to judge whether she really felt more comfortable after their little discussion or whether she was simply a good actress. "There's part of a message where someone phoned Ms. Blaisdell but didn't say anything. I think it was the guy she was supposed to meet the evening she was murdered. My guess is she hadn't arrived yet, and he was calling her to see if she'd changed her mind. When she wasn't home, he decided to hang up and wait a little longer."

"So how can I help?"

"I'm hoping this call was made from the same place where she called you. If so, you may be able to give me some clues to the location. There's music playing in the background, but it's too faint for me to nail it down."

She answered with a nod.

The message started with the familiar sound of an open phone line. Jenny listened intently, her head tipped to one side, her eyes closed. A babble of voices filled in the background along with what must have been a band playing. But it was too faint for him to make out much beyond the observation that the rhythm was lively.

"Yes," she gasped. "That's the same music."

"How can you be sure?" he asked, struggling not to pin too much on her response.

"Well, the band is unusual. Rhythm and blues edged with a country twang. Marianne said she was at a bar in Fell's Point."

He'd have to take her word for it.

"I'm almost positive that was the group playing in the background when Marianne called me! She said the place was a bar in Fells Point."

He started to get excited, then tempered the enthusiasm. "Of course, there's a time problem I didn't think about," he mused. "Why didn't he know she was already there?"

"It's possible he didn't recognize her." Jenny paused for a moment. "She didn't want people to know she was losing her vision, so she worked hard to look…normal. If he was trying to spot a blind woman, he could have missed her."

"That's a workable hypothesis," he allowed.

"So now if we take a tour of the local bars, we can find the place. Somebody must have seen them together."

"What do you mean—we?" he demanded.

She appeared to give him a look so penetrating that he had to lower his gaze. "You said you couldn't distinguish the music."

"I could have the tape enhanced," he argued. "A lab can filter out everything but the band."

But she must have picked up on the uncertainty in his tone. She was too damn perceptive for her own good. "How long will that take?"

"The way things are now with our budget cuts, at least a week."

"And you'll lose momentum."

"Maybe, but I'm not going to take you anywhere dangerous again."

"It's a public bar," she shot back.

"It was dangerous enough for Marianne. If another blind woman comes in, she's going to be damn conspicuous," he growled.

"I'll leave my cane in the car and hang on to you as if I can't walk a straight line by myself. They'll just think I'm another tipsy bimbo."

His breath caught as he remembered her body pressed to his. "It could take a long time to find the right place."

"Tomorrow's Saturday. We can both sleep late."

The image that sprang to his mind—of the two of them together in a bed—probably wasn't what she'd intended.

"Admit it," she pushed. "You need me if you want to follow up this lead before it gets cold."

He thought about arguing, but she'd boxed him into a corner. Or perhaps he wanted to be boxed—and wrapped and tied with a bow.

"All right," he growled. "We can give it a try, but you stay with me at all times, and if I catch a hint of trouble, you're out of there."

"Okay," she agreed, then gestured toward her jeans and T-shirt. "I can't go like this."

"Sure you can."

"It'll be better if I look like I'm dressed for a night on the town. Give me a few minutes to change."

Without allowing time for further discussion, she stood and hurried toward the stairs.

Alone, he contemplated his line about staying with him at all times, then convinced himself that he was accepting her offer because he was, indeed, worried about the trail getting cold.

Twenty minutes later he heard her coming back down the stairs and looked up automatically. When she stepped back through the doorway, he damn near lost his breath. She stood there in jewel-green stretch pants and a matching top with gold and silver sequins scattered provocatively across the breast and over the shoulders. Dangling gold earrings ending in a cluster of gold and silver balls moved gracefully as she walked. And a small gold purse hung from a spaghetti strap over her left shoulder. The only concession to comfort she'd made was that she wore low-heeled sandals.

When he failed to speak, she stayed in the doorway, looking a bit uncertain. "So, will this do?"

"Oh yeah," he answered, his voice thick. He cleared his throat. "I mean, uh, you look very together."

A tiny smile flickered at the corners of her lips, and he suspected she could guess the effect she was having on him.

She used her cane to make her way down the steps and follow him to his car. Then she quietly laid it on the floor of the back seat and he started the car.

The silence of the next five minutes was broken only by the sound of a light rock station on the radio.

He took his eyes off the road several times to see her stroking the edge of the leather seat with her fingers the way she'd stroked the cutlery at the restaurant.

"This car is nicer than the one you had the other day," she finally said.

"That was police-department issue. This is mine."

"What is it?"

"A Celica. I picked it up secondhand. The engine needed some work, but a friend of mine did it."

"Oh."

The silence stretched again until she murmured, "So, aren't you going to offer me any candy?"

"Uh—sure." Fishing in his pocket, he brought out one of the cinnamon disks.

When she opened her hand, he pressed the candy into her palm, lingering for a moment, captivated by the feel of her skin against his.

"You're always prepared," she observed.

"With candy, anyway."

She unwrapped it, and he watched it disappear into her

mouth. Then she held out the wrapper. Again, he accepted the opportunity, stroking his finger lightly against hers. He felt her shiver and wondered if she was really brave enough to hang on to him the way she'd promised. He definitely hoped so.

She cleared her throat. "So tell me, you said you liked my shirt when you came in. I've got several with cartoons. Which one was I wearing?"

His head swung toward her. She looked a bit quizzical.

"Monsters destroying New York."

"Oh, right." She grinned, her white teeth flashing in the semi-darkness.

He did too, then realized she couldn't see the expression. "How do I let you know I'm sharing the joke?" he asked softly.

"You just did."

The ice was broken once more. For several heartbeats she turned her hand up and touched her fingers to his, and his blood raced.

He took his eyes from the road several times to look at her. Despite his best intentions, he was getting pulled in deeper, like a swimmer who couldn't fight a riptide. And he didn't have the strength to stop it from happening.

"That outfit looks great on you," he said huskily.

"Does it?"

"Yeah."

"Some of my friends help me shop. One of them—Sabrina— is kind of flamboyant. She made me get this, and picked the accessories, too. I wore it to her garden party last summer."

"She knows what she's doing."

"So do we look like we're going to the same party?" She found his arm, and ran her hand along the nubby fabric of the sleeve to the shoulder and then the notched lapel. "Sports jacket?"

"Yeah." -

"What color?"

"Black and gray. With a white button-down shirt, no tie, and gray slacks."

"Sounds conservative."

"I could stop home and get my leather jacket."

"You've got one?"

"Leftover from when I worked undercover narcotics."

She drew in a little breath. "It must have been dangerous."

"It was good experience," he answered quickly. One of the most harrowing of his life. He'd made it a kind of test. And he'd passed. But he wouldn't want to endure another two years of that hell again.

"I was worried about you," she softly repeated what she'd said earlier.

"I should have called." He said what he should have all along.

"You were busy."

"Not too busy to set your mind at ease."

They had reached Fells Point, and he slowed as he began to search for a parking place. There was nothing on Broadway, so he turned left along the harbor. A couple blocks down, he made a U turn in an alley, came back up the block and wedged the car into half a space in front of a stop sign.

"You must be lucky. There are a lot of cars circling around down here," she murmured.

"I'm pulling rank." Opening the glove compartment, he got out his police card, which he put on the dashboard.

"So are we ready?" she asked.

He turned toward her. "I want to make sure you know what you're getting into. The crowd can be kind of rowdy on a warm night."

"I've got protection."

"It's all relative. I once saw a guy come down Thames

Street carrying a huge, round cake he was holding up in the air over his head the way waiters carry trays. He stopped dead in his tracks and pitched it into the crowd."

"You're kidding."

"Nope. So don't blame me if you get covered with icing."

"Sounds like a free dessert."

He laughed. "Actually, people *were* scooping it up off the sidewalk and eating it."

"Yuck."

He nodded, then added, "Agreed."

AS JENNY WAITED on the sidewalk, she resisted the impulse to wrap her arms around her shoulders. She'd never been down here on a Friday night, and she had no idea how she was going to manage. She was assaulted from all directions by a thousand impressions. The heavy warmth of the evening air. The sounds of people laughing, talking, shouting, walking. Car wheels moving against the pavement. She felt naked without her cane but she wasn't going to admit it.

"If we head toward Broadway, we'll pass a lot of bars and restaurants," Brisco said.

"Fine."

"Time to try out our act."

Maybe he was hoping she'd back out. Instead, she stood without moving, fairly vibrating to the sound of his approaching footsteps. Her breath caught as he slipped his arm around her narrow waist. All at once she was buffered against the swirl of activity around her. Brisco represented safety, security. Or he would have, if he hadn't been so sexy. Every nerve ending was aware of her body touching his. It was well-muscled, supple, masculine.

And responsive. To her. She'd boldly tested that in the car, and thrilled to the knowledge that the kiss the other evening hadn't been an aberration. Knowing she was turning him on made up a little for her own uncertainty.

"If this is gonna work, you've got to look like you're enjoying yourself," he warned, his voice as thick as the blood pounding in her temple.

"Okay." Before she could reconsider, she slipped her arm around him and settled more comfortably against his side. His breath caught the way hers had.

Then her breast pressed against his ribs, and she felt an electric charge surge through her. Neither of them spoke. They clung together as if for support, and she wondered if she was crazy to think she could pull this off with a man who aroused her so powerfully. She was in a world of chaos. Yet all the other external stimuli were pushed into the background by her awareness of Ben Brisco holding her against his side. She knew he felt the shiver travel through her body.

"Steady," he murmured.

"I'm fine," she lied.

"Let's try it. On the count of two. One…two." His right foot moved. So did hers. He took several small steps, probably shortening his strides considerably, she guessed. She followed as if he were leading her in some sort of strange folk dance. There was a grace to their movements, as if they instinctively knew how to maneuver together. She had just started to relax a little when the smell of beer wafted toward her and a big person in what sounded like high-heeled shoes brushed by, knocking her against Brisco.

"Watch where you're going, buddy," he growled.

"That was a man? In high heels?"

"Cowboy boots," he said as he steadied her. "Maybe this isn't such a good idea."

"We've hardly given it a try," she argued, knowing she'd be disappointed if the experiment ended before it had really begun.

"Tell me if you want to quit." His movements weren't

quite so smooth as he steered her around the corner onto Thames Street.

Suddenly, there were a lot more people and more noise. Excitement. A big outdoor party. Most of the revelers were reasonably behaved, yet a few were not. She could tell when they passed, by the way Brisco's arm tightened protectively around her. If he let her go, she'd be lost.

"Lots of people," she murmured. She neglected to say that she wasn't comfortable in crowds. So she pushed everything but him into the background. He was enough to make her giddy.

"You're doing fine."

They ambled up the sidewalk, and he brought them to a halt in front of what seemed to be a popular bar, judging from the noise level inside.

"No cover. No minimum," a deep male voice said.

Jenny turned away from the speaker, hiding her face against Brisco's neck.

She felt him react, not anything she could define but a subtle change in him that she was starting to recognize.

"You got a band?" Brisco asked, his hand sliding along her bare arm, raising goosebumps.

"Rock."

"Maybe we'll be back later," he said before addressing her, "Come on, honey."

"You're the boss," she answered throatily. As they started off again, she felt dizzy. She'd never imagined herself glued to a man like this on a public street. But it was for a good reason. She had to look as if she fit in. Apparently, so did Brisco. As they walked, his lips nuzzled her ear, and she almost lost her footing.

"Careful," he murmured.

She wasn't being careful. Just the opposite. But she was going to play this through. For Marianne. No. She wouldn't lie to herself. She was getting high on being this close to Brisco. And she was certain the feeling was mutual—even though neither one of them was admitting it out loud.

They passed another bar where music blared from the interior. Brisco stopped and brought his lips close to her ear, his breath warming her several degrees. "Sound familiar?"

She listened for half a minute. "No."

"You're sure?"

"It's nothing like it."

"There's another place a couple of doors down. It's called Three Sheets to the Wind."

"I suppose that's a charming reference to Baltimore's nautical heritage."

"Right." He led her several yards farther along the sidewalk. As they approached the entrance, all she could hear were people talking and laughing. Another strike out. Then the band began to play, and she went very still.

"What?" Brisco asked instantly.

"I think…this could be it."

"How sure are you?"

She listened for another minute. The beat was very similar to what she remembered. But there was something different about the quality of the sound.

"What's the place look like?" she asked.

"Nautical decor. There's an old-fashioned diving suit in the window. The sign is on a ship's steering wheel. There's a porthole in the middle of the door."

"Could we go inside?"

"I'd rather not have you in there." The words were brusque, short, certain.

Jenny struggled to keep her protest quiet but insistent. "Marianne called me from the pay phone. I want to hear what the music sounds like from wherever that is."

Brisco hesitated for several seconds. Then he sighed. "All right."

Inside, the atmosphere was thick with cigarette smoke and the smell of beer. The noise from the band felt like it was going to shatter her eardrums.

"You want a table?" a woman asked. "'Cause you can't come in here just to use the john."

Jenny held her breath as she waited for the answer.

Long seconds passed before Brisco said, "Uh—a table."

The room vibrated with closely packed humanity. Although Brisco steered a course through the crowd, it was impossible not to brush against furniture and bodies.

She breathed a sigh when he announced, "We're here."

After finding the edge of a small table, she eased into a seat, practically jammed up against the wall. She was also jammed up against Brisco, who tried to move his leg away. Apparently, there was nowhere else to put it. She was left with the new stimulation of his knee against hers. She moved her leg a little, just for the pleasure of turning up the heat building inside her.

"Tight fit," she murmured.

"Uh-huh."

She hadn't thought his voice could get any thicker. She'd been wrong.

When the waitress came by to take their orders, he asked for a Coke. Jenny did the same. Around them, most of the patrons were drinking beer, and the smell made her stomach twist into a knot. She hadn't touched beer since high school. In fact, it was associated in her mind with her worst memories.

"YEAH, THIS PLACE is pretty raunchy," Brisco whispered and she realized her expression was probably as tightly knotted as her stomach.

She tried to relax. "Not Marianne's kind of place."

"Maybe it's the wrong one."

"Maybe it wasn't so crowded on a weeknight."

He made a noncommittal sound.

She brought her attention back to the band. Despite her previous comment about needing to hear the music from inside, she was pretty sure this was the place from which her friend had called. But she suspected that if she said so, the evening would come to an abrupt end and she wasn't ready to give up the thrill of being this close to Brisco. He'd told her he'd known who he was kissing. If she hadn't believed him when he'd said it, she did now.

The Cokes arrived, and she took a couple of small sips to moisten her dry mouth.

"Damn," Brisco muttered. "I see a guy a couple of tables away I busted for possession."

"And you don't want him to spot you," she murmured.

"You got it."

Before she had a chance to reconsider, she angled her body around and brought her hand up. Slowly she moved it forward until it was pressing the side of his face. Maybe it hid his features. Maybe it only gave her the excuse to touch him the way she'd wanted to since they'd sat down.

He drew in a breath, then answered, "Right," in a tone that gave her permission to go farther. Which was lucky, because once her hand settled against the scratchy surface of his beard, she couldn't stop herself from stroking it. Almost imperceptibly, he moved his face against her fingertips, sending warm currents racing through her. She'd never behaved like this. She'd never wanted to. Yet Brisco did something to her that made her want to throw propriety—and caution—to the wind.

Her pulse hammered as his hand curved around her back, tight and strong. She felt a surge of excitement that increased the sense of recklessness.

"So, do we fit in with the crowd?" she asked.

"Oh yeah," he growled, moving so that the other side of his face pressed against her cheek. Her heart lurched inside her chest. All she had to do was turn her head slightly, and her lips would brush against his. Then she could taste him again. That heady taste more intoxicating than wine.

She knew she shouldn't do that. Yet she wasn't sure what she would have done if Brisco hadn't taken the decision away from her. Oh so slowly, giving her time to pull back, he turned his head. She stayed where she was, thrilled by the first brush of his lips against hers.

It was a very light contact, yet heat coiled through her. Heat that had been building all the time they'd been walking up the sidewalk, all the time she'd been in his arms.

"Jenny." Her name came out as a strangled set of syllables.

His lips moved lightly against hers. Then he took several nibbling bites that she felt all the way to her toes.

Her eyes closed as his teeth played with her lower lip and his hand slid up and down her ribs. Fire raced across her skin. She forgot where they were, forgot everything but the taste of him. His tongue teased the sensitive flesh of her inner lips. She dared to do the same and gloried in his fevered response.

Her hand stroked under the lapel of his jacket. Absently she noted that his shirt was crisp oxford cloth—over strong muscles.

She didn't realize her other hand had slipped into his lap until she became aware of another tactile sensation—rigid male flesh straining against the fly of a pair of pants.

Instantly she snatched her hand back as if it had come in contact with the surface of a hot stove.

"Damn," he said. She could hear him sucking in several deep breaths.

She hoped it was too dark for him to see the blush spread-

ing across her cheeks. She could hardly believe what she'd
been doing in a public place—even if the last part had been
an accident.

They sat in silence for several seconds, then Brisco pushed
back his chair and stood up. "Where's the telephone?" he
asked someone.

"Back that way," a woman directed.

"Come on." His fingers laced with Jenny's, and she struggled to her feet.

It was disorienting to stand. Her head was fuzzy from the
cigarette smoke and the blaring music. She held tight to
Brisco as they wove between tables, her nerves jangling.
Once she hit the back of a chair. "Watch where you're going!"
a man called out.

"Sorry." She cringed, wishing she could escape from this
place that had turned into a nightmare. Too many people. Too
much noise. Too many feelings surging through her. All she
had to do was tell Brisco she was about to crack up, and he'd
whisk her outside, she told herself. Yet she wasn't going to
admit she was out of her depth.

The journey though the boisterous crowd seemed to take
forever. *One more step. It's only one more step,* she told
herself over and over. Finally they turned a corner. Magically,
the noise level decreased a bit, and she tried to shake off the
feeling of disorientation.

"The phone's at the end of the hall, past the toilets." Brisco
unlaced his fingers from hers, and panic leaped in her chest.

"Don't let go of me," she gasped.

He cupped his fingers around her arm, and she had to stand
rigidly to keep from trying to sink into him. "The hall's
narrow. We'll have to go single file. Are you okay?"

"Yes," she lied. To bolster the falsehood, she took several
small steps forward along the uneven floorboards, fervently
wishing she had her cane. It was her early-warning system,

and without it she felt exposed. However, she had no problem discerning that she was right outside the rest rooms; the offensive odors repelled her. With each step she took, her feeling of foreboding increased. It was like the morning she'd been afraid Marianne was dead.

The hot, fetid air seemed to press in around her, and she stopped short. This was the place. She knew it. And she wanted to get out now.

"Brisco?" she whispered.

He didn't answer, and to her dismay, she realized that she'd completely lost track of him. She didn't want to shout his name and call attention to herself, so she sped up, knowing she'd run into him eventually—unless he'd ducked out the back. And she was sure he wouldn't leave her here on her own.

Just then a whoosh of air and an intensification of the unpleasant smells announced that a door to one of the restrooms had opened. In the next moment, a man barreled into Jenny, pushing her against the wall.

She couldn't see him, but she sensed him as a massive presence. Automatically she reached to steady herself and encountered a handful of his shirt. It was covered with metal studs. Another cowboy.

"Why, sweetie pie, I didn't know you cared," he murmured, his hand suggestively moving up the front of her body, his speech slightly slurred.

"Sorry." She tried to wiggle away. He kept her captive, and she felt her throat closing.

"Please. Let go of me," she croaked.

# *Chapter Eight*

An angry shout reverberated through the narrow space, and footsteps pounded toward Jenny. Brisco's voice seemed to bounce off the walls of the airless hallway. "Take your freakin' hands off my girlfriend."

"Sure. I didn't mean any harm. She's the one who bumped into me," the voice whined.

Brisco's arm curled protectively around Jenny's shoulder, but he still addressed the stranger. "Get moving before I take you out in the alley and teach you some manners."

"Sure. Sure. No harm done." The man's footsteps beat a hasty retreat down the hall.

"Come on."

Jenny was shaking as Brisco clasped her hand and led her a few yards farther down the hall to a spot where the air was cooler and less fetid. Turning, he pulled her close, wrapping her in his strong embrace, his hand curving around the back of her head so that her face was pressed against his chest. Eyes closed, she nestled against him, letting his scent and the warmth of his body blot out everything else.

"Are you okay?" he asked softly.

"Y-yes." *Now.*

His hand soothed over her shoulders, bringing back a measure of calm. "What happened? I was taking a look at the phone booth. When I glanced back, that jerk was crowding you against the wall."

"I guess I was in his way when he blasted out of the men's room."

"That's hardly an excuse for manhandling you," he grated.

"Well, he probably thought I was alone."

"I'm sorry. I should have waited for you."

"It's not your fault. I should have kept up with you."

"But you couldn't without your cane," he said with a self-accusatory note in his voice.

Her head jerked up. "That's true. I couldn't. But I don't expect you to remember—"

His hand lightly touched her cheek. "I'm sorry. I forgot about it at first. I guess I was bent on getting out of here as quickly as possible."

"It's not the only reason I stopped."

"What else?"

She tried to put the uneasy sensation she'd experienced into words. "It was like…I suddenly felt anxious. The way I did the other morning when I tried to call Marianne and all I got was her answering machine."

"It must have been the music," Brisco murmured as he combed his fingers gently through her hair, sweeping it away from her face.

"I guess." She wasn't convinced that was all.

"So it's the same music you heard in the background when she called?" Brisco asked, his focus still on the original mission.

"Yes."

He breathed out a little sigh. "Let's head home."

A moment ago she'd wanted to get out of this place. Now she felt as if a door had slammed in her face. "I thought we were going to ask some questions."

"*I'm* going to ask some questions," he said. "When I'm back on duty."

"But—"

"I can't make you part of the official investigation. Besides, I've put you in enough danger."

"I'm fine."

"Sure. I left you alone for five seconds, and you got pawed by a drunk. Come on." He turned her and steered her back toward the noise of the main room.

The route to the door was more direct, and they were outside quickly. On the sidewalk, she breathed in the cool night air. But Brisco didn't give her time to enjoy it. Turning left, he steered her back the way they'd come. He still held on to her but the earlier feeling of intimacy was gone. It was as if he was deliberately putting distance between them—if not physically, then mentally. When they reached the car, he opened the door and she slid inside. Probably he regretted making out with her in the bar, she decided a few blocks later when he hadn't made any attempt to renew the conversation.

They rode in silence, giving her plenty of time to think about her behavior. If he hadn't called a halt, they could have been arrested for an R-rated performance in a public bar. If people were still arrested for that kind of thing. Or maybe the cops would have extended Brisco professional courtesy.

She gave a little snort.

"What?"

"Nothing."

"You were obviously thinking about something," he pressed.

"About making out in public."

His foot bounced on the accelerator, but he didn't comment. Moments later, he slowed the car, then turned to the right. As the vehicle began to bounce up a rutted track, she realized they'd reached her driveway. It hadn't been re-surfaced in a long time, and tires had dug two deep gashes in the gravel—giving Brisco the excuse of concentrating on his driving instead of answering her.

He pulled into the parking area and cut the ignition. Then she heard him shift in his seat. She wanted to reach for him, at least to lay her hand on his arm. But she sat very still, waiting for whatever he'd decided to say.

"It shouldn't have gone that far," he finally muttered.

"You're sorry again."

"Police detectives aren't supposed to get personally involved with witnesses."

Jenny knew the safest thing would be to let the subject drop. But somewhere along the line she'd decided to take a chance. "What if I weren't a witness?" she asked.

"It's complicated."

"You wouldn't want to get involved with a blind woman."

"That has nothing to do with it!"

"Right. You haven't noticed."

She heard him swallow. "Okay. What if…uh, I knew you? From before?"

Every muscle in her body tensed. "What do you mean?"

"I went to Howard High School—when you did. You wouldn't remember me. We moved to the area when I was a sophomore. I'm a year younger than you…."

She'd felt dizzy and disoriented at the bar. Now her head was spinning again. But the accompanying sensations were a lot less pleasant.

"So you know all about me. And you didn't think that was relevant?" she asked, gripping the edge of the car seat as if it were enough to steady her.

"Oh, come on. You turned up as a witness in a murder investigation. Knowing you wasn't relevant when I was interviewing you. In fact, if I'd said something about your background, you might not have been so cooperative."

"I—" She stopped, because she honestly didn't know if he was right.

"Exactly when was I supposed to tell you?" he asked.

Suddenly she was on firmer ground. "Before you kissed me," she answered back.

"You know damn well I wasn't in any kind of shape to be thinking things through."

Her ears heard the words, but her roiling mind had disconnected from the conversation. For twelve years, she'd cut herself off from everyone who had known the other Jenny Larkin. Call it habit or reflex or anxiety, but she wanted to keep it that way. Automatically, she opened the car door and stepped onto the gravel parking area, listening for the tinkling of the wind chimes on the porch. Their soft music was like a beacon in a storm, guiding her to a place of safety.

Behind her, she heard the other car door open. So she sped up as she crossed the parking area and stumbled when she reached the steps.

"Jenny."

Ignoring him, she grabbed frantically for the railing and recovered before she fell.

"Wait! You can't just leave like this," Brisco called out, his voice closer—too close.

Afraid he was going to grab her with those strong hands of his and forcibly keep her from leaving, she practically sprinted up the stairs.

"Don't!" he called, and she could tell he had stopped at the bottom of the steps. Thank God.

She didn't answer. She didn't want to be with him another minute, and it appeared that at least he had sense enough to leave her be. Scrabbling through her bag, she found her key and thrust it in the lock. Then she was inside. She closed the door with a mighty shove and leaned against it, panting. Praying that he wouldn't follow.

After a long moment she heard his footsteps recede. Then a car door slammed and the engine started. Finally there was only the crunch of gravel as he backed up, reversed and drove away.

She stood with her back pressed to the door for a long time, her breaths coming in uneven spurts and her mind circling like an animal trapped in a cage. So he'd known her in high school. He knew!

Sometimes for months at a time, she managed not to think about that part of her life.

Her fists clenched into hard knots. Stiffly, she made her way to the living room and dropped into an overstuffed chair. She felt cold all over.

"I'm sorry," she whispered, not even sure whom she was addressing. Maybe her grandmother. Maybe Craig Coopersmith, the boy she should never have dated.

She didn't want to remember the girl she'd been. But she was powerless to slam shut the floodgate of memories Brisco had opened. Maybe it started when her parents had died and she'd gone to live with Gran. It had been a good relationship, but not perfect, because Gran had been fearful of losing her, too. In turn, she'd been eager to please the one person left who still loved her.

All at once she couldn't sit still. Leaping out of the chair, she crossed to the steps and pounded up to her bedroom where she began to tear off the sexy outfit she'd worn for Brisco. She almost left the skirt and top in a heap on the floor. Then she imagined herself coming back and tripping over the clothing. With a sigh, she picked up the discarded items and took them to the closet. God, what irony. She was back where she'd started. Toeing the line. Only now she didn't have a choice. She rarely allowed herself to be angry. But anger seethed inside her as she yanked open a drawer and pulled out a pair of shorts and a T-shirt.

She was angry with Brisco for bringing it all back. And angry with herself for making it happen.

Her chest ached as she bent to exchange her sandals for socks and tennis shoes. Then she marched down the hall to the exercise room. Climbing on the bike, she began to pedal as she programmed the machine for a grueling series of hills.

Her legs worked furiously. But she couldn't stop the memories. In high school, something inside her had snapped, and she'd started testing limits, daring to leave her room a mess or not coming home on time for dinner. Then she'd gotten into a crowd where the kids were all too reckless for their own good. They all drank, a few girls got pregnant and some of the boys were caught stealing radar detectors from cars. Jenny had avoided the worst of it, but she'd been stupid enough to attend a party John Traver had thrown when his parents were on a weekend trip to New York.

The exercise bike started her up a steep hill at level six, but she was back in the nightmare of the party. Drinking beer. Making out even though she didn't really enjoy it. By the end of the evening, Craig said he was too wasted to drive. Hands on his hips, his face inches from hers, he'd given her an ultimatum. She was going to have to drive them both home if she wanted to get back that night.

That was her last memory of the evening. The rest was a blank she would never fill in. Later they told her she'd been driving up Lawyer's Hill Road. Witnesses said that she'd had the green light at Route 1, but an approaching car had failed to stop when the light in his direction had turned red. So technically, the accident hadn't been her fault. But a technicality had never salved her conscience. If she'd had her wits about her, she would have seen the speeding car and stopped. Or maybe she *had* seen him, and her reflexes had been too deadened to respond in time. All she knew for sure was what they told her later. The vehicle had slammed into the passenger side of her car, and the driver had died from the impact. Craig had also been killed outright. At least she hoped that was the way it had happened. She'd been hit in the face by flying glass and suffered internal injuries as well as a broken shoulder. Someone on the scene had pulled her from the car before it burst into flames.

Sweat dripped from her body as her long legs automatically pumped, and her breath came in harsh gasps. She was shaking, but she kept pedaling, her sightless eyes staring forward but her mind stuck in memories she would never escape.

She'd still been in the hospital when her class had graduated from high school two months later. A few of her old friends had tried to keep in touch. Most had been glad to put her out of their mind, because she was a painful reminder of how swiftly and terribly life could change.

Time had healed the physical wounds—except for the loss of her vision. The emotional damage had been greater. At first, she'd lain in bed feeling sorry for herself—yet sure that God had meted out a fitting punishment for Craig's death. Then a dedicated nurse had figuratively given her a swift kick in the butt. She could either be a burden to Gran and everybody else for the rest of her life, or she could make the best of the hand fate had dealt her. Outraged, she'd cursed and cried a lot. In the end she'd accepted the challenge. She'd gotten in touch with the National Federation of the Blind, which turned out to be right in Baltimore. She'd finished high school with a home tutor, then gone on to a training center for people who'd been blinded. She'd learned braille and computer skills and how to use a cane for mobility. And she'd completed four years of college at the University of Colorado. After that she'd gone out on job interviews and won a position—first in the records department of a bank, then with Birth Data.

Gran had died eight years ago. Probably she'd never recovered from the shock of what had happened to her granddaughter. That was another sorrow Jenny had to bear. But she'd learned to deal with pain. She'd learned to go on—and seem happy. She had lots of friends. She had a satisfying life. And she'd even dated a few guys. They'd all been blind, because she'd been comfortable with that. And they'd all made her feel accepted. They hadn't tried to dominate her as Craig had. But she wasn't very sure of herself around men. And none of them had set off sparks inside her. Although, she silently admitted, she really hadn't given any of them a chance.

Now there was Ben—so alive, so vital, so masculine. The intensity between them frightened and shocked her—and drew her to him. So she'd pushed to find out how he felt about the two of them. Maybe she'd even been secretly hoping he'd tell her it couldn't work out. At least that was safer than the unknown of a relationship. Safer than what had happened tonight. Any of it.

Finally, she was forced to stop pumping the bike. Her legs ached. So did her chest. What she needed was a shower and some sleep. But she wasn't fool enough to assume things would look better in the morning.

L. J. SMITH closed his eyes and leaned back in his ergonomic desk chair as he listened to the angry voice-mail message for the second time. The man on the other end of the line was so angry that he could barely speak two words without one of them being an obscenity.

"This is Havers. Listen, you S.O.B., I paid through the nose for some of your effing credit cards a couple of days ago. One of them is a piece of crap. The owner is dead. A woman named Marianne Blaisdell. We almost got our asses hauled into custody when we tried to use it. If you don't call me in the next twelve hours, I'm going to take action."

Smith's face contorted. For a moment he hesitated, then

he pressed the button that saved the message. He'd have preferred to erase it, but Havers wasn't going to go away. And he shouldn't. He'd get a refund on his whole order, an abject apology for the screwup, and an assurance that it would never happen again. Because in this business, when you lost your reputation for reliability, you lost your customer base.

Drumming his fingers on the polished wood surface of his desk, L.J. thought about his next move. The name Marianne Blaisdell was familiar. He'd seen it splashed across the front page of the *Baltimore Sun* a few days ago. She'd been murdered and her body dumped behind an empty row house.

Which left him with three undesirable possibilities. One of Techno Transfer's hackers had found her wallet with its credit cards and identification, figured California was far enough away for safety, and had decided to take a little shortcut in his work. Or the killer could have sold the credit cards to one of his guys. Both of those were pretty bad. But not as bad as the third scenario—that one of his employees was a murderer who was mixing business with pleasure, or whatever you wanted to call it.

Eyes narrowed, he opened the file that contained his personnel records. Most of his staff were quiet guys who spent as much time at home on the computer as they did at work. A couple had prison records; a few engaged in odd extracurricular activities but nothing that affected their work. Now he had to find the skunk in the woodpile. Somebody very dangerous—or reckless—or dumb. It didn't matter. Whatever had gone down, he'd have to terminate the guy. He'd done it before and he was fully prepared to do it again to keep his business functioning smoothly.

SCREECHING to a halt just short of the parking area in back of his Canton row house, Ben cursed silently under his breath. The kids next door had been building forts out of packing crates again and they'd left the debris scattered around his trash cans. Sighing, he got out of his car and cleared away enough of the mess so he could squeeze past. He'd complained to the boys' mother before and discovered she was overworked, underpaid, and struggling to keep food on the table since her husband had taken off for parts unknown. After that, Ben didn't hassle her too much and he spent some of his own limited time with her sons. But they still had problems he couldn't solve.

Not surprising, since he couldn't solve his own.

He sighed again as he unlocked the back door and turned on the kitchen light. He didn't see the dishes in the sink. Instead he flashed on an image of Jenny the way she'd looked as she'd dashed away from the car and up the steps as if she was afraid he might follow.

Eyes closed, he stood very still trying to wipe out the disturbing picture. It was replaced by the panicked expression on her face when he'd first come to the Birth Data office. He slapped his fist against his palm. He should try to get some sleep. But he knew that it wouldn't do him much good to lie down. He'd only see Jenny's face behind his closed eyelids.

His eyes opened and he looked around the kitchen, fixing on the dirty dishes. As he washed them, the smooth movements of his hands belied his inner turmoil. He was angry with himself. When he'd started to talk about going to Howard High, he hadn't fully understood what he was doing. But the drive home from Jenny's had given him plenty of time for self-analysis.

He slammed a mug into the soapy water and grimaced as hot suds splashed his shirt. He prided himself on his analytical mind and his sense of control. He'd never felt as out of control as he'd been ever since he'd heard Diangelo mention Jenny's name. He'd been helpless to stop himself from butting into the investigation, and helpless to govern his behavior when he was around her. All he had to do was get close to her and he started acting like an adolescent at the mercy of his hormones. Even now, remembering the taste of her lips or the electric moment when her hand had accidentally strayed into his lap was enough to make him hard again.

He understood what had happened, all right. The need to get the truth out in the open had become a pressure cooker building up steam inside his chest. Finally, he'd blurted out his confession and told Jenny he knew her, knew about the accident, because he simply couldn't go on lying after the way they'd turned each other on. He had to know if there was a chance for a real relationship between them. And the only way to do it was to come clean. He'd been prepared to tell her the rest of it, too, until she'd leaped out of the car and run away. Talk about picking the wrong moment. Now he wondered if he would get a second chance and whether he'd only screw up again.

JENNY HAD GONE to bed, but she'd known she couldn't sleep after that last scene with Brisco. Lifting her watch from the nightstand, she checked the time. Four-fifteen in the morning. She was going to be a zombie tomorrow. Thank God she didn't have to go to work.

Swinging her legs over the side of the bed, she stood and donned the pair of sweatpants she'd hung on the back of her closet door.

The bare floor was cold against her feet, but she didn't bother pulling on slippers as she made her way to the small room downstairs where she kept her computer. To her chagrin, she found that she'd forgotten to turn off the machine. It had been running the whole time she'd been down at Fells Point.

Unfortunately that wasn't the only thing she'd forgotten, she realized with a little groan. Her cane was still in Brisco's car. Luckily she kept a couple of spares in the closet.

When Brisco found the one she'd overlooked, would he try to return it? She stopped short as she imagined him knocking on the front door the way he had earlier in the evening. Then she lowered her head into her hands. She didn't want him knocking on the door. He'd lied to her, even if it was a lie of omission. Probably it would be better if she never saw him again. She'd tried to believe that as she'd lain awake in bed. Yet she wasn't sure she was being honest with herself. She wasn't sure of anything where Ben Brisco was concerned. Maybe she was simply a coward, and he'd given her the perfect excuse to break off a relationship that frightened her. On the other hand, she did know one thing for certain. She'd been the one to encourage Marianne to start meeting people on-line. So she was at least partially responsible for what had happened to her friend. When Craig had died, there was no way she could atone. She was in the hospital herself, trying to cope with the enormity of waking up blind—and finding out it was a permanent sentence. But this time was different. There was something she could do for her friend. She could help catch Marianne's killer. Even if Ben Brisco wanted her out of the loop.

She imagined coming to him with more evidence, and she felt her face glow as she heard the timbre of his voice when he praised her. The daydream expanded to his telling her he couldn't solve the case without her…. With a shuddering sigh, she cut off the fantasy before it could really form. What was wrong with her? She was doing this for Marianne, she reminded herself, not because she cared what Ben Brisco thought or how he felt about her.

With decisive movements, she reestablished the link with World Connect. She knew that Marianne had been thinking about a Caribbean cruise. According to the status scan, there were presently twelve people in a chat room discussing cruises.

At four-thirty in the morning?

Jenny knew she could read the bulletin boards without revealing her name and number. But she couldn't remain anonymous in a chat room. She'd have to disclose her identity—but only to a small, specialized group of night owls, she told herself. Taking a deep breath, she typed in her name and number and asked what ports of call were best for a first timer.

A guy named Scott told her how much he liked the Western Caribbean. A woman named Tina said she'd had more fun in Bermuda. Then a man named Fred jumped in to ask if Jenny was planning to travel alone.

"With a girlfriend," she quickly typed.

"So when are you going?" he asked.

"I'm not sure. I'm just starting to investigate the possibilities."

Fred named a couple of party ships, then asked, "Do you like to dance?"

"Love it," Jenny answered with what she figured was the right response.

"So did my late wife."

When she deliberately didn't pick up on the personal comment, he was ready with another question.

"Are you and your friend from Baltimore?"

Startled, she reared back from the computer. Instead of answering she said she had to get ready for work and signed off quickly. With jerky motions, she shut down the machine and sat with her shoulders pressed against the chair back as she reviewed the conversation. She hadn't mentioned where she lived. Did he have some kind of specialized equipment that gave him information ordinary subscribers lacked?

There'd been no way she could have anticipated anything like that. She wished she'd stuck to her original plan and stayed out of the chat rooms.

# Chapter Nine

The watcher hiding under the branches of the maple trees fifty yards from Jenny Larkin's house smiled to himself as he saw her pad past the window in a T-shirt and panties. She didn't have a clue that he was getting an eyeful. He could step out from under the trees and walk right up to the back door if he wanted, break the glass, go inside, and do anything he wanted. But he wouldn't make his move yet. Not until he knew for certain that nobody else was going to show up. Like that cop from the other day.

Taking a last drag on his cigarette, he stubbed it out and ground it into the dark soil with the heel of his running shoes. He was back on track. And he wasn't going to make another mistake like the one a few nights ago. It had been a stroke of genius to check out the records on research projects at that association for blind people. That was how he'd found out that Jenny Larkin was using the same computer system as Marianne Blaisdell. After the robbery attempt, Randolph Electronics had scooped up Blaisdell's machine, and he'd figured he couldn't make the delivery after all. But he'd kept checking around, because he hated to disappoint a customer who would pay sixty thousand bucks for one computer.

A hot, syrupy feeling had spread through his chest when he'd seen her and realized she was the bitch who'd damn near put his eye out with a screwdriver. His face still stung where she'd slashed him. But he was going to get even.

The back door opened, and she came outside. He went very still as he watched her take several deep breaths.

She tipped her head to one side, and he wondered if she'd come out for a little fresh air. Then she began to tap her cane along the surface of the wooden deck. She was heading for a metal trash can but she wasn't carrying any trash. He waited while she took off the top and dipped inside. She came out with a plastic container full of rice or something. He considered moving closer to get a better look but didn't. If she couldn't see, she probably had a great sense of hearing. But he had the upper hand, he reminded himself. He had twenty-twenty vision. And when he started chasing her, it was going to be fun watching her trip over rocks and roots and catch her hair in the tree branches as she tried to get away. Maybe he'd let her think she had a chance. That would add a little spice to the game.

His eyes never left her. She was heading toward a bird feeder, and he finally realized it was birdseed in the container. She was going to feed the little buggers.

He took a step forward. He was almost out from under the trees when an old sedan came up the driveway, and he froze. A gray-haired woman got out, and Larkin turned immediately toward the sound.

"Hester?" she called out

"Sorry I'm a little late," the old lady answered. "Traffic was backed up at Route 1."

Larkin finished filling the feeder. "That's okay. It gave me a chance to take care of the wild life. I'm going to need some more birdseed. Let me put it on the list and get my pocketbook. Then we can leave for the grocery."

"Your garden is so pretty," the woman named Hester murmured.

"Thank you."

"There are a few weeds along the edge of the path here. Do you want me to get them?"

"Thanks. I'd appreciate it." Larkin put the plastic container back in the trash can and set the lid firmly into place.

"Are you all right?" Hester asked as she tossed some unwanted greenery into the woods.

"Of course. Why do you ask?"

"You look a little upset."

"Well, I've had a few…untoward…things happen lately. But nothing serious. And nothing to do with you."

"So do you want to go anywhere else beside the grocery?"

"No. That will be fine."

Then they both went into the house.

The man in the bushes gave a satisfied little sigh.

He considered waiting until they'd left and grabbing the computer. He'd get his money and be finished with the job. But she'd know the machine was missing—and then the place would be crawling with cops. It might be weeks before he could get his revenge, and he wasn't about to wait that long. He wanted her to understand that she'd brought her punishment on herself by tripping him up at Blaisdell's.

BEN PULLED a candy out of his pocket, then grimaced when he saw the flavor printed on the wrapper. Passion fruit. After stuffing it into the ashtray, he concentrated on finding a parking space near Three Sheets to the Wind.

This morning he'd donated the remainder of the cinnamon ones to the secretary's candy dish and started on an assortment of exotic mixed fruit that he'd picked up the week before at Harborplace. The tart flavors had seemed like the perfect contrast to the cinnamon he'd shared with Jenny—until he'd discovered that passion fruit was part of the mix.

Damn, he was hurting, and it hadn't gotten any better after six hours of tossing and turning in bed.

After shoehorning his car into a space halfway down the block, he reached in his breast pocket and pulled out the picture of Marianne Blaisdell and Duke Wakefield he'd slipped from an album in her bureau drawer. It was a couple of years old, because the photographic record of their life together had ended abruptly. In the photo she looked wholesome and hopeful—a far cry from the woman whose battered body had turned up in a weed-choked backyard. Wakefield looked like a jerk.

There'd been no point in talking to the day staff, so he'd waited until the end of his shift when he should be on his way home.

Inside the bar, the evening crowd was still small. It would swell when the band arrived.

Ben flashed his badge at the lean, mustachioed bartender. Then he got out the picture of Blaisdell and her ex-husband. "Have you seen either of these people around?" he asked.

The man shook his head and went back to polishing glasses, so Ben began to canvass the waitresses. On the third try, he hit pay dirt with a dishwater blonde whose black uniform was two sizes too small.

The woman looked at the picture for only a few seconds before nodding her head. "I've seen her. I don't know him."

"In here?"

"Yeah. Either last week or early this week."

"How do you remember her?" Ben asked.

"She seemed out of place—nervous—like a crowded bar wasn't her scene. You know what I mean?"

"Was she alone or with somebody?"

"Alone—at first. She relaxed after she hooked up with a guy."

"He picked her up?"

"I'd say they'd arranged to meet."

"What were they doing?"

"They had some drinks and talked. Then they left."

"You're sure it wasn't him?" Ben asked, tapping the picture of Duke.

She shook her head.

"But you could describe him? You've seen him around other times?"

"He comes in here sometimes." She pursed her lips. "He was here last night."

That got Ben's attention. "Last night? What does he look like?"

"He's got different looks." She laughed. "Real different."

"How do you mean?"

"I guess he thinks he's a master of disguise. Sometimes he's got long blond hair. Sometimes it's shorter and dark. Sometimes he dresses like a biker—in leather. Sometimes like he just got off the early shift at Domino Sugar. Sometimes like a cowboy." She thought for a minute. "Yeah, last night he was Jesse James. Western shirt with fancy studs across the front. Boots."

"Yeah, Jesse James," Ben repeated. "What time was he here?"

"Same time you were. Left just before you did."

"You've got a good memory for faces."

She nodded.

His mind flashed back to the man who had barged out of the rest room. He'd been big, with long blond hair that didn't exactly go with his cowboy outfit. My God, could he have been the same one who'd killed the Blaisdell woman? He shuddered as he remembered the way he'd crowded Jenny against the wall.

"Anything else you can tell me about him?" Ben asked. "Eye color? Scars?"

"I can't give you those kinds of details. It's dark in here."

"Then how are you so sure it's one guy with so many different looks?"

"I don't know." She gave a little laugh. "Bad vibes. I started looking at him—noticing."

"Helen," someone called from the back, and the woman stood up straighter.

"Gotta get back to work," she said. "Unless I can serve you a drink."

"No." Ben got out one of his cards. "If you think of anything else, let me know."

She looked at the card, slipped it in her pocket, and took several steps away. "Sure," she called over her shoulder.

Ben left with a mixture of feelings. Maybe he finally had a murder suspect. But it wasn't going to be easy to ID him.

As he walked back to the car, he thought about what kind of man would spend his life wearing various disguises. He might not have a strong identity. Or he might hate the person he was supposed to be. Maybe playing games was easier than staying in touch with the real world. Or his mug was recognizable, because he had a record as long as the Statue of Liberty's arm. Too damn many variables.

He turned the key in the lock and opened the car door. Of course, there was another interesting line of speculation. Like, for example, what if Jesse James was the guy who had met Blaisdell through World Connect? Would he have more than one alias on the system? Just like he had more than one physical persona? That would make it even harder to catch the bastard.

SUNDAY MORNING, Ben took the kids next door fishing and managed to relax for a few hours. Then he went back to the Blaisdell case. At least that was better than sitting and brooding about Jenny, he told himself as he booted the special software that had arrived from World Connect.

The computer service was anxious to determine if one of their customers was stalking victims through the system and had agreed to cooperate with the Baltimore Police Department. They'd given him monitor access and sent the utilities that would allow him to track the usage of every subscriber over the past few weeks.

He'd spent Saturday night and most of Sunday afternoon familiarizing himself with the arcane instructions, which were obviously written for computer geeks, not police detectives. Finally, he felt comfortable enough with the system to give it a try.

Using his modem, he connected to the company headquarters in Boston. While the software and the main computer talked to each other, he unwrapped the tuna sub he'd picked up for dinner, but didn't have the appetite to eat any.

If Jesse James was from the Baltimore area and he'd met Blaisdell through the service, then the place to start might be with subscribers in the region.

When the computer signaled that Ben could proceed, he called up the member list. The register that appeared on the screen began with people who had signed up in the past few weeks. Well, he didn't need that, since both Blaisdell and the presumed killer had met each other on the system earlier. He was about to scroll past the names, when one caught his attention, and his heart leaped into his windpipe.

Jenny Larkin. Son of a bitch! Jenny Larkin had gone out and gotten herself a membership. And he'd bet his last passion-fruit candy that she wasn't researching background information on adoptees for Birth Data.

Forgetting that he'd planned to check the list of area members, he went right to another feature of the utility and typed in her ID. Seconds later, up popped a list of services she'd accessed along with the dates and times. She'd started on the cooking bulletin board. Then she'd read messages posted by the recently divorced and gone on to literature. As he looked at the time signatures, he realized she'd been on the service when he'd knocked on the door the other night! And she hadn't told him anything about it because she'd known he'd be mad as hell.

Before they'd gone to Fells Point, she'd simply been looking at bulletin boards. Later that night while he'd been tossing and turning in his bed, she'd gone into a chat room and posted her ID for everyone on World Connect to see.

The conversation had been at four-thirty in the morning. Was there a way to retrieve it? Pawing through the three-hundred-page reference manual, he found out that the material was held in a restricted buffer for forty-eight hours. By the time he finished reading the exchange, he was angry enough to spit nails.

He'd warned her to stay out of the investigation. He'd told her it could be dangerous. A grisly image leaped into his mind. It was Marianne Blaisdell, the way she'd looked when they'd found her dead in the alley, her face reflecting the pain and fear of her final agonizing moments.

LIEUTENANT FREDERICK Henry hummed softly as he booted his computer. While he waited for the World Connect software to go through its routine, his fingers lightly stroked the keys. Just a light caress to remind him of the pleasures that awaited this evening. He'd been on the system for four hours last night, chatted with several women. Women who couldn't sleep. Women who were looking for company on a computer network after midnight. A few of them had been aggressive—pushy. He didn't like that. It reminded him too much of Meema and her constant commands and warnings. Especially after Mom had split.

He remembered when that had happened because it was the day before the Halloween parade at school. A lot of the other second-graders had fancy costumes their mothers made. He'd been going to wear a sheet because he didn't have anything better. Mom had said she'd get him something from the dime store, and he'd been so happy, for once. As usual, she hadn't kept her promise.

He gritted his teeth. Those days were gone forever. He could be whoever he wanted. He wasn't a sniveling little kid. He had money, and skills, and all the women he could handle.

Mom had bailed out, and Meema had gotten worse. After that he'd spent as many hours as he could away from the house. A lot of the time at the public library. That's how he'd gotten into reading. It was magic when you could learn all about the lives of fictional characters and forget about your own miserable existence.

Things had changed for the better when he'd gotten big enough to hit back. He'd made Meema afraid of him. God, how he'd loved seeing the old bitch tiptoe around her own home. The home she'd told him so many times she would kick him out of if he didn't behave.

It was a shame he'd missed the chance to strangle her. But she'd had a heart attack and died in her sleep. He was seventeen by then. Incredibly, she'd named him the beneficiary on her insurance policy. Probably to spite Mom. So he'd lived in her house for a while. He'd already gotten into computer hacking—and figured out some ways he could make money through his modem.

Then he'd had his first love affair. With a waitress at the local diner, Nadine Packard. He'd told her he'd seen both his parents shot to death—like the poor kid in *Cold Fire* by Dean Koontz. She'd been so sorry for him. He'd enjoyed stringing her along, seeing how much bull he could feed her, until his hands had ended up around her neck one evening while he was bonking her.

What a rush. Of course, he'd had to leave town. But he'd

covered his trail. And the police had never tracked him down, or connected him to any of the others. Marianne Blaisdell was the eighth. Now he was planning his next conquest. Of the women he'd been talking to on-line, the one who interested him most was Jenny Larkin, perhaps because she'd been a little nervous—and cautious. He could always tell, and that was a turn-on. Or perhaps it was the sixth sense he'd developed for knowing when a woman had a secret.

While they'd been chatting, he'd used his special interface to the network software to find out her location. My, my. She lived right in the Baltimore area. That would make it easy to get together with her. Since she wasn't right in the city, he could have his fling with her, and the city police wouldn't even be involved. Perfect.

Would she like the story he was using? He'd given her a hint already. But she'd been too shy to respond. He smiled. He'd work the conversation around to his dead child next time. A real tragedy. Sweet little Jenny ought to respond to that.

BEN DIDN'T GIVE himself time to think about his motivation. He shut down the program, turned off the computer, and climbed into the car.

He didn't listen to the radio. He simply hunched grimly over the steering wheel, temples pounding, mind frantic. All he knew was that he had to keep Jenny from suffering the same fate as Marianne Blaisdell.

When he reached Jenny's house, he screeched to a halt inches from the porch, jumped out of the car, and took the steps two at a time. Then he started banging on the door so hard it shook.

No one answered for half a minute, and a moment of sanity broke through his anger as he wondered if the darkened house meant Jenny really wasn't home.

Then the porch light came on.

"Wh-who is it?" Jenny's voice asked.

"Brisco. Open up."

The bolt slid back. He turned the knob, surged inside and slammed the door shut behind him before she had time to ask what he wanted. He was breathing hard as he stood facing her, every muscle in his body tight.

Maybe she couldn't see him, but she backed away, her face pale in the dim light.

"What in the hell did you think you were doing?" he demanded.

"Wh-what do you mean?"

"Getting yourself on World Connect. Getting into a chat room and letting people know who you are."

"All I did was—"

He'd had the whole ride over to let his fear and anger build. Now that he could finally confront her, blood pounded in his ears so loudly that he could barely hear what she was saying. With a harsh expletive, he crowded her against the wall.

"Ben please—"

"What if someone came after you? I mean like the guy in the cowboy shirt last night. What if he grabbed you and took you some place where he could do anything he wanted?"

"I—I—"

"But he doesn't have to take you anywhere. He could come here, just like I did, and break the door down. Because you're so far out in the country, only the racoons and squirrels are going to hear you scream."

He had never been so furious in his life. Never been so wild with terror. He caught her hands and held them in one of his while he tipped her head up and stared down into her rigid face. She was frightened. He wanted her to be damn frightened. As flat-out terrified as he'd been when he found out exactly what she was doing on her sweet little home computer. He wanted to make sure she'd never try a stunt like that again.

Her lips trembled. "Ben, you're scaring me," she whispered.

"*I'm* scaring you? Don't you understand? This isn't a game. You think somebody on World Connect murdered your friend. Now you're flirting with strangers on the same system. Inviting them to switch their interest to you."

"I'm not—"

"Don't lie to me! I've read the transcript of your conversations. Suppose you were talking to the murderer? Or suppose he was one of the other people in the chat room. It doesn't matter which. He could find you. He could do anything to you. Anything."

He wanted to shake her until her teeth rattled. Somewhere in the back of his mind, he was flabbergasted at his wild-man behavior. He was acting like a caveman claiming his mate. But terror ruled him. Terror that something unspeakable might happen to her. That he might never hold her again, kiss her again.

She tried reflexively to push him away, but he didn't let her go. He slid his hands into her hair, tilting her head first one way and then the other. She was so vulnerable. God, what if he lost her? Something inside him snapped. He couldn't stop himself from lowering his mouth, the barest touch of his lips to hers. As he did, he let out a low, anguished groan that came from the depth of his soul.

She went very still. "Ben?"

He struggled to suck in a strangled breath, to get enough control of himself to speak coherently. "Jenny, don't you understand?" he growled. "All I could think of was what happened to your friend—and that maniac getting you, too." He wrapped his arms around her, pulled her to him, as if somehow he could keep her safe. But he couldn't, because she was an adult woman, bent on making her own decisions, unaccustomed to deferring to anyone else.

She was quivering against him. And it filtered into his consciousness that she might not want this, that, in fact, she'd sent him away the night before. His hands dropped away from her. "God, I'm sorry. I have no right to—"

She cut him off before he could finish. "Ben. Oh, Ben." As she spoke his name, her hands came up to clasp his shoulders, her fingers dug into his flesh. Then she arched into him, bringing her body tight against his. Emotion surged through him again. Only this time was different from the frantic need to yank her out of harm's way. This time he knew that she wanted the contact as much as he did. Tenderness overwhelmed him, tenderness so acute that his eyes misted. All his life he had been searching for this woman. Miraculously she was in his arms, wordlessly saying that she wanted him as much as he wanted her. He found her lips with his again. When she didn't pull back, he felt his chest expand.

Her hands left his shoulders to move up and down his back, restless, seeking. She made a low, erotic sound in her throat that turned his blood to fire in his veins. Each time before, he'd felt that their kisses were stolen, that the sweet pleasure might end at any moment. This time she opened her lips for him, inviting him inside. And he accepted the invitation, exploring the silky texture of her lips, the line of her teeth, the tip of her tongue.

They drank greedily from each other. Hard kisses. Softer kisses. Nibbling kisses. Long, deep kisses that made him weak at the knees. He cupped her head, his fingers exploring her luxuriant hair and under it the long, elegant column of her neck and the perfect curves of her ears. He needed more. He needed everything she was willing to give. Remembering the sweetness of her breasts, he shifted her to the side and stroked the enticing roundness.

This time, she wasn't afraid to tell him how it made her feel. "Oh… Ben…that's so good. So good." Then a little cry welled from her throat as he found the hardened nipple with his fingertips.

He wanted her so much he could barely function beyond a physical level. He ached to pull her hips tightly against his and let her know exactly what was happening to him. Yet somehow that sweet, pleading sound penetrated the fog rapidly filling his brain. He knew that if this didn't stop now, he was going to scoop her up in his arms, carry her to the couch and make love to her.

His hand lifted away from her, and she whimpered in protest.

He sucked in a ragged breath. "Jenny, sweet, we have to stop."

"No, we don't."

The protest almost shattered his sanity. "You're angry with me, remember."

She gave a sharp, surprised laugh as if she'd just recollected how they'd parted Friday night. "Ben, I want—"

"So do I." He kissed her cheek, brushed her damp hair back from her brow. He had been unsure of his intentions when he'd come here. When he'd taken her in his arms, he'd quickly discovered precisely what he wanted. It went far deeper than assuaging a temporary urge. He wanted her in his life—permanently. He needed to know for certain that she was his. And he'd wanted her to understand that he would never do anything to hurt her—or take advantage of her.

"But I didn't come prepared," he whispered. "I can't protect you. And I'm not going to take any risks with you."

She drew in a shuddering breath. Lowering her head, she nodded against his shoulder.

"Are you okay?" he asked in a voice that wasn't quite steady.

She nodded again.

Lacing his fingers with hers, he led her toward the couch. On the way, he bent to turn on the lamp on the end table.

"Sit," he said, and she obeyed.

He should probably take the chair, but he couldn't deny himself the pleasure of sitting beside her, looking at her flushed cheeks, her lips swollen from his kisses. Yet the uncertainty in her eyes made his heart contract. He wanted her so much and he wanted her to understand what he was feeling. It was everything he could do to keep from dragging her back into his arms and damn the consequences. But there was too much at stake to let momentary pleasure rule.

"I shouldn't have done that," he muttered.

"Which? Scared me silly? Or kissed me?"

"Either," he answered with a grimace. Somewhere along the line, he'd managed to forget exactly how it had started. Now he took a deep breath and tried to justify his Neanderthal behavior. "I'm sorry. I was so damn upset when I saw you'd been in that chat room that I—I went berserk."

"Well, that's something, anyway."

"I'm serious. You are not to do that again. Do you understand?"

"How did you know I was in the chat room?"

"Stop changing the subject. I want your word you won't do anything so dangerous again."

She raised her chin defiantly. "I can't give it to you."

"I won't have you risking your life!"

"It wasn't like that. I was just talking with a few people."

"Your friend thought it was innocent enough, too. But I've seen pictures of what he did to her body. It's not very pretty. And it wasn't a quick death."

Jenny sucked in a strangled breath.

"Jesus, I'm sorry," he said. "I wasn't planning to say that. But I'll do whatever it takes to keep you out of danger."

"Why?"

"Because I care about you," he growled, wishing he dared to say more.

He watched her hands twist in her lap.

"Jenny, since I walked into your office, I've been on a roller coaster. I'm not exactly acting like myself. Things are happening too fast. And I don't like the lack of control."

"I feel that way too," she admitted. "First I'm giddy. Then I'm angry. Then you scare me spitless. And *then* I'm ready to—to jump into bed with you. That's where we'd be now, if you hadn't stopped. Believe me, that's not my normal mode of behavior."

He found her hand, folded her fingers around his and brought them to his lips. "It wasn't easy to stop." Even now, simply touching her was doing things to his equilibrium.

She gently stroked his lips, sending shivers over his skin. "You're a good man, Ben."

That was his cue to tell her the rest of what he'd started to say last night. He swallowed hard, but couldn't get the words out. If she knew him a little better, knew how he really felt, the rest of it wouldn't matter so much, he told himself.

She moved a little closer and lowered her head to his shoulder. They sat like that for several minutes.

"So if you won't take me to bed, will you let me fix dinner?" she finally asked. "I mean, if you haven't eaten."

"I haven't."

She gave a little laugh. "I guess I'm not much of a seductress."

"Oh, yes you are. But all I'm going to take is dinner."

"Then how do vegetable quesadillas sound?"

"Wonderful."

She stood, and he followed her into the kitchen. Lord, he'd come out here so mad he couldn't see straight. Now she was cooking for him, as if everything was settled between them.

"Can I help?"

"Maybe. For now, just sit down and keep me company."

He was curious about how she managed things like cooking. So he relaxed into a pressed back wooden chair and watched as she opened a pantry door. Inside he saw rows of jars and cans, all neatly fixed with braille labels. Stooping, she took out onions from a bin on the floor. Then she brought baby carrots, sweet red pepper, and a jar of salsa from the refrigerator.

She washed the vegetables and assembled them on a large baking sheet with sides. He saw it acted like a tray, keeping everything within reach as she cut the vegetables on a board and felt around for any stray pieces. Then she carefully transferred them to a skillet. "Could you bring the olive oil? It's in the pantry. On the left. At eye level," she said.

He brought the oil, and she slowly poured a little into a small measuring cup, using her finger to check the amount. The oil went into the skillet.

After stirring the vegetables for several moments, she cleared her throat. "So how did you know I was in the chat room Friday night?" she asked in a tone that he knew was supposed to be conversational, but he heard the edge of tension below the casual words.

"I have special tracking software supplied by the company."

"The guy I was talking to—Fred—knew I lived in Baltimore," she said suddenly, a little catch in her voice.

He sat up straighter. He hadn't read the end of the conversation. "Did you provide that information to the new members' list?"

"No."

"Then it looks like Fred is accessing protected system files."

"Oh—"

"I'll check his account when I get home."

"I, uh, have some other names and numbers, too. Especially someone named Oliver from the literature bulletin board. He was having an argument with some other people, and Marianne was backing him up."

"Okay," he answered, trying to sound half-appreciative.

She turned her back to him, concentrating on the food. Then she spooned out a piece of onion and tasted it. "Not quite done."

He wasn't going to let her off the hook until he got the answer he wanted. "Do you understand why it was dangerous to go in there?" he asked.

"Yes."

"And you won't do it again."

"Yes. Could we drop it now?"

"Jenny—"

"Ben, please. You've made me realize I was in over my head. Okay."

"Okay."

A bell rang to announce the oven was preheated. "The flour tortillas and the grated cheddar are on the middle right in the refrigerator."

While the tortillas warmed in the oven, she cleaned up the work area, carefully feeling along the counter surface to make sure she hadn't missed anything. It was all an impressive demonstration of her abilities, and he felt a surge of pride that took him by surprise.

The timer rang, and she swiftly assembled the quesedillas.

A few minutes later, they were sitting down to eat.

"You're a good cook," he said after his second bite.

"It's an easy meal. Maybe next time I'll dazzle you with my beef burgundy."

"I'm impressed."

"I only do it for special occasions."

He wolfed down half of one quesadilla.

"How did you learn to cook?"

"I always liked it. When I was little, my grandma let me help her in the kitchen. I started off putting spices into canned soup and graduated to my own concoctions—and some of her old-favorite recipes. Then, after the accident, I had to learn new techniques. I was at a rehabilitation center for the blind for six months."

"Your grandmother? You lived with her?"

"My parents were killed in a boating accident."

"I didn't know that. How old were you?"

"Eight."

"That must have been…bad."

"It was. But Gran gave me the love and stability I needed."

He was about to ask another question when she asked one of her own. "How did you become a cop?"

"It's a long story."

"I'd like to hear it."

He took another bite before answering. "Well, I guess it goes back to when I was a teenager. I didn't feel very good about myself. I was too concerned with what other people would think. So I tried to conform."

"Like me," she murmured.

"It's probably a common condition."

"What didn't you like about yourself?"

"I wasn't very strong. Or athletic. And I wasn't able to buck the crowd. Before my senior year, I decided to mold myself into someone I liked better. I started jogging and working out with weights, and changed my body." He laughed. "Stronger, better, faster. At first I was tempted to pick fights with guys who had pushed me around. Then I realized that what I really wanted to do was help people."

"Clark Kent," she murmured.

"Well, not exactly. I went to the U. of M. and took criminology. Then I applied to the Baltimore police force."

"Why Baltimore?"

"It's where the action is. More of a challenge than the suburbs."

"How long have you been on the force?"

"Eight years."

"Do you like it?"

Again, he took another bite of dinner before answering. "I used to be pretty idealistic. More and more, I get the feeling we're losing the battle."

"But you keep at it. Like the little Dutch boy with his finger in the dike."

He laughed. "It's not just me. I work with a bunch of dedicated guys."

"You were married," she said suddenly. "What happened?"

"Lots of things. We were wrong for each other, so I started focusing too much on my job."

"Oh."

"I'm different now," he said quickly. "The job is important. But I keep it in perspective." He pushed back his chair, partly because he didn't like the turn the conversation had taken. He'd picked Brenna for her looks. Then he'd been disappointed when she hadn't lived up to his expectations. "It's getting late. I don't really want to leave, but I should let you get to bed."

Standing, he carried his plate and glass to the sink. She followed with hers.

"Let me help you with the dishes."

"Most things can be rinsed and put in the dishwasher." She pulled the door open, then leaned to turn on the water. Because she didn't know he'd raised his arm, her breast brushed against him. It was like a jolt of electricity sizzling through him.

He'd been careful not to touch her since they'd left the living room. Now he couldn't stop himself. She made a little sound as he pulled her toward him. Then his lips lowered and his mouth found hers again. He wanted to kiss her hard. He tried to keep it gentle. But it quickly deepened to passion as he angled his mouth one way and then the other.

They were both trembling when he lifted his head.

"I shouldn't have—"

She gave him a little smile. "I didn't exactly protest."

"Remember why we can't let this get out of hand," he warned, his voice gravelly.

"I'm trying. But, Ben, I've never felt this way before."

"What way?"

"So hot and shivery and needing—"

"Ah, damn."

"It's not that way for you?" she asked, lowering her head.

He stroked his thumb across her reddened lips. "It's exactly that way for me."

"Then—"

"Let me do the right thing. Okay?" he asked in a gritty voice.

She gave a long, reluctant sigh. "If you'll promise to come prepared next time."

"Ah, sweetheart." He could barely breathe.

She managed a strained laugh. "Now that I've got your attention, I was going to ask you a favor."

"What?"

"There's supposed to be a spotlight out back, but the woman who takes me shopping says it went out. I got a new bulb, but I haven't put it in."

"Are you worried about intruders?"

She hesitated. "I'd feel better with the light on."

He studied the tense lines of her face. She wasn't telling him everything, but he wasn't going to swing into another interrogation—yet. "I can do that, sure."

Her tone became brisk. "You'll need the step stool and a bulb. They're in the pantry."

He looked out the window. "I'll get the flashlight from my car. It's kind of dark out there."

"As a matter of fact, I have one—in case someone needs it. The kind you plug into a wall outlet."

"Great." After gathering the necessary equipment, he headed for the back door. Before getting to work, he moved the light in an arc on the ground—and stopped abruptly to examine something that shouldn't have been there at all.

# Chapter Ten

Ben was outside longer than she expected, and she waited tensely for his verdict. She hadn't been telling the whole truth when she asked him to fix the light. But she hadn't wanted to sound paranoid, either. Hadn't wanted to voice her vague fear that someone was watching her.

As she listened to him working on the light, she stroked her fingers against the edge of the countertop.

He was finished. But instead of coming inside, he moved away from the house, and she felt tension pool in her middle.

His footsteps were heavy as he came back across the porch. Something was wrong. She knew from his walk. No, she'd known all along. "Is the light working?" she asked.

"Yes."

"Good." She waited.

"Tell me why you were worried about somebody being out there," he demanded.

She gulped. "I—I thought I smelled cigarette smoke a couple of times when I went out. But it was very faint. Maybe I was mistaken."

"You weren't mistaken," he said sharply. "There was a cigarette butt on the ground near the back steps. And I found some farther away—in the woods. Somebody has been staking out your house."

She felt for the edge of the counter and pressed her fingers against the hard surface. She hadn't wanted to believe it. Yet he was right. She'd already suspected.

"The one near the door is dry. Since it rained this morning, it has to be from later than that. I don't suppose you remember anything else. Any noises outside?" The question was low, urgent, insistent.

She tried to remember anything specific but could come up with nothing. "No," she whispered. "That's why I convinced myself I was making it up."

"The ones under the trees are wet."

"Oh," was all she could manage.

"I found footprints, too," he informed her tensely.

"What kind?"

"Running shoes. They lead away toward a spot where I think a car was parked. Somebody has been here off and on for several days."

Chilled to the bone, Jenny ran her hands up and down her arms.

"I'm going to spend the night here," he told her in a tone that assumed no arguments.

"No." It appalled her to believe she was in any kind of danger. She'd spent years making this house into a place where she felt entirely comfortable and secure. Now someone was threatening that security. "Ben—"

He reached for her hand, held it tightly. "Your fingers are icy."

"I—"

"Come on. We might as well sit down."

She let him wrap his arm around her and lead her back to the living room. His embrace was like a circle of warmth. When he didn't follow her onto the couch, she turned her face questioningly toward his.

"I'll be with you in a minute."

She heard him moving around the room, lowering the venetian blinds. Then he switched off the lamp. When he came down beside her, she wanted to burrow against him. But she didn't, because she preferred him to think she wasn't in danger of going to pieces.

He stroked her arm. "This is an isolated location. Anybody could come up that driveway and—" He stopped abruptly and began again. "I'm not leaving you alone until I know it's safe."

"Nobody's here now." She was trying to argue past her terror.

"They could come back. Jenny, is there anyone who would want to hurt you?"

"I can't think of anyone. Except—"

"Who?"

"Duke Wakefield. Marianne's husband. He was angry at me for encouraging her to leave him."

"All the more reason I'd like to find him," Ben muttered.

"Do you think he'd hang around here? Watching me?" she asked in a low voice.

"I don't know anything about him—except that he moved out of his apartment. And he didn't have much to do with the neighbors." He looked around the room. "I can sleep down here."

"I have a guest bedroom."

"I'd like to be on the first floor where I can keep an eye on things better."

She heard him kick off his shoes. Then there was a rustling sound followed by something metallic hitting the table beside him.

"What's that?"

"My gun. I figure I might as well get comfortable."

He pulled her to him, his fingers stroking her shoulder and her hair. He didn't go any farther. She knew why. They'd been too close to doing something imprudent all evening, and he'd been going to leave. But now he was too worried about her. She listened to his breathing. It was quick and unsteady. All she had to do was turn her head and find his mouth with hers, and she could force the issue that had simmered between them.

"I'd better go upstairs," she murmured.

"That would be smart." But he didn't turn her loose. Instead, he pulled her closer. To her surprise, he lay back so that they were stretched full-length on the couch with her half on top of him.

"What are you doing?" she asked in a breathy voice.

"Torturing myself." He finished the sentence with his lips moving over her face and his hands shifting her so that she was draped over him. There was no mistaking his obvious arousal. The imprint of his body seemed to burn into hers, sealing them together with heat.

She'd never felt this alive, this vital. The blood in her veins had turned to fire as his hand slipped under her shirt and played across her back.

"Ben—"

"Shh." His lips nibbled along her cheek. "Let me tell you what I'm thinking, here, while I can still talk coherently. I'm off early tomorrow, so I can give you a ride home from work. And if you still want to make love with me—we can."

She couldn't hold back a frustrated moan that came from deep inside her.

He shifted her to the side so she was no longer on top of him.

She ducked her head and pressed her cheek against his neck. "Ben, I— In high school when a girl wouldn't go all the way with a guy, there were other things.... I mean..."

He gave a long, shuddering sigh. "Is that what you want to do?"

"If you do."

"It's been a long time since high school—and I didn't like it much back then. I don't want to settle for less than the real thing with you, sweetheart." He cuddled her against him. "But if you want me to make you feel better, I will."

Her face heated, partly because she wasn't sure what he meant. In her experience, it was women who made men feel better, not the other way around. "What about you?" she murmured.

"I told you what I want. I could say it a lot more explicitly, but I don't think it would do either of us any good at the moment."

She could hear the yearning and frustration in his voice. Tonight she'd learned a lot more about him. And not just physically. He wanted to protect her—every way a man could protect his woman. The realization stunned her, made her longing more acute and more bearable, all at the same time.

"If you can wait, so can I," she whispered.

"Ah, Jenny."

She found his hand and knit her fingers with his. "Let me stay here for a while."

"I like holding you."

She liked being in his arms, even if she couldn't have what she wanted tonight. She thought she was only resting, that she'd be far too tense to fully relax. But being with him felt so safe that she drifted off to sleep.

SHE WOKE with a start, disoriented and fearful. The slamming of a door had broken through the barrier of sleep. For a moment she didn't know where she was. Then she felt the texture of the sheets and the familiar thickness of the pillow beneath her head and knew she was in her own bed. She was wearing the T-shirt and sweatpants of the night before.

Firm footsteps came up the stairs, and she clutched at the

edge of the blanket, waiting. Then he walked into the room, and she knew it was Ben.

"You're awake," he said. "And I see I've startled you. I'm sorry. But I didn't want to call out, in case you were still sleeping. It's pretty early."

"I heard the door slam."

"The wind took it out of my hand. I was outside."

"Looking around?"

"Yes."

"And?" she asked, sensing that she wasn't going to like what she heard.

"There are fresh tire tracks on an old dirt road that runs parallel to your driveway."

She nodded tightly.

"It's good I'm coming back here with you tonight."

"Yes. But not because I was looking for a bodyguard."

He moved toward her, and she felt the bed shift as he sat down. She reached for his hand; his fingers wrapped around hers and held. He smelled like her soap and the shaving cream she kept in the shower.

"I hope you don't mind if I borrowed some of your stuff," he said, and she knew he'd caught her sniffing.

"Of course not. I have a vague memory of your carrying me up here."

"I thought you'd be more comfortable."

She leaned forward and found his shoulder with her cheek and then her lips. Tomorrow, she thought with a little smile, she'd wake up beside him. He nuzzled his lips against her hairline.

"Mmm."

"I'll get dressed and get you some breakfast."

"I made coffee. Chocolate raspberry. You have quite a collection."

"An indulgence."

"I'll give you a ride into town."

"Then I'd better call my van pool before I take a shower." He stood, and she climbed out from under the covers.

"I'll be downstairs," he said, and she couldn't help smiling.

"What?" he asked.

"I'm learning to read little changes in your voice. I think you're as nervous about being in my bedroom as I am about having you here."

"Right." His footsteps departed, and she quickly gathered up the things she needed and headed for the bathroom.

JENNY HUMMED while she waited for the printer to finish a batch of mailing labels.

"You're in a good mood," Erin said, stopping by the door.

"I've got a heavy date tonight."

"With Ben Brisco?"

"Uh-huh."

"Good for you."

The conversation was cut off by the ringing of the phone. It was Cameron Randolph. "I'll let you talk," Erin whispered. Then her footsteps departed.

"I'm sorry to bother you," Cam got quickly to the point. "But I have a little problem."

"How can I help?"

"I feel rotten about doing this, but I'd like to take back the experimental computer you're using at home."

"Oh, Cam. It's such a perfect system for me. What's wrong?"

"I've heard a disturbing rumor that someone is trying to steal the prototypes and pirate the technology before I can get them to market."

"Oh no. I'm sorry."

"I've already had the one at Marianne Blaisdell's picked

up. I'd like to bring yours back here where no one can get to it."

"I understand. But I hate to give it up." She let out a little groan as the implications sank in more fully. "All my software's on it."

"I've already thought of that. So what I'll do is trade you for the one you were using before. I can send Terry Richardson out to transfer your files to the old machine. But it would help if you could be there and tell him which stuff you need."

"What time?"

"He's on a pretty tight schedule. Can you get off around two? I can send a car to pick you up."

"If it's okay with Erin. Can I call you back?"

"Sure."

After clearing her early departure, Jenny phoned Cam back and confirmed the appointment.

"You remember Terry has a key to your house," he said. "Would it be okay if he got started before you arrived?"

"Yes."

After hanging up, she tried to call Ben. He was out of the office, so she left a message that she'd meet him at her house. Too bad they wouldn't get a chance to stop at the store, she thought. But there should be enough groceries in the house to make him a decent meal. If he felt like eating. She wasn't sure she could eat anything until later in the evening.

"WE COULD USE some help with this investigation," Ben told the woman in the wrinkled housedress. Her name was Sheryl Dyson, and her friend had called the homicide division to report that she'd said she knew something about the dead woman in the backyard across from her house.

"I didn't see nothing."

The women's bony hand clutched at the placket of her

dress, and her small black eyes slid away from Ben. Damn it, he knew she was lying.

"Your friend told us otherwise," he reminded her, trying to strike the right note of firmness and persuasion.

"Nelly? Now what call does she have to blab about me to the police?"

"She wants us to solve the murder. Catch the man who did this. Now, if you know anything about him, you'd better tell me."

"I don't know nothing," Sheryl insisted.

Ben thought about taking her down to headquarters. A half hour stewing by herself in a windowless room or a barrage of questions from him and Diangelo might get her talking. But she looked too frail to hold up under that kind of pressure.

With a sigh, he snapped his notebook closed. "I hope you sleep okay tonight. I hope for your sake another woman doesn't get murdered." He handed her his card. "If you change your mind, give me a call."

She slipped the card into the pocket of her housedress, and he saw a flicker of hesitation on her face.

"What do you want to tell me?" he asked.

She crooked her finger, motioning him closer. "You can't trust nobody these days," she mumbled.

"You can trust me."

Silence stretched, and he was sure he wasn't going to get anything out of her. But she surprised him.

"He was dressed up," she whispered.

"You mean in evening clothes?"

She snorted. "Not hardly. He looked like one of those guys who comes around and reads the gas meters. In a gray uniform. But I know he wasn't for real."

"How did you know?"

"Because he had on the wrong kind of shoes. My boy Roger had that job, and he used to complain to me that they wouldn't let him wear tennis shoes. Or whatever they call them now. Running shoes, I guess. Whatever they're called, they're not part of the uniform. But that was what this guy had on."

"Thank you for telling me," Ben said. "Can you describe him?"

"He had one of those gas-company caps pulled down over his eyes, so I didn't see his face. I guess he was a big man. Tall. Wide shoulders."

"His hair didn't stick out of his cap?"

"Not so you'd notice."

Ben asked more questions, but didn't get much of a description. "Thank you for helping," he finally said. "I appreciate it."

"I don't want anyone else killed," Mrs. Dyson mumbled.

He walked back to his car. She hadn't given him much to go on, but it was more than he had expected.

His face was grim as he started downtown. But his expression softened when he allowed himself to think about Jenny. A quick glance at his watch told him he had three more hours before he could pick her up. Three more hours before he could forget about murders and lying witnesses and lose himself in her sweetness. Last night she'd tempted him to the brink of his resolve. He'd come within a breath of accepting her offer. Now he was glad he hadn't. Because he wanted the real thing with her. Hell, he wanted everything. But there was still a chance he could lose her. If he didn't handle things right.

JENNY WAS DOWNSTAIRS and waiting for her ride at the appointed time.

A car pulled up in front of the building, and a window hissed down. "Ms. Larkin?"

"Yes."

"I'm Rich Mazel."

He didn't sound terribly friendly.

"Thank you for helping us out," he said as she climbed into the comfortable sedan and fastened her seat belt.

"Well, I'm sorry to lose the computer," she admitted as they headed out of the city. Then she thought about the cigarette butts Ben had seen on her property and wondered if someone was casing her place for a robbery. "But I wouldn't want anything to happen to it while it's in my possession."

Mazel murmured something in the affirmative.

"So, do you like being a driver for Randolph Electronics?" she asked to make conversation.

He gave a sardonic laugh. "Actually, I'm an executive in the research division. I'm just pinch-hitting."

"Oh." So that was it. He'd been pressed into service to drive the blind woman home.

The radio was turned to an oldies station, so there was no need for more conversation. At least they kept up a steady pace. As they pulled into the parking area in front of her house, Mazel made a little noise of approval. "Good. The van's already here."

"Well, thanks for the ride," she said as she reached for her cane. Then she hesitated. She hated being uneasy about going into her own house. But after last night, she was nervous.

"Do you need any help?" Mazel asked.

"Uh, could you come with me? I'd like to verify that it's really the technician from Randolph."

"It's our van. Who else would it be?"

"Yes, I understand, but—"

He heaved a sigh. "I really have to get back. I've got an important meeting in half an hour. But if you want me to go check out the place for you, I will."

She worried her lower lip between her teeth. He obviously wanted to get back to work now that he'd fulfilled his driving assignment. And she was probably being overly cautious. After all, there was no one here but Terry Richardson.

"No. I'm fine. Thanks for taking the time out of your busy schedule to bring me home," she said, trying to keep any trace of sarcasm out of her response.

He grunted, and she thought about informing Cam of his rudeness. Maybe she would. Almost as soon as she stepped out of the car, he pulled away. And she was left standing uncertainly in the parking area.

BEN'S PORTABLE PHONE beeped, and he reached to press the button. "Brisco."

"You have a call from Erin Stone," his secretary informed him. "She says it's important."

Erin? Had Jenny changed her mind and gotten Erin to call him with the bad news?

His fingers were clammy as he punched in the number. It seemed to take an eternity for the call to be transferred.

"Mrs. Stone? This is Ben Brisco," he began.

"Detective Brisco. I'm worried about Jenny."

"What's wrong?"

"She's on her way out to her house to meet a technician from Randolph Electronics. They phoned here a few minutes ago to see if she'd left. He was supposed to call the office from her house, but he didn't check in."

"She's on her way out there?" he asked, stepping on the gas. "Yes."

"I'll be there as soon as I can."

Hands gripping the wheel, he made a U-turn and headed out of the city. It was nothing, he told himself. She was all right. She had to be all right. But he couldn't stop his pulse from racing as he turned on his siren and floored the accelerator.

JENNY SLOWLY CLIMBED the steps, her footsteps ringing hollowly on the old boards. Almost reluctantly, she felt in her bag for her key.

Then she pushed against the front door and found it ajar. Wishing Terry had locked it behind himself, she called his name.

He didn't answer.

"Terry?"

As she stood in the doorway, a sense of uneasiness gathered around her like a storm about to break. Something—

Something was wrong. It took a moment to realize what was bothering her. Then it hit her with the force of a wrecking ball shattering a brick wall. The air was tainted with the acrid smell of cigarettes. Here, in her house. Did Terry smoke? She was sure he didn't.

Her mouth went as dry as cotton. As quietly as she could, she started to back out the front door. But it was already too late.

"Hello again." The harsh voice was grating. "We've been waiting for you."

The hairs on her arms stood on end as footsteps came across the floor straight toward her. It was someone heavy. Someone walking on his heels. Like the man from Marianne's house.

For an awful moment her body seemed paralyzed. Then she turned and dashed down the steps, almost stumbling when she reached the parking area. She no longer had her pocketbook, but her hand still miraculously gripped her cane. Swinging it in front of her, she banged against something large and metal. Probably the van. Dodging to the side, she caught her leg on the edge of the bumper and cried out in pain. But she didn't slow her pace as she veered toward where she expected to find one of the paths through the garden. She knew she was moving much too fast for safety, yet the footsteps following her drove her.

They crunched behind her. Keeping pace. But they weren't gaining on her. Maybe he couldn't run very fast. Maybe she had a chance. But where could she go?

Misjudging the path, she plowed into the branches of a small tree and cried out as the twigs snapped against her face, then caught in her hair. With a little sob, she pulled away and corrected her course, veering toward the woods, she hoped.

She was running through a nightmare landscape where rocks moved into her way and trees reached to grab her. But she had to keep racing on.

Behind her, she heard him laughing, and a sick, strangled feeling rose in her throat, almost choking off her breath. She knew in that terrible moment that he was playing with her, enjoying the chase, because he could catch her any time he wanted.

Yet she couldn't give up.

"Haven't you had enough?" he called out. Suddenly the steps were closer. A hand plucked at her shoulder. Screaming in terror, she sped up, stumbled, and caught herself with the cane.

"Careful. You don't want to hurt yourself," he taunted, his voice swelling with satisfaction. Her breath came in little sobs. He laughed again and let her get a little farther down the path before tangling a hand in her hair and pulling her roughly to a stop.

She screamed again, this time in pain. "No! Let me go."

"You didn't really think I'd let you get away, did you?" He spun her around to face him.

She didn't waste her breath on more pleas. With all her strength, she turned and struggled in his grasp, beat her fists against his chest. This time she had no weapon. And her blows fell on a body that was as solid as an oak tree.

Reaching up, fingers curled, she scratched aside thick, straight hair and tried to get at his eyes. He caught her hands in one of his.

"Not this time, you don't, you little hellcat," he spat out. His body had the same distinctive smell of sweat and smoke she remembered from Marianne's. But this time he wasn't in a panic. This time she hadn't taken him by surprise. Because he'd been watching her, planning this.

"I let a blind woman make a fool of me once. You're not going to do it again," he snarled.

# Chapter Eleven

All too quickly he brought her struggles to a halt. Her body was immobilized, but she could still twist her head. Shifting to find a better angle, she found the edge of his palm and sank her teeth into his flesh. With a low curse, he delivered a swift blow to the side of her head. The impact brought a galaxy of stars showering down in a black void. In the moment before she blacked out, she realized it was the first thing she'd seen in years.

She woke slowly, in stages, too disoriented to think clearly. There was a ringing in her ears, and time drifted past her like water flowing through a brook. She was in some sort of hot, cramped space where it was almost impossible to move. By shifting her body, she finally brought her hands together and touched her watch face. To her relief she found it was probably only about fifteen minutes since she'd first walked in the front door of her house.

She'd only been unconscious for a few minutes, but that was long enough to have drenched her body in perspiration and turned her limbs to lead. In fact, even the effort to find out the time sapped her strength. For long minutes she lay curled on her side, panting, her head still ringing from the whack the intruder had given her. The air around her was close and stale as well as hot, and her cheek rested against a scratchy surface that smelled like oil. Lifting her hand, she felt a curved ceiling inches above her head. It was marred with several large indentations.

At first, her fogged brain failed to put the sensory data together. It came to her suddenly that she was in the trunk of a car, probably an older American model. Testing the theory, she felt with her feet and hands and found the wheel covers. When she pushed against the roof, it wouldn't budge, nor could she work the catch from the inside. Panting, she fell back against the coarse blanket on which she was lying. It was hard to breathe, harder to move. She was trapped. But at least she was alive.

God, what if he'd left her here to die?

A scream rose in her throat. Somehow she kept it locked inside her. He might still be out there, and she didn't dare risk letting him know she was awake.

Her worst fears were realized when she heard footsteps crunching on gravel. A convulsive shudder racked her. He was coming back to finish what he'd started. Well, she wasn't going to let him do it without a fight. With deadly concentration, she scrabbled over the floor of the trunk, trying to find something she could use as a weapon when he lifted the lid. But there was nothing.

Agonizing moments ticked by as she lay in the stifling heat. He was playing with her again. Waiting for the right moment to open the trunk. Instead, she heard the left rear door of the car open. The vehicle shifted as he set something heavy on the back seat. Again, she tensed, but he only went around to the driver's side. The engine started, and the car moved forward.

Where was he taking her?

The car bumped down the ruts of the long driveway, throwing her around in the trunk. Each time she tried to brace against the walls of her moving prison she was pitched in another direction. When the car came to a screeching stop, she decided they must have reached the road. At least the ride should be smoother from now on, she told herself.

In the distance she could hear a police siren. Not an ambulance or a fire engine. They sounded different. Hope bloomed, then faded as her captor stepped on the accelerator, and the vehicle sped away from the noise of the siren.

HIS HANDS fused to the steering wheel, Ben tore down the road toward Jenny's house. Ahead of him, he could see a dark-colored car speeding in the other direction. If he'd been in the city and if he wasn't on another mission, he would have given chase. Now his mind had only one focus—to make sure Jenny was all right.

Turning in at her mailbox, he took the narrow, rutted drive as fast as he dared. He screeched into the parking area behind a gray van with Randolph Electronics on the back door. Gun drawn, he approached the vehicle, but there was no one inside. So he turned and made for the steps.

When he saw Jenny's open pocketbook lying on the front porch, he cursed silently. Carefully, he opened the front door. The hall was empty. So was the living room. Then he saw a shoe protruding from beyond the kitchen doorway. His heart stopped, until his eyes told him it was a man's shoe. Not Jenny's. Thank God.

He was in the kitchen in seconds and kneeling beside the man. There was blood on the floor around his head and a large lump on the back of his head. A quick check of his neck showed a pulse. He called for an ambulance and Howard County backup. Then he searched the house for Jenny. Bedroom, exercise room, kitchen, basement. The chance seemed bleaker with each empty room. In his gut, he knew he wasn't going to find her anywhere in the house. But he had to look.

TRYING TO KEEP track of the route her captor was taking, Jenny clung to the illusion that she was doing something constructive. The car turned left. Then right—almost certainly at Route 1. She struggled to imagine where they were going as the sedan sped up, changed lanes, made another turn. But her head was too fuzzy for her to remember more than a few turns. So why bother? She probably wasn't going to get the opportunity to tell anyone about it.

To tell Ben, she corrected. Oh, God. Ben. He knew she'd gone home to meet the Randolph technician. Would he call? What would he do when she didn't answer?

She wished she believed in telepathy as she tried silently to send him a mental message. *Ben, he's got me. Find him. Find me. Please find me, Ben. Because I've never been so terrified in my life. Ben, please, I need you.*

She said his name over and over—asked him to come to her rescue. But it was the only thing she could do to give herself a measure of hope.

The vehicle came to an abrupt stop. So did her heart. It started again in double time as she waited for whatever was going to happen. Cars whizzed past. Then a larger vehicle— a truck—shook the car as it sped by. They were on the shoulder of a road. A road with traffic. Maybe she had a chance.

When the driver's door opened, every muscle in her body went rigid. As she heard a key scrape in the lock of the trunk, she curled her hands into claws. Before she could bring them into position, he had whipped up the lid and pressed something cold and metallic to the back of her neck.

"It's a gun," he growled, "in case you can't tell."

She braced herself for the impact of a bullet.

"I don't want to shoot you. So don't give me any trouble," he whispered. "Nod if you understand."

She nodded, the barrel of the gun playing with the hairs at the base of her neck.

The wind gave a sudden shriek, finding her heated body and turning the sweat on her skin to ice.

"Come on." His large hand closed around her upper arm, and he started to drag her from the car. Then, incredibly, she heard another vehicle coming to a stop right behind them.

She felt his body shift as he shoved her roughly back into the trunk and pulled the blanket over her. "Say a word, and I shoot both of you," he said in a voice only she was meant to hear.

"You need some help?" a pleasant male voice called.

"No, the, uh, groceries in the trunk shifted around. I've got to pack them better or I'll break something."

"A bridge is a bad place to stop," the stranger commented.

"Tell me about it."

There was a long pause during which she could feel tension radiating from the hand that held her fast. He wasn't lying. He was going to shoot unless the man drove away.

*Leave,* she silently urged the driver of the other car. *Leave before you get us both killed.*

As if he'd heard her mental plea, the other man started his car up and drove off.

Her captor leaned into the truck. "That was close," he said in a more relaxed, almost conversational tone. "Got to hurry before someone else comes along and spoils things. Hope you have a nice time."

Confused, she didn't struggle when he pulled her from the trunk. Was he going to let her go, after all?

Her muscles cramped painfully, and she wavered on stiff legs. Grabbing her arm, he steadied her.

"This way." He turned her to the side and nudged her forward until she felt a curved barrier press into her middle. The railing.

Grateful for the support, she started to anchor her hand around the top. He pulled her fingers away. "I wish you could look down and see where you are," he said. "Or maybe it's more interesting this way. The same as when you took me by surprise with that screwdriver. Bye-bye."

In one swift movement, he pushed her up and over the railing, and she went sailing through space.

A scream tore from her throat as she plummeted like a rock dropped from a tower.

It was over before she had time for another scream. Her feet hit first. Hit something yielding and cold. The first contact was followed by a stinging pain as she plunged into—

Into water.

Instinctively she held her breath as she rocketed down, the water rushing past her like slick, deadly silk. The momentum of her fall carried her into the depths. Terror was mixed with clinical detachment. There was no way she could make it to the surface alive. But some reserve of inner strength, some will to fight for her life, made her kick her legs and flail her arms. With agonizing slowness, the downward spiral halted, and she began to struggle up.

Kicking, clawing her way, she rose through the resisting water. But it was agonizingly slow. Too slow. Her lungs were on fire, about to burst. She couldn't hold her breath much longer. It was going to be over soon.

Just when she was about to drag in water, her head broke the surface, and she took a thankful gulp of air before going under again. This time she didn't sink as far. Struggling upward again, she lifted her face toward the sun. Droplets splashed at her mouth and nose. But at least she could snatch in small breaths of air.

Her sodden shoes were dragging her down. Automatically, she kicked them off, as she struggled against shock and the terror squeezing its icy fingers around her windpipe.

BEN KEPT DRIVING, broadcasting a kidnapping report and a lookout for the speeding car, angry that he could give almost no details. The best thing he could hope for was that a state trooper might catch the bastard exceeding the speed limit.

He was heading down Route 104 when he caught a snatch of traffic on the Montgomery County police frequency. A motorist had reported a suspicious incident on Route 29. A car had been stopped at the bridge over the reservoir between Howard and Montgomery counties, and it looked like the man on the bridge was about to dump something in his trunk over the side.

Something—or someone? A deep and awful panic twisted in his insides. Not Jenny. He couldn't do that to Jenny.

There was no concrete reason to believe it was true. He didn't even know for sure if it was the same car. Yet a picture of the dark water far below the bridge loomed in his mind. In it, a woman was struggling frantically with no idea of which way to swim to safety. He told himself he'd conjured the image out of his own fear. No one could be sadistic enough to toss a blind woman off a bridge into deep water. Yet he'd learned a long time ago to trust his intuition. The panic clawing at his vitals threatened to tear through his flesh. The only way to ease the pain was to press the car's accelerator to the floor. He sped down the road, siren blaring, praying he could get to the bridge before it was too late.

SHE WAS IN DEEP water. She didn't know where. Or how far she was from shore.

Her teeth began to chatter, and tears of fear and frustration burned in her eyes. The cold water felt as if it were seeping into her body, turning her to ice.

She was going to drown. There was no way out. Then she clenched her fists in fierce determination. He'd thrown her in here because he knew she'd be terrified and disoriented. He was sure she would drown—perhaps after she floundered around in terror for a while. But she wasn't going to let him win. She was going to swim to shore. She had a date with Ben tonight and she was damn well going to keep it.

Clenching her jaw, she stopped the chattering of her teeth and tried to think where the shore might be. At first she thought of trying to judge the current. It would flow parallel to the bank, wouldn't it? If she swam across it, she'd reach dry land. Holding as still as she could, she tried to feel the movement of the water. But the reservoir was too still for her to make the judgment.

Despair threatened to swamp her. Her arms and legs were getting numb, and she knew that she couldn't stay in the water much longer. Then she heard a car cross the bridge and realized there was another way.

At first she could make out nothing but the vehicles passing far above her. Then she detected the sound of water lapping against rocks. Against the shoreline. Thank God.

Her hands and feet tingled with cold as she began to swim with a modified crawl stroke that kept her head out of the water. At first she had to keep stopping and listening for the lapping of the waves. Finally the rocks were close enough for the sound of the water hitting them to be distinct above her stroking arms and kicking feet. Changing the angle of her body, she found she could touch the muddy bottom.

With a grateful sob, she clawed her way up the submerged incline, banging her knee on a boulder as she made it to dry land. Finally, she sprawled on the bank, panting and shivering, her hair streaming with water, her clothes sodden. For several minutes all she could do was lie there gasping in air.

BEN SCREECHED to a halt at the Howard County end of the bridge, where a patrol car was already stopped.

The officer looked up questioningly as he trotted along the shoulder.

"Ben Brisco, Baltimore City police," he identified himself. "I called in the kidnapping."

"Well, if this incident is connected, the guy's long gone. I didn't spot anything suspicious in the water, but it's hard to see with the sun coming at you."

Ben shaded his eyes and squinted at the reservoir's surface, afraid he would see something, afraid he wouldn't. When he detected nothing beyond the glint of sunlight on the rippling surface, he wasn't sure whether to be terrified or relieved.

"Sounds like the motorist who called had an overactive imagination," the Howard County officer commented.

Ben nodded, but he continued to scan the area below. He was about to turn away when he saw a flicker of movement on the rocks above the water. His heart in his throat, he made out the form of a woman clawing her way up the hill. A woman with long, honey-brown hair.

"Jenny!" He started down the steep slope, half sliding, half climbing. "Call an ambulance," he flung over his shoulder.

Her head rose, and she appeared to be looking in his direction. Then she was scrambling toward him.

"Jenny, don't move" he gasped out as he barreled toward her. "I'm coming."

"Ben!" She ignored him, her movements more frantic as she changed course toward the sound of his voice. When she stumbled on a rock in her path and cried out, his anguished cry echoed hers. But she struggled up and kept moving. They met several feet farther down the slope, and he pulled her into his arms.

She was cold and shaking, her clothes sopping, her teeth chattering and she looked half-drowned. But she was alive. And she had made it out of the water and climbed two-thirds of the way up the hill under her own power.

He held her close, trying to transfer some of his warmth to her chilled body, trying to shelter her as best he could.

She reached up, running her hands over his face, stroking his cheeks, his eyebrows, his lips. He realized with a strange sense of rightness that he was doing the same thing with her, as if touch had become his most compelling way to make contact.

"Ben, it's really you. You found me."

He cradled her close and crooned low, soothing words, as much to reassure himself as her.

"What happened?" he croaked when he had enough control to speak.

"He…he was in the house when I got there. He hit me and I blacked out. I woke up in the trunk of the car."

"I think I spotted him just after he left your access road. But I didn't know what was happening."

"He threw me over the side of the bridge. Into the water. Ben, it was the man from Marianne's house. He wanted to— to punish me for getting the better of him," she finished with a little sob.

He curled his body protectively around hers, even as he uttered a string of curses. If it was the last thing he did on this earth, he'd get the sadistic bastard.

"I—I swam to shore," she gasped out. "I wasn't sure which way, then I listened for the sound of the water lapping against the rocks."

Lord, would he have had the presence of mind to do that? "That was pretty damn smart," he growled.

"I wasn't sure I could make it."

"You did it," he whispered, amazed at her strength and endurance even as he said the words. "You did it."

The wail of an ambulance pierced the air. Ben looked up the slope, wondering how they were going to get a stretcher down the incline. "Can you walk if I help you?"

"Yes."

Slowly, gently he helped her upward toward the road. Then the medics arrived and brought her the rest of the way. When they started to load her into the ambulance, her face turned frantically toward him, and she stretched out her hand. "Don't leave me."

"I won't."

A DETECTIVE NAMED Glen Patton from the Howard County police department arrived a few minutes after they'd brought Jenny to the emergency room at the county's General Hospital.

"I'd like to get a statement from her as soon as possible," the detective said after Ben told him what he knew.

Ben bit back a sharp answer. Usually he was the guy who pressed witnesses to talk. Now all he wanted was for Jenny to get some rest, but he knew enough not to interfere.

The nurse came in and said that the doctor had finished his examination. Ben charged through the door and saw they'd taken away Jenny's wet clothing and dressed her in a hospital gown. A sheet covered her legs. He wanted to rush to her side, but with a curious detective looking on, he contented himself with asking if she was all right.

"Yes," she answered in a slightly shaky voice.

"Detective Patton from the Howard County police is here," he told her. "He wants to ask you some questions."

"I'll do my best."

As Patton pressed her for information, Ben decided it was good Jenny couldn't see him, because he was so angry it took all his willpower to keep from bashing his fist against the wall.

"Was there a sexual element to the assault?" Patton asked.

"No," Jenny answered.

Ben watched her face. He thought she was telling the truth. Thank God.

"I don't suppose you can give me a description of the man who abducted you?" Patton muttered.

"I can tell you some things. He wasn't too tall. About three or four inches taller than I am."

"How do you know that?"

"His voice came from a little above my face. It was a tenor voice, with a slightly gravelly quality. He was smoking in my house. He probably smokes too much."

"Anything else?"

"Well, his footsteps are heavy. And when he picked me up, his arms were big and his body was chunky. I banged against his chest with my fists. It was solid. I'd say he works out. And he was wearing a knit polo shirt, if that's any help."

"Everything you can tell us helps."

She thought for a minute. "His hair is straight—and low on his forehead. I tried to scratch his eyes and had to push it out of the way. And, uh, his brows are thick."

Ben had forced himself not to interrupt, but he couldn't maintain the professional detachment another second. "Why didn't you wait for me?" he asked.

Her head jerked toward him. "I— Randolph Electronics was in a hurry to pick up their computer. They told me Terry would meet me there—" She gasped. "Terry—is he all right?"

"He's in the hospital with a blow to the head. I guess that's the perp's specialty," Ben growled. "When he's not thinking of more creative methods."

"But he's going to be all right?" Jenny persisted.

"I can check for you," Patton said. Apparently he'd gathered that the other two people in the room might appreciate some privacy.

When he left, Ben said, "I shouldn't have interrupted."

Ignoring the apology, Jenny hurried to explain what had happened. "Rich Mazel, the man who gave me a ride, had to get back to the office for a meeting. He said the Randolph van was right there, and…he acted like I was crazy hesitating about going into my own house."

"I'll make sure Randolph hears about that," he snapped.

"He didn't know. He thought—"

"Stop making excuses for him! He was in such a hurry he could have gotten you killed."

He saw she was on the verge of tears. "Jenny," he said softly, moving toward her. "It's not your fault. The last thing you need is for me to give you a hard time."

At that moment the nurse, whose name tag identified her as Sally Watson, came back. "We're ready to take Miss Larkin to a room in the medical wing."

"Isn't she all right?' Ben clipped out.

"We're keeping her for observation. I'm sure she'd like some help washing the reservoir water out of her hair."

His gaze shot to Jenny.

"I'm capable of taking a shower by myself," she said in a strained voice.

"Of course you are, dear," Ms. Watson said before addressing Ben again. "We'll let you know when she's nice and clean and ready to see you again."

Jenny's face was rigid. Ben wanted to yank Ms. Watson into the hall and point out that if Jenny had been able to extricate herself from a watery death trap, she could damn well take her own shower. But he supposed the nurse wouldn't be any more responsive than the waitress who hadn't believed which one of them had spilled the water. And if he gave her a tongue-lashing, she might take out her feelings on the patient. So he addressed himself to Jenny. "I'll be waiting for you when you finish."

She nodded tightly.

As soon as Ms. Watson took Jenny off in a wheelchair, Patton reappeared.

"Terry Richardson is going to be all right," he said.

"Good." Wearily Ben propped his shoulder against the wall. Now that Jenny was out of his sight, he was suddenly exhausted. But he needed to give Patton the big picture, so for the next fifteen minutes he briefed him.

"Thanks. I appreciate it," the detective said when he was finished.

"I'll send you a copy of the file."

Ben looked at his watch, hoping he could see Jenny soon. To his relief, Patton departed, and he was free to head for the medical wing. All he wanted to do was be alone with her. He needed to hold her, to kiss her, to make sure she understood why he'd gotten upset—and that he wasn't mad at her. And he needed to tell her about Richardson. She would worry until she knew he was okay.

He was striding toward the nurses' station when his beeper sounded. Phoning headquarters, he found that Diangelo had some important news. What timing.

He wanted to be with Jenny, but he knew he couldn't pass up the opportunity his partner was offering him. He asked Nurse Watson to explain to Jenny why he had to leave, then he sped back to the office. Two minutes after he walked onto the sixth floor of headquarters, he was standing at the one-way mirror outside a dingy interrogation room where Duke Wakefield sat slumped in a hard wooden chair.

"Thanks for waiting," he told Diangelo.

"I figured you'd want to be in on it. Besides, it's never a bad idea to let a guy like him stew in his own juices."

Ben nodded as he studied Marianne Blaisdell's ex-husband. He was short and chunky, with a ruddy complexion and deep-set brown eyes beneath a high, sloping forehead. He looked scared and nervous as he rubbed his fingers across his week's growth of beard. Sweat plastered his thinning hair to his head.

But that didn't mean he was guilty of killing anyone. An hour alone in an interrogation room could unnerve even an honest, upstanding citizen.

Ben looked at the arrest report and rap sheet. Wakefield had been stopped for a minor problem with his vehicle in West Baltimore and brought in for questioning about his wife's murder. There was also an outstanding warrant for nonpayment of alimony. They could use that if they needed it. Unfortunately, he'd been collared about the same time Jenny was being kidnapped. So he hadn't been at her house that afternoon. But maybe they could get something out of him if they pretended he was on the A list for Blaisdell's murder.

"Want to do a good-cop, bad-cop routine?" Diangelo asked.

"Yeah. You act like you want to nail him to the wall. I'll be his savior."

When Diangelo opened the door, Wakefield looked up belligerently. "You don't have any right to hold me like this—" He stopped abruptly as his eyes shifted between the two detectives. Ben had the instant impression that his presence had unnerved the man—as if they were old enemies—yet as far as Ben knew, they'd never met.

"You know why you're here?" Diangelo asked.

Wakefield slumped down in his seat, his shirt collar riding up around the lower part of his face, and shrugged.

"We'd like to ask you some questions about your wife's murder."

He kept his head down. "Don't know nothin' about that."

"You can save us all some time if you make a confession," Diangelo snapped.

"You arresting me?" He gave Diangelo a direct look. The effect was spoiled as his eyes shifted away.

Diangelo shook his head. "No. But we can hold you on

the alimony warrant. You kill her so you wouldn't have to pay?"

"You got it all wrong, man," Wakefield whined. "Why don't you go after the real guy and turn me loose?"

Ben joined the conversation. "I don't think you did it. But I need some help here. You understand?"

Wakefield barely nodded. It wasn't the response Ben expected. Most guys in his position would have jumped at the offer of aid and comfort.

"It was just bad luck you got picked up for that equipment violation," Ben tried.

The man's Adam's apple bobbed, and he pressed his lips together.

Ben's eyes narrowed. What was going on here? He gave Diangelo a nod. "Be right back."

The other detective looked momentarily surprised, then tore into Wakefield without missing a beat. Ben closed the door and looked through the window again. There was a definite change in the man's demeanor now that he was alone with Diangelo. He should be more uptight, because he'd been left to the tender mercies of the bad cop. Instead, he appeared to have relaxed a notch.

It didn't make sense, Ben thought, as his eyes flicked between the drama inside the room and the arrest form. Earlier, he'd skimmed over the specifics of the arrest. Now he noted that Wakefield had been stopped for a broken tail-light on his pickup.

He'd seen a pickup truck with a broken taillight. Another scene flashed into his mind. Jenny in the street, a blue truck bearing down on her. A blue pickup.

He went back to the report. The truck was blue. Presumably Wakefield knew Jenny was a friend of his wife. It wasn't any kind of conclusive evidence, but he could add another fact to the chain of suppositions. The driver of the truck had seen Ben dash into the street and grab Jenny. If it was Wakefield, he'd have good reason to be nervous about confronting him again, particularly now that he knew he was a cop—and assigned to his wife's murder case.

Ben's brow furrowed. Jenny had said Wakefield hated her for encouraging Marianne to get out of a bad marriage. Was he mad enough to try and run her down? Maybe, under the stress of hearing about his ex-wife's death. It made more sense than someone out for a random act of violence.

Laying down the file, Ben strode back into the interrogation room. Again Wakefield tensed, and Ben knew in his gut that his speculations were on the money.

He leaned close to Wakefield's face for maximum intimidation. "I've been trying to figure out why you looked so familiar, and I've put the pieces together. You know I can nail you for an attempted hit-and-run murder." That wasn't exactly the truth. It wouldn't be true unless the man confessed. But there were no rules against bluffing in the interrogation room.

"You ain't got nothing on me," he muttered.

Ben tapped the arrest form. "I've got the license plate of your pickup right here."

"So?"

"The first three letters match the letters on the license of the pickup that tried to run down a woman last Tuesday on Johnson Street."

The man behind the table hunched farther down in his seat.

"But I'm still willing to cut a deal."

"Like what?"

"Like I won't go after you for the hit-and-run if you come clean with us on your wife."

"I didn't kill her. I loved her! That's why I was after that Larkin bitch. She was the one who told Marianne to leave me. She was the one who pushed her into dating other guys. She was the one who got her killed."

The tirade stopped abruptly as Wakefield realized what he'd given away.

"You loved her?" Ben asked into the silence. "You had a pretty funny way of showing it."

"Okay. I was freaked when she started going blind. I mean, anybody would be. We needed her income, you know. And how was she going to keep her job? How was she going to take care of the house and all? But I missed her, and I looked out for her. I used to park at the end of her street and watch her house. That's how I know she spent so much time with that Larkin bitch."

"Did you follow her around, too?" Ben prompted.

"Yeah. Like the night she went to that bar, Three Sheets to the Wind. I hung around outside. She went in by herself and came out with this big blond guy." Wakefield looked at Ben. "You're not conning me, right? If I tell you what I know, you'll take care of that thing on Johnson Street?"

Ben nodded tightly. "It's up to the state's attorney. But I'll tell them you cooperated. What else do you remember about the guy she met in the bar?"

Wakefield thought for a moment. "He had long hair. Cowboy shirt, boots, jeans."

The same guy the waitress had described, Ben thought. The one who liked to change his appearance.

"Did you get a look at his face?"

"Yeah."

"Did you follow them?" Diangelo asked.

"I wanted to. But you know how the traffic is at Fells Point. By the time I got back to my truck, they were gone."

"If we bring in a police artist, can you describe him?" Ben asked.

"Yeah." He hesitated. "But you gotta protect me, you know."

"Sure."

Duke was almost eager to talk now. "Well, I saw him before, when I was worried about all the debts I was piling up after I lost Marianne's income and the court said I had to pay alimony to boot. I was thinking about, you know, maybe figuring out a way to get some of the stuff I needed. And a friend pointed out a dude who could supply me with a credit card—using some kind of high-powered computer technology, you know. I'm pretty sure it was the same guy."

"You're saying he makes computer-generated bogus credit cards," Ben clarified.

"Yeah. Only when I asked about the price, it was too damn much."

"You tried to run down a blind woman for breaking up your marriage, but you walked away from Marianne's killer." Ben struggled to contain his anger.

"He's dangerous," Duke shot back. "Bad news."

Ben turned away in disgust.

## Chapter Twelve

Ben glanced at the bright morning sunlight oozing through the grimy windows of the sixth-floor squad room—then at his watch. Jenny was being discharged at eleven. He'd have to hustle if he wanted to be on time to pick her up.

He'd stayed at headquarters until early in the morning—first wringing every shred of information he could out of Duke Wakefield, then waiting while Wakefield and a computer operator made a composite sketch of the man from the bar. Next Ben had logged on to the Baltimore police department system and paged through the fraud case files. After a couple of hours of digging, he'd discovered there was an ongoing investigation of an outfit called Techno Transfer that specialized in supplying counterfeit IDs, credit cards, and ready-made backgrounds. Listed among the long string of fraudulent transactions was an unauthorized use of Marianne Blaisdell's credit card.

Ben had slapped his fist into his palm and shouted "Yes!" Then he'd gone home for a couple of hours of badly needed sleep.

Now he scanned the information on Techno Transfer again. Six months of investigation had determined there were eight experienced computer hackers working for the illicit company. Did one of them like to dress up in a bunch of different outfits and change identities on World Connect?

The lieutenant in charge of the investigation had agreed to apply for a search warrant of Techno Transfer immediately. While they were looking for evidence of fraud, they might scoop up the killer. Meanwhile, Ben had put in for a couple of days of emergency leave, because until the murderer was safely behind bars, there was no way he was going to leave Jenny alone again.

He should be bone-weary, he thought, as he got up and stretched. But the prospect of folding Jenny into his arms had a wonderfully rejuvenating effect. Maybe she wouldn't feel well enough for what they'd planned. But if he could only hold her, that would be enough.

After briefing Diangelo on the new angle, he made one more call—to Randolph Electronics—and spoke to Cameron Randolph. His angry words about Rich Mazel were met by a quick apology.

Then Randolph cleared his throat. "As it happens, I was planning to call *you*. I understand you were having trouble using Marianne's computer."

"Yes, I couldn't figure out the operating system."

"It was more than that," Randolph informed him. "Someone overwrote most of the directory." He explained that whoever it was had tried to make it impossible to get at the data on the hard disk. But they had people working on it.

As interesting as Ben found the information, he told Randolph he'd be back in touch. He didn't want to be late for Jenny.

Half an hour later when he stepped off the hospital elevator, he was surprised to meet Erin Stone.

"What are you doing here?" he asked.

"Jenny's getting dressed. She called and asked me to bring her home." Perhaps it was an unconscious gesture, but she moved so that she was standing between him and the hallway to the patient rooms.

"I was planning to do that," he answered with more calm than he felt.

"You didn't say anything about it to her."

"I—" He stopped, realizing suddenly that she was right. He'd tried to phone her after finding out when she was going to be discharged but the line had been busy. Then he'd never had another chance to call. "I've been busy," he finally said. "Trying to get a lead on the bastard who killed Marianne and dumped Jenny off the bridge."

Erin continued to study him. "Jenny had a rough night."

"I would have been here if I could."

Erin barely nodded.

He swallowed hard. "Look, I know you're very protective of Jenny—because you like her and you think she needs special handling. She doesn't. She's a fully functioning adult who hates being treated differently because she's blind."

"*She* called me," Erin insisted.

Ben met Erin's steady gaze. "I care about Jenny as much as you do. You can trust me to do the right thing."

"You're saying I should get out of your way?"

"Yes. I'll take Jenny home."

After several seconds, Erin nodded. "All right."

Ben didn't wait for her reply. He'd already headed down the hall to Jenny's room and knocked on the door.

"COME IN," she called out.

The person entering the room wasn't Erin. It was Ben. She'd know his walk anywhere, and she felt her heart lurch inside her chest. She'd waited for him to call last night, waited to hear from him in the morning. Finally, she'd given up waiting and phoned her friend. But now he was the one who'd arrived.

After a moment of silence, she cleared her throat. "Ben?" As she tipped her head up, she suspected that her expression was guarded. He'd been angry with her yesterday. She wanted to come right out and ask if he'd changed his mind about the two of them, but she didn't have the guts.

"How did you know it was me?"

"Well, I don't believe Erin's gained sixty pounds and lengthened her stride in the past twenty minutes."

"Yeah. Well, I sent her back to the office." He moved toward her, stopping a few feet away. "You're looking good. No one would know you went for a surprise swim yesterday afternoon."

"I feel fine," she murmured. Except that her heart was thumping so wildly she could hardly breathe. Last night when reaction to her ordeal had set in, she'd needed him, and he hadn't been there. Now here he was, walking into her room as if they'd planned this.

"I should have gotten back to you," he said in that way he had of reading her mind. "I got wound up in the investigation. I think I've narrowed the list of suspects down to a handful. And the department's ready to move on it."

She blinked. "You had a breakthrough?"

"Well, Duke turned out to be a big help. For the record, he's the lunatic who tried to run you down outside the federation. We brought him in after a routine traffic stop. You were right. He blamed you for helping to break up his marriage. And he was thrown off balance by Marianne's death."

Jenny shuddered. "He would have killed me if you hadn't been there."

He moved closer, laid a hand gently on her shoulder. "Do you want to press charges?"

"No."

"Why not?"

"Maybe I did help break up his marriage."

"Marianne made her own decisions," he shot back.

"But I—"

"You've had a rough time lately," he said thickly.

"Yes," she whispered, leaning into him, finally relaxing a little. It was wonderful to breathe in his familiar scent, wonderful to feel his arm strong and firm around her shoulder.

His knuckle gently stroked her cheek. "Let's get out of here. I'll get your bag." He picked up the overnight bag Elizabeth Egan had brought the evening before. Elizabeth worked part-time at Birth Data and was also a graduate student at Hopkins.

Standing, Jenny took Ben's arm, and sensed him edge protectively toward her. It felt good. She allowed herself a moment to stroke the nubby fabric of his sports jacket. She imagined they made an odd-looking couple—with him dressed for the office and her wearing the yellow running suit Elizabeth had picked out because it was both comfortable and cheerful, she'd said.

In the parking lot, he opened the passenger door and then climbed behind the wheel. She heard him slip the key in the ignition, but he didn't start the car immediately. "What are you doing?"

"Looking around."

"For what?"

"Habit."

Did he think the man who had tried to kill her was lurking nearby? She felt a tight, choking sensation. She didn't want to think about what had happened yesterday. She wanted it to be over. And she wanted to know where she stood with Ben—exactly where she stood. It was hard to draw in a full breath, and she could hear her words come out in a rush as she said, "I'd like to stop at the drugstore on the way home."

He swung toward her. "Are you okay? Did the doctor give you a prescription or something?"

"I wanted to pick up some condoms—unless you already remembered to get them."

He didn't answer, and she felt her heart plummet. Well, better to know now.

"You're sure about that? I mean, you just got out of the hospital," he said in a strained voice.

"I'm sure."

He reached for her and kissed her fiercely. When he finally lifted his head, she nestled her cheek against his shoulder. "Ben, I wouldn't have gotten out of that reservoir alive if it wasn't for you. I told myself we had a date, and I was damn well going to make it."

"Jenny," he whispered, his lips playing with her hair and his hands stroking her neck and shoulders.

She longed to touch him too. And she did, feeling the recently shaved skin of his cheeks, the hard muscles of his shoulders and upper arms. When she slid her hand over his drumming heart, he clasped her fingers.

"I needed you last night," she whispered.

"I needed that, too." The words rumbled low and intense in his chest. "But Diangelo called to say he had Duke Wakefield in custody. He knew I wanted to be in on the interrogation. He gave us some information that links Jesse James to an outfit called Techno Transfer. I spent the morning getting Fraud to speed up their timetable for raiding the place."

"I guess you *have* been busy." She tipped her face toward him. "Who's Jesse James?"

"That's what the waitress at Three Sheets to the Wind calls the cowboy. I want him behind bars where he can't hurt you or anyone else again."

She burrowed closer, craving his warmth. "Last night I couldn't stop thinking about what it was like when he threw me into the water," she whispered. "I went down so far, I thought I'd never come up."

"Sweetheart, I'm so sorry I wasn't there."

"It's okay…now."

He held her for a few more minutes, murmuring words that sent shivers of anticipation across her skin.

"Drugstore," she finally managed.

"Right. There's one in the Wilde Lake Village Center."

It was only a short ride away. After pulling into a parking space, Ben cut the engine. "I won't leave you in the car."

She chose to put a positive interpretation on the statement. "I'll be glad to give my opinion of what product to buy."

"Based on what?" he inquired in a slightly thready voice.

"Well, I don't know much about condoms. I guess you'll have to read me the features on the labels," she answered cockily.

"This should be interesting."

He climbed out and came around to her side of the car. "There's a flight of steps leading up to the store."

"I'll be as graceful as possible. I wouldn't want to call attention to our mission."

She heard Ben laugh and gave him a little grin.

"YEAH, VERY FUNNY," muttered the man following Larkin and the cop. Pulling into a parking lot on the other side of a service road, he cut his engine. Then with a quick twist of his wrist, he also turned off the directional mike that had let him listen in on their stimulating conversation. He hadn't gotten the first part—when they'd been sitting in the hospital parking lot—because of some damn interference. But as soon as they'd started moving, he'd begun picking them up loud and clear. It didn't sound like he'd missed too much.

From his vantage point, the watcher could see them climbing a flight of steps. Well, Little Miss Goody Twoshoes had certainly fooled him. He'd thought he was messing with a chaste blind girl. Now he knew she was hot to jump into bed with lover boy. And the cop—Brisco—was hanging around so he could get into her pants, damn him.

Lips pursed into an angry pout, he climbed out of his car and walked with his arms folded tightly across his chest. A lady carrying two grocery bags gave him a curious look, and he ducked his head. When he raised it again, the happy couple had gone into the drugstore. He went alongside the building and in the front entrance.

Pretending interest in the greeting cards, he made his way slowly toward the back of the store, where he could see them. Snatching up a Father's Day card, he stared at the sappy sentiment, but anger made his vision blur.

He was furious with Larkin for getting out of that reservoir. And furious with himself for dumping her over the side of the bridge instead of simply putting a bullet in her brain. He had let his ego interfere with business—telling himself it would be fun to play with her for a while and then watch her flounder in the water. That was his first mistake. He hadn't been able to watch. He'd had to drive away. His second mistake had been thinking that she couldn't possibly get out alive. No, his third, he admitted. He never should have let her chase him out of Blaisdell's house with that screwdriver. If he'd whacked her then, he would have had the computer, and been on his way—instead of being left with this mess. It had been a matter of honor to finish her off. Now it was a matter of necessity because she could probably identify him. It was too dangerous to leave her on the loose.

"IS ANYONE LOOKING at us?" Jenny asked, fighting acute embarrassment. Was she really in a drugstore with a man, all but announcing to the world what they were going to do? Still, the embarrassment was tempered with a giddiness she hadn't felt since—well, since Ben had held her at his side for that memorable stroll in Fells Point. Then she'd been intoxicated by his closeness. Now they were getting ready to move a lot closer.

She longed to know where he saw the relationship going. With all her heart, she wanted it to last a lifetime, but she wouldn't make any demands. If he felt that something permanent with her was too much of a commitment, then she'd still have the memories of their time together. And she wanted that time, more than she'd ever wanted anything in her life.

He interrupted her musings to answer her question. "A little old lady with horn-rimmed glasses is looking at us like we're about to rob the place."

She flushed. "Really?"

"No."

"Ben, don't tease me."

"I'm nervous."

"You?"

"Let's just say I'm glad we have the back of the store practically to ourselves."

"It's too bad we can't order through the mail."

"We can. But we'd have to wait for delivery."

"Not acceptable."

"So what's your pleasure?" His voice was husky. "They've got about three hundred different choices."

"Such as?"

"Well, latex, natural lamb skin. Lubricated, or unlubricated. Ribbed…"

She was too embarrassed to ask what that meant.

"Extra long. Shocking pink. Strawberry-flavored."

"Flavored?"

"Only in specialty stores with black paint over the windows. Or by mail order in a plain brown wrapper."

"Um." She tried to sound nonchalant. But she knew her face was going to stay beet-red until they left the store. Maybe longer.

"Then there's the quantity."

"You're enjoying this, aren't you?"

"It has its points." He leaned down and gave the spot

behind her ear a quick kiss, sending bursts of electricity along her nerve endings. "We can get a three-pack. A twelve-pack. Twenty-four. Forty-eight."

"Forty-eight sounds like a commitment," she heard herself say. "But if you only get three, you might have to go out for more."

He made a strangled noise.

"Go for twelve," she whispered. Her hand was sweating, but she didn't pull away to wipe it. Her whole body was hot. "Your favorite brand," she tossed out.

"I think you have a distorted picture of my life-style."

"Do I?"

"I'm pretty selective about women," he confessed.

"Oh," she managed. There was a wealth of implications in his words.

SHEESH! Twelve. It looked like the cop wasn't planning to leave anytime soon. Maybe he could just follow them home and surprise the two of them in bed. That would be a hoot. The lovebirds naked and defenseless. This time he wouldn't screw up. He could snatch her right out from under lover boy. Except that the cop probably slept with his gun under his pillow.

He'd have to hang around until they came up for air. Maybe she'd send Brisco out for groceries. Then he could slip inside and grab her. Have some more fun. And finish it right there. That would give the cop a nice surprise when he came back home and found her.

"I HATE TO HURRY you, but a horny-looking teenage couple came in. I think they'd like us to move along so they can make a selection."

"Then pick something, so we can get out of here."

"Okay." He reached forward, and she heard him remove

a package from the shelf. Then he led her toward the counter, and she stood stiffly while he made the purchase.

"What did you get?" she asked when he climbed into the driver's seat and closed the door.

"Plain vanilla. No fancy features."

"So, what kind of expression is on your face now?" she asked. "Smug?"

"Try lustful. I'd give you a long, passionate kiss, but I'd better stay in shape to drive."

"Hmm. What kind of shape are you in?" she teased. She'd thought she was too reserved to play this kind of game, but she was finding out what a rush anticipation could be.

She got more than she'd bargained for.

"Since you asked…" Taking her hand, he carried it to his lap.

When her palm encountered his erection, she gave a startled exclamation. She'd never realized how much it would turn her on to touch his rigid flesh.

He muttered something incoherent, and she felt his body tremble as she gave in to her desire to stroke him. Caressing him made her feel suddenly hollow, as if her own body would never be completely whole until he filled her.

"Jenny…ah, Jenny." His trembling hand lifted hers away from him. "Bad idea," he growled. "Let's get out of here."

The key turned in the ignition and the engine started. That was the last sound in the car till they turned into the rutted tracks of her driveway.

Ben got out and came around to her side. She was on familiar ground, but she kept hold of his arm as they climbed the steps. Now that they were finally here, desire curled through her. Every sense was focused on him, every thought on what they were going to do.

"Do you have the key?" he asked, and she realized they'd been standing in front of the door for several seconds.

"Yes." She fumbled with the purse Elizabeth had brought.

"Let me." Her heart was pounding as his fingers brushed hers. He opened the door, and they walked into the front hall, their footsteps echoing on the floorboards. All at once she was unsure of herself. Would they go right up? He shattered her romantic illusions with a low, policeman's command. "Wait here, I'm going to check out the house."

"What?"

He took her firmly by the shoulders and moved her against the wall. "I'll be back as soon as I make sure everything's okay."

Then he was gone, and she was left standing frozen and brittle—feeling as if she would shatter.

As she heard him move stealthily down the hall to the kitchen, all the raging desire and sweet anticipation that had been building inside her evaporated. Instead of making love to her, he'd left her parked by the door while he checked the house for enemies.

She clasped her hands over her shoulders to keep them from shaking. She felt so damn frightened and disappointed—and she wasn't sure which was worse. Ben climbed the stairs, and she wanted to shout for him to come back in case there was someone upstairs waiting—like the night at Marianne's.

It was difficult to keep drawing in air and expelling it from her lungs. Trying to stand as still as possible, trying to stop her body from trembling, she strained her ears, listening for sounds of a scuffle—imagining Ben slumping to the floor again.

## Chapter Thirteen

She couldn't hear him, and fear leaped inside her. She was dizzy with it, sick with it. This had all happened before. Only last time…last time… Her brain wouldn't complete the thought. Finally she heard him at the top of the steps. It was him. She knew it was him. At least she hoped to heaven she wasn't fooling herself. He started down, then slowed as he drew near the bottom. She imagined she heard the sound of his gun being slipped into his holster.

He halted a few feet from her. "The house is secure."

She squeezed her hands into fists. "I wanted—" She stopped abruptly, afraid she'd break down if she tried to tell him all the things she was feeling. She suspected they were splashed across her face, anyway.

A long sigh eased out of him. "I'm sorry I frightened you."

The joy had gone out of the morning. The mood between them was shattered. Worse, she felt as if they were standing on opposite sides of a chasm instead of only a few feet from each other.

"Do you want to sit down? We can go into the living room." She heard disappointment mixed with resignation. She couldn't stand to hear either. What was wrong with her? Why was she shoving away the very thing she most wanted? And for the wrong reasons.

"Ben," she said on a sob, stretching her hand toward him. He closed the chasm, taking her fiercely in his arms.

"I was scared. It's so awful when you don't know what's going on—and you start imagining the worst."

"I know, sweetheart, I know," he crooned.

"Do you have to be so damn understanding?"

He gave a low laugh. "I thought that's what women are always saying they want."

Miraculously, she found she could laugh with him. As she did, the last of the frightened, disappointed feelings left her.

His voice was soothing. "I'm not going to take any chances where you're concerned ever again."

His hands slid up her back to her shoulders, where he began to knead her tense muscles. Closing her eyes, she melted against him, lulled by the brush of his lips against her hair and the magic of his tender caress.

The warmth she'd felt earlier came flooding back through her. She made a little sighing sound. His hands closed around her, lifting her, pressing her against his body.

"So tell me what expression is on your face," he teased.

"Happy. Turned on—if that's an expression. Perhaps a little worried."

"Let's explore that last one," he suggested as he rocked her body against his, the friction drawing a gasp from her lips. Luckily he was still holding her, because she wasn't sure her own knees would have held her up.

She hid her face against his shirtfront, breathing in his wonderful, unique scent.

"Tell me what you're worried about," he insisted.

"I don't want to disappoint you in bed."

"You couldn't."

"I—I don't have much experience," she whispered. "I—I haven't had many relationships. It, uh, didn't seem worth the effort. Sex was never like in books. No fireworks. I figured I just wasn't going to feel that way. Until I met you."

She heard him catch his breath. "This time is going to be different," he promised.

"It already is."

"Let's go upstairs." He laughed. "While I can still walk."

"I'm not sure I can."

"No problem." He swung her into his arms and strode across the foyer. After the initial surprise, she wrapped her arms around his neck and held on while he carried her up to her bedroom. When he set her down, the edge of her knee brushed the bedspread, and she knew exactly where they were standing.

"That was pretty decisive," she whispered.

"Yeah."

She knew from her limited experience how the rest of it would go—fast and to the point. But that was all right, because she longed to feel him shudder in her arms when she gave him the ultimate pleasure.

She heard him shrug out of his sports coat and toss it onto the chair. Then he surprised her with a request.

"Jenny, would you take off my shirt for me?"

She reached out, found his broad chest covered by crisp oxford cloth. She could feel his heart thumping as she slid her hand to the shirt buttons.

He stopped her for a moment by lifting her hands to his lips and kissing each in turn. Then he brought them back to his chest, and she began to slide open the shirt buttons, her fingers touching warm skin and crisp hair as the fabric parted. She couldn't resist slipping her hand inside, burrowing into the crinkly hair. When her fingertips brushed against a flat nipple, he caught his breath.

He felt good. Wonderful and sensual. And touching him brought a wanton heat to her own body.

His rapid breathing and wildly beating heart told her that he liked what she was doing. So when the shirt was out of the way, she traveled the path her hands had taken with her face and lips.

He bent to nibble at her ear. "My turn."

She was suddenly shy again, but she could deny this man nothing. "Yes," she whispered, nodding against his heated skin.

He must know how she felt because he didn't take a direct approach. Slowly his hands slipped under the back of her knit shirt and splayed against her flesh. Then they slid up and down her ribs, touching the sides of her breasts. She shivered, wanting more. He gave her tiny, provocative kisses as he unhooked her bra and pushed it out of the way. When he took the weight of her breasts in his hands, she couldn't hold back a satisfied cry. He seemed to know what would feel good, what would drive her higher and higher so that all she wanted was more and then more still.

She hardly noticed when he pulled her shirt over her head. All she knew was that she was gloriously free in his arms, moving her naked breasts against his chest, crying out with the rasp of his hair against her sensitized flesh.

He clasped her to him, restricting her freedom of movement. "I want the pleasure of watching your face when I touch you in all the places that feel good."

She was beyond knowing what to expect from him—beyond knowing what to expect from herself.

"I want you stretched out on that bed," he whispered. "Beside me. With nothing between us."

A shiver went through her.

"Does that frighten you?"

"A little. But it makes me…hot."

"Good." Again he took her hands and this time he brought them to the buckle of his belt. "But first I'd like some more help."

He waited patiently while she undid the belt and the metal hook at the top of his slacks before moving to the zipper, vividly aware of his rigid flesh behind it.

She felt him stop breathing as she moved her hands to his hips, slipping them inside his slacks and under his shorts, caressing his strong muscles. She wanted this, wanted him naked so she could love him. It was as simple as that. So she hooked her thumbs over the edge of his pants and pushed her flattened palms down his slim flanks. He exhaled the breath he'd been holding then, telling her how much he liked what she was doing. Using his feet, he kicked the pants the rest of the way off and out of the way. Her hands slid up and down his hips and thighs, learning his superb body.

There was one more place she needed to touch, one more part she needed to know. When her fingers brushed that hard shaft, he went absolutely still. She closed her hand around him, measuring his hot, rigid length and heard him utter an exclamation that was more groan than anything else.

His forehead settled against hers. "Ah, Jenny, sweetheart, that feels so good. Too good."

He stepped back from her, and before Jenny could miss his touch, his hands were back on her, removing her remaining clothes.

"Lord, you're so beautiful," he whispered. "You'd better let me lie down before you knock me off my feet."

She was the one who was having trouble standing. Just in time, she felt him bend to pull down the covers. Slipping between the sheets, she moved aside to make room for him.

He came down beside her and gathered her to him. She snuggled against him, wrapped in his embrace, his scent, his warmth. She had never imagined this much joy.

He kissed her eyelids and her cheeks before taking her mouth in a hot, deep kiss, and she discovered that there was more.

"Let me love you, Jenny."

"Yes."

She thought he would part her legs and move between them, and she waited for the warm sensuality to change to insistent male urgency. Instead he pressed his lips to the thrumming pulse point at the base of her throat before sliding them lower, kissing the tops of her breasts and finally finding one distended nipple.

"Oh, Ben. Oh," she gasped in pleasure as he took it into his mouth and sucked. She gasped again as his fingers mirrored the erotic touch with the other side. A small explosion seemed to go off inside her, and she arched into the caress.

He murmured low erotic phrases against her skin as his hand slid slowly down her body, giving her time to know where he was headed. When he cupped his fingers over the mound at the juncture of her legs, she tensed. But the tension changed into melting desire as he began to caress the exquisitely sensitive flesh.

Again she called his name. Then she could only draw in panting little breaths as the gliding strokes of his fingers turned her molten. He took her to some high plane she had never visited before, then higher still. Until her body writhed and her hands moved restlessly, beseechingly over him.

"Ben, please—" she pleaded, not even knowing what she sought.

"Yes," he murmured. "Oh, yes."

When his hands left her, she whimpered. He told her that he was getting the condoms he'd set on the night table. Then he was back with her, over her, gently moving between her legs.

She felt his touch and started to tense, afraid she wouldn't find pleasure in this part of their lovemaking. Her first surprise was his tender kiss as he surged forward and into her. Then he went absolutely still.

"Ben," she gasped.

"Did I hurt you?"

"No. Oh, no."

"My sweet Jenny." He kissed her as he began to move. At first it was a slow sensuous rhythm that tuned her body to his, then faster, as hot currents surged through her. Frantically she moved against him, desperate for something she couldn't name. She felt as if she were on the verge of exploding. Her heart hammered, her body was drenched in sweat, vibrating with pleasure almost beyond bearing.

She would die if she didn't—if she didn't—

"Ben, I need—"

His hand moved between them, stroking as he had before. Then, with a sudden convulsion, her whole body tightened and released over and over on wave after wave of ecstasy so intense that she sobbed out his name.

She heard him shout something incoherent as he went rigid above her.

Jenny clung to him, lost in a haze of rapture as little aftershocks of pleasure still quivered through her. Ben rolled to his side and took her with him. The physical storm had left her limp, the emotional storm was even more intense. "I didn't know…." was all she could manage.

He kissed her damp brow. "Well, now I feel damn cocky."

She giggled. "I guess you should."

An arrogant male laugh vibrated in his chest as she cuddled against him. "You must be exhausted. I am too. I only got a couple of hours sleep last night."

"So what are you like in bed when you're fully rested?" she murmured.

"You'll find out later." Reaching down, he pulled up the covers that had slipped to the bottom of the bed. "I'll be here when you wake up."

L. J. SMITH GLANCED at the door, then back at the kneehole under his desk. Bolted to the right side was an easy-to-access holster that had come in handy during business meetings back in the early days of Techno Transfer. He hadn't used it in a few years, but this afternoon he'd loaded it with a .357 Magnum in preparation for his conference with Arnold Heiser. Heiser was one of the most talented hackers working for him, but also one of the most dangerous. A couple of times another fellow in the office—Billy Compton—had tried to pick a fight with Heiser. He'd walked away in cold silence. After the second incident, Compton hadn't come back to work. Smith was used to a certain amount of staff turnover. He just wasn't sure that particular departure had been voluntary, or even whether Compton was still alive—even though he'd electronically transferred the remaining balance in his bank account to another institution. L.J. had ignored his nagging suspicions because Heiser was so good. Now he couldn't afford that luxury.

He turned to his computer and scanned his file on Heiser. Probably the man thought he'd wiped out his tracks, but L.J. knew a good deal about him. He was from Oklahoma City. He'd had a mediocre school record—and a couple of minor scrapes with the law. He'd kept to himself. No school sports. No after-school clubs. But he had taken a job as a bag boy at the local supermarket to make his spending money. The family had been lower-middle-class. There were two kids. The other was a sister who was fourteen years older. The parents were in their mid-fifties by the time Arnold was born. Pretty late for a pregnancy, Smith mused. The father had died the year after that. When Heiser was eight, the big sister had run off with a small-time hood and never reappeared.

L.J. paged down to the newest information, stuff he wished he'd dug up earlier. The week Heiser had left Oklahoma City, a woman who worked as a waitress at a diner near his home had been found dead in a rural area east of town. There was no conclusive proof that Heiser had done it. But the woman had been strangled—the same as Marianne Blaisdell, whose credit-card information had ended up in the Techno Transfer database.

The door opened, and L.J. glanced through the window into the outer office. It was Heiser, right on time and looking pleased to be there. The rest of the staff had the evening off because L.J. had told them that the electric company had scheduled a power outage, so there was no point in hanging around.

That gave him plenty of privacy for his chat with Heiser, who thought he was coming in to get a bonus for his excellent performance.

JENNY STIRRED, suddenly aware that she was cold. Irrational panic seized her as she felt over the bed for the large, male body that had been keeping her warm.

Ben wasn't there, and she started to get up, then realized she was naked—except for her watch. She was still wearing it, and it told her the time was late afternoon.

Heat flooded her as she recalled her lovemaking with Ben. She'd never thought she was capable of such sensuality, but he had proved her wrong—the way he'd challenged so many of her assumptions. He was a skilled lover. She had sense enough to realize that. But she had responded so deeply, so totally. And she knew that would be impossible unless... unless she loved him.

The realization shook her. She'd been afraid to open herself so completely. But it had happened anyway. She'd been helpless to deny her feelings for Ben. She hugged the knowledge to her heart, wondering when she would have the courage to tell him, wondering when she'd lose the edge of worry that tempered the joy.

Footsteps sounded on the stairs, and the tempting aroma of food drifted toward her. Snatching at the covers, she pulled them above her breasts just before he stepped into the room.

"Hi." His greeting held that smile she'd come to savor so much.

"Hi." She'd bet her expression matched his.

"How are you?"

"Wonderful."

"Glad to hear it. I brought us some supper."

"I eat a lot neater when I'm sitting at a table."

"I thought about that. But I wanted to keep you in bed." She blushed.

"For carnal purposes," he clarified, his tone deepening. "Remember, you're the one who said a three-pack wouldn't be enough."

Her face was burning now.

"But first I intend to feed you. It's canned split pea soup. Carrot and celery sticks. Ham sandwiches on whole wheat. Iced tea."

"Sounds great. Would you hand me the robe hanging on the back of the closet door? So I can get up for a minute."

"I don't mind the view."

She wished she could stop reacting so blatantly. "I'm not exactly used to this kind of thing."

"I see."

"So what are you wearing? Or are you walking around my house naked?" she suddenly asked.

"Yeah, since I was planning to come back to bed."

"Oh, Lord."

She heard him laugh as he put the robe into her out-stretched hand. "Okay, I'm turning around so you can put it on."

"No cheating," she warned.

"No cheating."

She made a quick trip to the bathroom, then returned to the bed and heard him fluffing up the pillows.

"Climb in and I'll put the tray on your lap."

She followed directions. As he leaned over her, she caught the warm, familiar scent of his body.

"Naked, huh? So how do you look?" she asked boldly.

"One thing about hooking up with you, I don't have to worry about appearances, do I? I've been told my face wouldn't win a beauty contest."

"Right. You're lucky beauty-contest winners don't cut it with me. But I'll bet women take a second and third look at your body. Give me a picture."

He cleared his throat. "Well, I lift weights three days a week, and I run. My stomach's still flat. I think you know my shoulders are pretty broad and that I've got a fair amount of hair on my chest. It's dark. The same as on my head. And I'm five-ten."

"I think we're skirting the parts in the middle," she said, shocked that she could be so brazen.

"If we get into that, we're not going to get anything to eat—food, anyway," he muttered. "And I'm hungry. So I'm going to get my supper."

Before she could react, he turned and left the room.

She suppressed a giggle. While he was gone, she felt the contents of the tray, discovering where everything was.

Ben came back and claimed the other side of the bed.

"So, did hunger get you up?" she asked after taking a sip of the soup.

"Partly. I also checked in with my office."

"And?"

"Probably Jesse James used the Techno Transfer software to tap into World Connect."

"I should have asked before—what's Techno Transfer?"

"An outfit that specializes in computer-generated false IDs and stolen credit numbers. I'm almost positive the man who killed Marianne works for them."

She swallowed painfully. "Oh."

"I'm sorry I brought it up," he muttered.

"I'll feel a lot better when he's behind bars."

"I'm not going to leave you alone until he is."

"How? I mean—you have to work, don't you?"

"I took some personal leave."

"Ben, you didn't have to do that."

"I wanted to," he said gruffly.

They ate in silence for several minutes, and she sensed that he was still unsettled.

"My cooking's not as fancy as yours," he finally said.

"It's fine."

"It's hard for me to remember to put everything back in the right place. But I'm getting used to your kitchen. You'll find most things where you left them. Except for the dirty dishes in the sink."

"You cooked. I'll clean."

"It's only about twenty minutes from here to my office."

She wondered where the string of observations was leading.

"Your house needs some repairs. Like the back window that won't open. And the trim that needs painting. I could do them."

"You don't have to do all that for me."

"I'd want to." He cleared his throat. "If we got married."

She'd been caught in the act of picking up her soup mug. It clattered back onto the tray. Was it possible he'd said what she thought? "Wh-what?"

"Will you marry me?"

"Ben, we hardly know each other."

"You think it's a bad idea? Too soon? Am I crowding you?"

"I love you," she said thickly.

He lifted the tray from her lap and set it on the bedside table, along with his own. Then he turned and gathered her close. "Maybe I didn't say it right. I love you. I want to marry you." His tone had turned mock playful, yet she sensed the urgency behind the words. "If you don't say yes, I'm going to use every erotic technique I can think of to arouse you to a fever pitch of sexual need—and keep you that way until you tell me what I want to hear."

"You'd resort to torture?" she managed to say.

"Yeah, I would."

"I'm too weak to withstand torture."

His hand cupped her breast. "Last chance," he warned.

"I guess I'd better say yes."

He hugged her fiercely, rocking her in his arms. "Okay. I pushed you pretty hard. But I swear you won't be sorry."

"Ben, knowing you love me makes me so happy. But are you sure you don't want more time to think about it? I mean, being married to me will—will mean extra responsibilities for you. I can do a lot of things but I still need help with shopping and I can't drive and—"

"Shhh." He silenced her with a finger pressed to her lips. "We'll work out the details later. I just want to know I have you for keeps."

She was still overwhelmed by the proposal, but she nodded against his hand.

"When did...did you decide that?" she whispered, needing more confirmation that she wasn't dreaming, that he'd offered her what she wanted most in the world.

"When I saw you soaking wet, climbing up the hill from the reservoir," he answered thickly. "I knew then what it would mean to lose you." He sealed the assertion with a long, deep kiss.

"I can't keep my hands off you," he growled as he began to touch her again in ways that made her tremble.

A few minutes later, he demanded, "So was I the only one lying awake at night? Did you maybe entertain some secret fantasies about marrying me?"

"Yes," she admitted in a whisper.

"Good. And did you have fantasies about this?" He took her hardened nipples between his thumbs and fingers, squeezing gently until she moaned with pleasure.

"I didn't know how much I'd like that."

"Well, we'll have to find out what you like best, won't we?" he asked with a smile in his voice.

He devoted himself to that project until she was incandescent with desire.

When he told her it was time to get the package of condoms on the bedside table, she grabbed his hand. "Don't."

"You don't want—?"

She sucked in a shaky breath and let it out in a rush. "Don't use one." She felt him go absolutely still. "Something I did fantasize about was having your baby. If we're getting married, then it should be okay."

He swore under his breath.

She struggled to hold back her disappointment. "But if that's going too fast for you…"

"No." He turned his hand and knit his fingers tightly with hers. "It was part of my fantasy, too. The whole enchilada. Married to you. Making babies. Us having a family."

Moisture gathered in her eyes. He brushed away the tear that began to slide down her cheek. His kiss was tender, then passionate as he eased back beside her on the bed and began again to teach her how much pleasure a man and woman could give each other. Only this time it was different—better, more intense—because she knew he loved her.

## Chapter Fourteen

Ben sat at the kitchen table watching Jenny make hamburger stroganoff for supper. He had a feeling she was showing off, demonstrating again how efficient she was in the kitchen. But he already knew she was incredible and that he'd never regret asking her to marry him. Really, when you thought about it, the decision wasn't so rash. He'd had a crush on Jenny since high school, though he hadn't been able to do anything about it then. She'd been in his mind for years. When he'd found her again, all the old feelings had come surging back. Only now she was a mature woman who had fulfilled the promise of the girl he'd known. More than fulfilled it—because the things that had happened to her had made her stronger and more adept. It had only taken a little while to realize he'd be a fool to let her go again.

He cracked his knuckles, and she half turned to give him a little smile.

"So now you're slowly letting me discover your bad habits."

"Right."

"Are you hungry?"

"Yeah. You should be, too. I think we both worked up an appetite over the past couple of days."

She blushed.

"I'm grinning at you," he informed her. "It's a wicked grin—based on fond memories of keeping you in bed all day."

"You like to say things that will embarrass me, make my face turn red."

"And your neck. And shoulders. And—" He peered at the vee of skin visible at the top of her button-down shirt.

"Stop!"

"Maybe I shouldn't have let you get dressed."

Without bothering to answer, she turned back to the skillet. He stretched out his jean-clad legs and crossed them at the ankles. He thought about how good he felt, happier than he ever could remember being, then his beeper went off.

"I'll be right back," he told her as he trotted toward the office. He'd been expecting a report from Diangelo on the Techno Transfer raid.

"Well, did they hit the place?" he asked his partner.

"Yeah."

"What took so long?"

"There was a problem with the paperwork for the search warrant. Anyway, it didn't go down the way you figured."

Ben gripped the receiver.

"For starters, the guy in charge—L. J. Smith—is dead. It looks like some of the employees came to work, saw the body, and split. So Fraud was only able to scoop up three of them."

"Not the one we wanted, I assume."

"I don't know for sure yet, but I wouldn't bet on it."

Ben scowled. He'd been so damn close. Now they were back to square one.

"I suppose Smith didn't keel over from a heart attack."

"One shot in the chest. Another to the head, just to make sure. The M.E. says it happened sometime yesterday. There was a gun in a holster under the desk but he never got a chance to use it." Diangelo sighed. "Sorry. I knew you were hoping we were going to wrap this up."

"Murphy's Law," Ben muttered, already thinking of alternate plans.

When he returned to the kitchen, Ben was glad Jenny couldn't see his face. But she read his mood somehow.

"What's wrong?" she asked as he pulled out a chair and sat down at the table.

"How do you know there's something wrong?"

She turned from the stove and appeared to fix him with an analytical stare. It was all he could do to keep from lowering his eyes.

"You left in a hurry like you were expecting a present. When you came back into the room, your walk was slow and heavy as if you were carrying an enormous weight on your shoulders."

"You've got me pegged." He let out a long sigh. He didn't want to spoil the rest of the afternoon, but his police training was too ingrained to lie about her being in danger. He told her the details.

"I'm probably going to be working overtime to bring in the killer. Is there someplace you could stay until we catch the killer?"

He saw her swallow and suspected she was trying not to panic. Yet when she spoke, it was to protest his suggestion.

"I don't want to impose on any of my friends."

"They won't see it that way."

"Ben, I won't be comfortable at someone else's house."

"It's only for a few days."

She folded her arms across her chest. "Stop pushing me. I—" she gulped "—I promised myself I'd never again let a man talk me into something that felt wrong!"

He studied the rigid lines of her face. "You can't let what happened twelve years ago be the basis for every decision you make," he said, perhaps with more exasperation than he should have allowed himself.

"Excuse me?"

"I assume you're talking about Craig Coopersmith persuading you to drive."

"Yes," she whispered.

"This is entirely different. He was drunk the night of the accident. And he was abusive. You tried to argue with him, but he made it practically impossible for you to say you wouldn't drive home. He didn't care about what happened to you. I do."

She stood with her hands on her hips, her eyes narrowed. "How do you know all that?"

Too late he realized he'd said too much.

"How do you know?" she shot at him again.

"I was at the party."

"And you neglected to tell me that important fact?"

"I was going to tell you that evening when I brought you home from Fells Point but you jumped out of the car before I had a chance."

"You've had plenty of chances since then."

He slicked a hand through his hair. "I was waiting for the right time," he muttered.

"Speak up. I have to rely on my ears. I can't see the expression on your face. I can't judge how much you're hiding. So you were at the party watching me drink? Watching us fight? What?"

He thumped his fist against the table top, and she jumped.

"Okay. You want to hear it all? I'll tell you the whole story. Every damn detail. I was at the party watching you all evening, wishing I was your date, wishing you liked me instead of that jerk Craig Coopersmith—because I knew I would have treated you a lot better than he did. I was in love with you. I wanted to be the one you were kissing. But it was hopeless, because you were older than I was. You didn't even know I was alive. When Craig started saying you were going to have to drive I could tell you were embarrassed and worried. Probably you didn't want to lose face in front of your friends. I wanted to butt in and say I'd take you. But I knew that would have been even more embarrassing for you."

She seemed to be too stunned to say anything, so he continued.

"You may feel guilty about what happened that night. But so do I, because I shouldn't have let you leave like that. When I heard about the accident the next day, I went out speeding in my car and damned near wound up wrapped around a tree. I told you I made some changes my junior year in high school. Well, *you* were the reason. When I got back from driving around like a maniac I vowed I was going to be a better person. That I'd never let something bad happen to someone else because I was afraid of getting cut down. Almost every decision I've made since then goes back to the night I let you leave the party. Do you understand?"

She didn't answer. He didn't know whether he was getting through to her. And he didn't get a chance to press the point, because at that moment the smell of charring beef suddenly filled the kitchen. Jenny snatched the pan off the burner and it clattered into the sink.

"Don't," he shouted when she reached for the water.

It was already too late. A cloud of steam rose and sizzled in her face as he jumped from his chair.

She coughed as he pulled her back and turned off the faucet. He pushed back her hair. She hadn't burned her face, thank God. "You're okay." When he tried to take her into his arms, she stiffened.

"It's too much right now. It's all…too much. I've spent the past twelve years trying to forget the night I killed Craig Coopersmith."

"You didn't kill him. It wasn't your fault!"

She ignored him. "And you keep bringing it back to me. Maybe this just won't work."

"I won't let you think that! The accident wasn't your fault. You had the right of way. And even if you hadn't, Craig forced you to drive."

"Don't make excuses. I made the decision to get behind the wheel. If I'd been sober, maybe I would have stopped when the other car jumped the light."

He had to convince her, so he gripped her by the shoulders and went on in a rush of words. "You cut yourself off from all your friends. But Craig wasn't worth it. He was no good for you. Any fool could see that he was taking what he could get. Is he the one who convinced you that sex was something guys enjoyed and girls did because they were being accommodating? Or was it worse than that? Did he say you weren't any good at it? Is he the boy who kept you from making love all these years? Is he the one who kept you from loving anyone?"

She sucked in a sharp breath. "So is that why you got involved with me? Because you felt sorry for needy little Ms. Larkin?"

"Of course not! I got involved with you because I couldn't help myself. You were everything I always wanted, and I couldn't stay away from you."

It was clear she wasn't listening to him anymore. "I need to be alone," she said in a strangled voice.

"Jenny," he pleaded, but his hands dropped away from her. In his rush to convince her, he'd told her too much—things he'd thought over the years, conclusions he'd come to since they'd met again. He should have kept them to himself until later.

She was standing with her hands clenched in front of her and her jaw so tight it looked like it would shatter. Seeing her that way made his insides knot. He wanted to hold her and kiss her until she understood how he felt about her. But he knew she wouldn't yield to a show of force.

"Okay. I'll be in the office checking out World Connect to see if—" He stopped, shaking his head. Everything he said seemed to lead to a topic better not discussed. He supposed it was lucky she couldn't see a picture of his former wife. Because if she did, she'd realize Brenna looked a lot like her. Only she hadn't been Jenny, and it hadn't worked out. But there was no use bringing that up. It wouldn't help any more than the other stupid things he'd blurted out.

"I—I'd like you to leave," she said.

"I can't do that." He heard his voice crack and knew that if he kept talking much longer he was going to sabotage his image as a strong male.

"This is my house."

"That's true. But I'm not going to leave until I know you're safe. We'll talk about it when you're not so upset."

Turning on his heel, he left the room, his footsteps ringing hollowly on the wooden floor. The light from the computer screen glowed at him as he stopped at the office door. It would be dark in another hour, he thought. That didn't make any difference to Jenny, but it might to the killer. No matter how she felt about the two of them, he wasn't going to leave her until he knew she was safe—here or in another location where nobody could get to her.

DEEP IN THE SHADOW of the pine trees, the watcher lowered his binoculars and uttered a few choice words. He'd been here half the day and nothing had changed. It looked like the damn cop had moved in. Jenny Larkin's personal protection service. Was she paying him, or was he just enjoying the benefits of her bed and board?

He snorted, then reached for the pack of cigarettes in his

pocket. Before he lit up, he stopped. The other day he'd seen her standing in the front hall sniffing the smoke. If he smoked, he could give himself away again.

It didn't look like she or the cop was going anywhere. Maybe he'd check them out with the directional mike he'd turned off because the sappy dialogue was making him sick. If everything was the same, he could stop at the sub shop for something to eat.

The watcher started to turn toward his car when he heard a door open. Wait a minute. It was too good to be true. He held his breath, watching in fascination as she stepped out onto the deck. Alone. Without her private bodyguard.

A slow smile spread across his face. "Come here, baby!" he murmured as she took a couple of steps away from the house. "Come a little closer before that cop realizes you're missing."

BEN SAT in front of the computer trying to do something constructive. But all he could think about was Jenny and how he'd screwed things up with her. He'd made a mess of it from the start. Or had he? Maybe it wouldn't have worked out any differently if he'd come clean with her from the beginning. She'd only have had more time to build up her defenses.

But now his pain was like a fresh knife wound—sharp and stinging. Because he'd kissed her. Made love to her. Opened his soul to her. She'd told him she loved him and wanted to have his baby. Lord, what if she were already carrying his child? he thought with a mixture of longing and anguish. He squeezed his eyes shut, unable to stand the thought of losing her now that what he wanted most in the world was shimmering in front of him. Yet when he reached for it, it moved out of his grasp.

He should give her the time she wanted. But he was too nervous to stay away from her when their whole future was hanging in the balance. Maybe he'd think of something to say, something that would make her understand how much he loved her. Quietly he went down the hall toward the kitchen. He'd see how she looked before he said anything. Or maybe it was safer just to keep his mouth shut. But he had to see her. She might not even know he was there, and he could just stand and look at her.

The smell of charred hamburger drifted toward him, but when he looked through the doorway, the room was empty.

"Jenny?"

She didn't answer, and wild panic seized him. He charged into the room. The burned pan was still in the sink. How long had he been in the office? Twenty minutes? Anything could have happened.

Telling himself to stay calm, he checked the pantry. She wasn't there, either. He listened intently and heard nothing.

"Jenny?"

His heart in his throat, he dashed into the living room. It was as empty as the kitchen. He was about to start searching the upstairs when he glanced out the window. She was on the deck that wrapped around the side of the house, her hand gripping the railing and her face turned toward the woods.

Relief slammed into him like a tidal wave crashing into a shore line. His next emotion was anger. What the hell was she doing out there? He'd told her to stay inside, hadn't he? His hand was shaking as he pulled open the door and stepped outside.

He knew she heard him because of the way her shoulders tensed. Yeah, she knew he was there, all right. But she didn't turn around. He tried to control his tone. "You shouldn't be out here by yourself," he said.

"If you're going to stay in the house, then I need to be outside where I can think," she murmured, so low he could barely hear.

"I told you I'd keep out of your way."

"Yes, but I can't trust you anymore."

He raked an exasperated hand through his hair. He wanted to hold her, kiss her, force her to respond to him. "Please," was all he allowed himself.

"I can't turn off the way I feel."

"Neither can I."

She bowed her head.

"Don't throw away what we've made together because I used poor judgment."

She dragged in a long breath and let it out in a rush. "I told you, Ben. Maybe I'm not being rational. I can't think straight. All I know is that I need to be by myself for a while. I'm used to being by myself. So don't try to persuade me. I have to figure this out on my own."

He couldn't stop himself from pushing her to the limit. "What if you're going to have my baby?"

She made a little choking sound that brought a terrible, tight constriction to his throat. When she turned toward him, he saw that she'd been crying. His insides ached with wanting to cross the few feet of space that separated them. But he stayed rooted to the spot where he stood. "I love you. Everything I've done—everything you're holding against me—is because I don't want to lose you."

He saw her swallow hard. He wanted to tell her that if she was carrying his baby, then she didn't have a prayer of getting away from him because there was no way he wasn't going to be a father to his child. But he knew it would sound like a threat, and that would only make things worse. And he knew in some small compartment of his mind that he meant it as a threat.

While he scrambled for something more to say, the sound of a car on the gravel drive made them both jump. He reached for the gun tucked into the waistband of his slacks before he realized he didn't need it.

"Howard County police," he told her.

Some of the tension went out of her face.

The car came to a halt at the edge of the parking area. The uniformed officer got out and walked along the garden paths to the deck.

"I assume you're Ben Brisco," he said.

"Yes."

"Denton Kane. I've been assigned guard duty."

"I wasn't informed of that."

"We just got the word. You can check with our chief if you want."

"No. That's okay."

"Detective Brisco was hoping to take a break," Jenny cut in.

Kane touched his hat, then looked slightly flustered as he remembered she couldn't see him. "Miss Larkin?"

She cleared her throat. "Yes."

Ben's gaze shot to her. She was standing very still, her face turned away from him. Probably she was ecstatic that Officer Kane had intervened in their two-person drama.

"I can take the evening shift," Kane said. "You could report back in the morning."

"No need. I'll be going to work in the morning," Jenny said coolly.

Ben wanted to drag her inside and have a talk with her. If she wouldn't accept his protection, then she should go somewhere he knew she'd be safe. But he couldn't start an argument in front of Kane.

He sighed. "Okay. Give me a few minutes." Heavily he went back into the house and upstairs. Every room held a memory of Jenny that stabbed painfully at his heart. They'd used the exercise room together that morning. Then he'd shown her how much fun it was to shower together.

He looked critically at each location, picking up a towel

here, changing a weight setting there. When Kane checked out the house, he didn't want him figuring out what had been going on for the past two days. The sight of the unmade bed was worse than anything that had come before. He felt like a dagger was twisting in his chest. For a moment he couldn't move. Then he crossed the room and yanked up the covers, trying to ignore the signs that he and Jenny had been warm and cozy here only a few hours earlier. The box of condoms was still on the bedside table where he'd abandoned it at her request. Stiffly, he shoved the incriminating evidence into the top drawer.

He squeezed his eyes closed for a moment. Everything he wanted had been within his grasp. So close. Now he might be consigned to hell for the rest of his life.

He turned one last time to look at the room and spotted the discarded foil wrapper on the floor half under the bed. "Brisco, you're great at hiding evidence," he muttered as he wadded it up and shoved it into his pocket. He wanted to linger in the room. Maybe it was the last time he'd ever be here. But he figured Kane would wonder what he was doing.

Jenny and the officer were still outside, neither one of them saying anything when he came back out. Ben wished he could speak to her alone, but maybe it was better this way. Maybe they did need a cooling off period, since everything he said seemed to drive her farther from him.

He cleared his throat. "Well, goodbye Ms. Larkin. I'll keep you up on the status of the investigation."

"Thank you."

At least she hadn't told him to have Diangelo call.

There seemed to be nothing more to say, so he descended the steps and walked smartly to his car, trying to give a good imitation of a detective glad that he'd been released from extra duty.

# Chapter Fifteen

Jenny listened to Ben's departing footsteps. When the car door opened, she almost called out to him to come back. She almost clattered down the stairs and followed him. Part of her longed to feel his strong arms around her. Part of her longed to weep on his shoulder and listen to his quiet reassurances. But the part of her that had insisted on being self-sufficient for the past twelve years wouldn't let her give in to the weakness. She hadn't been lying to him. She was wounded by his failure to tell her some key facts. Maybe she understood his reasons, but she wasn't going to let him sweep her along on the course he'd set. She had to think things through for herself, or she'd never be sure that she hadn't been coerced. But that didn't make sending him away ache any less.

"Ma'am," a voice said, startling her. Feeling utterly alone, she'd forgotten someone else was with her, intruding on her privacy.

She wanted to make Kane go away, too, but she knew that would be foolish. "Yes?"

"Come inside."

There was nothing overtly threatening about the suggestion. Yet under the veneer of politeness there was a current of something in his voice that set her nerves on edge.

"If you don't mind, I'd like to stay out here for a little while."

His foot scuffed against the boards of the porch. "Not a good idea."

She searched for an excuse to keep her distance. "My bird feeders need filling."

There was a little pause. "I guess it would be all right for you to do that. But don't be too long. It's going to be dark soon."

She gave a mirthless laugh. "That doesn't make any difference to me."

"Right," he replied, sounding embarrassed. "But stay where I can, uh, keep track of you if I look outside."

"I will," she agreed. When she heard the door close, she let out the breath she'd been holding. She'd practically insisted that Ben leave her with this stranger. Now that she had her wish, she felt a gnawing uneasiness. The air seemed to hang heavily around her and she was having trouble breathing.

She imagined unseen eyes drilling into her and felt her skin prickle. Was someone out there in the woods? Was that the source of her disquiet?

Standing perfectly still, she took a deep breath of the air. It was sweet. No cigarette smoke. No one was here, she told herself. More than likely, Officer Kane was looking through the window as he'd promised.

She felt her emotions swing first one way and then the other. She was confused and she'd let herself get dependent on Ben.

She raised her chin. Deliberately giving Kane something to see, she slowly crossed the deck. But when she reached the edge, she hesitated. She wasn't a fool. Whoever had tried to kill her was still on the loose. Stopping abruptly, she debated going back into the house. With Kane.

She didn't like that option. Yet she didn't feel safe out here, either.

BEN DROVE SLOWLY toward his office, trying to come up with a plausible reason to head back to Jenny's. None came to mind, and his hands clenched around the wheel in frustration. Doggedly, he kept his mind off certain subjects. He'd go crazy if he didn't think Kane was competent. He'd go just as crazy if he let himself wallow in the mess he'd made with Jenny.

So he tried to focus on the details of the case. Techno Transfer. World Connect. They were related, but he didn't have the proof. And what about Cameron Randolph's revelation that the computer directory had been altered? Was that to hide Marianne Blaisdell's World Connect files? He sighed.

He thought about Jenny's description of the kidnapper. Then the various interviews he'd done—with Helen the waitress at Three Sheets to the Wind, and with Sheryl Dyson, the woman who'd seen the killer dump the body. She'd said he was dressed like a meter reader. Helen had said he liked to play cowboy and biker and factory worker. Were they both really talking about the same man?

Then Jenny had described her abductor as wearing a knit polo shirt. Pretty prosaic for a guy who liked to dress up all the time. Well, his clothes couldn't pin him down. And probably the blond hair was a wig while the meter reader's cap had hidden the real color.

But height would remain constant. The cowboy was tall, so was the meter reader. But Jenny had said the man who'd thrown her over the bridge was medium height. The same man who had attacked her at Marianne's. Could the boots have made that much difference or was she mistaken? He was still trying to come up with some defining detail as he pulled into the parking garage.

JENNY REACHED for the container she used to fill the bird feeders. But instead of opening the can, she stood, listening intently.

Around her, the wildlife was strangely silent. Usually she could hear the birds hovering in the trees chirping to each other as they waited for her to finish filling the feeders. But they were totally silent, and it came to her with a sudden chill that their absence might be a sign of danger. Because they were hiding from someone else, someone out here.

Reaching toward the railing, she retrieved her cane. Hoping she looked casual and unconcerned, she turned and started toward the door. She had taken only a few steps when she realized she was hearing heavy footsteps crunching through the dry leaves under the trees.

If it was Kane, he'd be walking across the deck. These steps were coming from the wrong direction. And it was someone walking on his heels. Dropping the container, she sprinted the final few yards to the house. But he swooped down on her before she reached the door.

The smell of stale tobacco smoke and sour flesh made her gag. Then a hand clamped over her mouth. It was covered by a thick leather glove so that there was no possibility of biting flesh.

A scream rose in her throat, but it came out only as a low gurgle through the barrier of his hand.

"Not this time," he growled.

The tone of his voice was almost enough to shatter her sanity. Somehow she managed to hold herself together. She must stay rational. She must think. Because this time he surely aimed to finish the job he'd started.

He continued to mutter as he dragged her through leaves and debris. She had nothing to lose by fighting, she thought as she struggled against him, bucking and lashing her body from side to side as he carted her farther from the house—farther from any hope of rescue. Her thrashing didn't seem to slow him down much. Where were they going? Probably to his car, hidden in the woods.

She bucked again, this time from terror as she imagined the trunk lid slamming down on her.

"Cut it out, bitch," he growled as his hands tightened painfully on her shoulders.

Ignoring the discomfort, she concentrated her energy into one desperate lunge that wrenched her mouth from his grasp. In that second of freedom, she let out a bloodcurdling scream.

"Damn you!" His curse was accompanied by a slap across the face that stung all the way to the bone. Then he hoisted her onto his shoulder and started to run.

Behind them, she thought she heard a door slam, then footsteps thumping across the deck.

A voice rang out behind them. "Stop or I'll shoot!"

The kidnapper didn't slacken his pace. "He's not going to risk a shot when I'm carrying you."

But he was wrong. A loud report split the air. It was followed quickly by another. A bullet whizzed past Jenny's shoulder, millimeters from her flesh. The man carrying her cried out and began to stagger, listing precariously to the right. Another shot sounded, and he yelped in pain.

Then he dropped her heavily to the ground. The breath was knocked out of her, and all she could do was lie there and fight for breath. Feet pounded past her. More shots split the air. Then everything was quiet as a tomb.

"Please. Tell me what's happening," she begged, struggling to a sitting position. As her hands flailed in the air, they slapped against tree trunks. Crawling through fallen leaves, she propped herself up.

"Please...what's happening?" she repeated.

After an eternity, Officer Kane answered her. "I'm checking him out."

She managed a muffled reply. Then, numbly she waited until footsteps came slowly back toward her. It was Kane. It had to be Kane. Yet she still cringed away from the unseen man.

"He won't hurt you again," the officer announced. "I got him."

Jenny let out a long shuddering sigh, torn between relief and a growing apprehension. "You could have shot me."

"If you could have seen what was happening, you'd know you weren't in any danger," he clipped out.

When he came down beside her on the ground, she tried not to cringe. Kane had fired at the kidnapper's back. At least that was what she thought. But, of course, she could be wrong. And wrong about the bullets whizzing past her so close that she could feel the breeze. Maybe she was too strung out to know what had transpired. Certainly, she wasn't going to start questioning Kane's judgment—at least, not while they were alone.

"Are you all right?" he asked.

"Yes," she managed.

"Good. Stay put while I call in a report."

Panic surged through her. She couldn't stay here. Not when she had no idea where the dead man was lying. "No. Don't leave me."

He hesitated for a moment. "Okay."

Hooking his hand under her elbow, he helped her to her feet. She hated hanging on to him but her legs were too unsteady to be reliable. It was a relief to feel the paving of the path, then the deck. He led her to one of the Adirondack chairs, and gratefully, she sank into its familiar contours.

"He's the one?" she asked. "The one who killed my friend Marianne?"

Seconds ticked by before Kane answered. "It appears so."

"Thank God."

"The name on his driver's license is Jack Colmers. Does the name ring a bell?"

"No."

"Okay. I'll be right back."

As he headed for the house, she made one further request. "Please call Detective Brisco."

"As soon as I report in to my unit."

The rubber soles of his shoes crossed the wooden boards. Then the door closed behind him, and she was left sitting in the chair, her teeth chattering.

She was chilled to the bone, and not just from the cooling air. She'd almost gotten killed, and she knew she would never be truly warm again until she felt Ben's arms around her.

God, she'd been a fool to send him away. For the second time when she'd been afraid she would die, the worst part was the knowledge that she would never see the man she loved again. Never feel his arms around her or his lips on hers. Never bear the child they both wanted. And never have a chance to give him everything he deserved. Her eyes filled with tears. She needed to tell him how much she loved him. She needed to tell him she understood what she'd almost thrown away.

It was several minutes before Officer Kane came out of the house. Ducking her head, she swiped her hand across her eyes.

"The crime scene men will be here soon. Meanwhile, Detective Brisco wants me to bring you downtown."

Relief surged through her. In the back of her mind she'd been afraid that Ben wouldn't want to see her.

"I brought you a glass of water," Kane said.

"Thanks." She reached out gratefully, and he pressed the tumbler against her fingers.

While she drank, she heard him take a nearby chair.

"Feel better?" he asked.

"Yes." She balanced the glass on the chair arm.

"I know that was rough on you."

She nodded. She didn't really want to talk to this man, but he had saved her life. "I didn't thank you," she said.

"No need. I was only doing my job." She caught an odd note in his voice but before she could analyze it, he asked another question.

"So Marianne Blaisdell was your friend?"

"Yes. Didn't your department fill you in?"

"I'm a uniformed officer, so I only got part of the picture. I was told Colmers was stalking you. Now it's over," he said smoothly.

"Thank God."

"But there's something else bothering you, isn't there?"

Her head jerked up. "What do you mean?"

"You look troubled. Like you've got a secret that's weighing you down."

"I—" She stopped, struck by his choice of words. They sent her mind reeling. Yes, she'd had a secret for twelve years. Her part in Craig's death—which she'd kept from everyone, even her close friends like Erin and Elizabeth. But Ben already knew, and he'd made her face it. She'd barely listened while Ben was talking, but somehow his words had sunk in. Now she was starting to see the whole pattern of her life since that night in a different light. All these years she'd felt guilty. All these years she'd made herself pay for her mistake by limiting her associations with people—with men, in particular. But if there had ever been a payment to make, she'd discharged it in full, and she could stop beating herself up.

"What are you thinking?" Kane prompted.

"Pardon?"

"You look like you're bursting to tell me the secrets of the universe."

"Well, it's not quite that profound."

"Oh?"

She gave a little cough. "I, uh, it's something I need to tell Ben."

"Ben. You know him pretty well, then?"

"Yes."

"I'd like to hear, too. I'm a specialist in secrets. Like a therapist. Secrets are poison that seeps into the soul."

His tone might be smooth and persuasive, but it raised goose bumps on her arms. She didn't want to confide in him. The way he was pressing her only made her long to get away from him as quickly as possible. She cleared her throat. "Don't take this wrong. But I don't think I know you well enough. And I need to get downtown."

He didn't move from his chair.

"I knew a man whose grandmother forced him to keep a shameful secret," he said suddenly. "See, his mother was a bad girl who got pregnant and went away to have the baby. Then the family moved to a neighborhood where nobody knew them, and they all lived together. Only the big secret was that the girl who was supposed to be his sister was really his mother. And the woman who was supposed to be his mother was really his grandmother. He told me all about it."

Jenny nodded, not paying all that much attention to what he was saying because she was too caught up in her own problems. "It helps some people to talk about their lives," she murmured as she stroked her finger along the edge of the chair. She'd never been one of them. But now she needed to talk to Ben.

"That would mess a kid up pretty good, don't you think? Especially if his grandmother hated him and made his life hell. Because his mother was stupid enough to get pregnant with him."

"Uh…yes," she answered, trying to cut the conversation short by not showing much interest.

"I can see you're in a hurry."

He sounded piqued. Why should he be annoyed that she didn't want to confide in him? After all, he was practically a stranger. Did he get some sort of pleasure from prying confessions out of people? "Let me get my purse," she said. "And my cane."

"I took the liberty of bringing the purse," he answered. "Your cane is on the ground where you dropped it. I'll get it."

She waited nervously, thinking about his preoccupation with secrets. He was strange. The prospect of riding downtown with him wasn't very appealing. She considered waiting for someone else to arrive—until she remembered there was a body lying on the ground.

As they started toward the cruiser, his words echoed in her head. *Secrets are poison that seeps into the soul.* She knew she'd heard that before. But where?

She was still trying to remember as Kane opened the door for her and she slipped into the passenger seat of the police car. He didn't immediately open the other door, and she wondered what he was doing.

Restlessly, she moved her legs, and her feet tangled with something. When she reached down to move it out of the way, she realized she'd grabbed the front of a shirt. A western-style shirt with metal studs in a pattern across the front. She'd felt a shirt like that not very long ago. In the nightclub when she'd bumped into the man coming out of the bathroom.

Could that be a coincidence? she wondered with a sickening lurch in her stomach. And why was the shirt on the floor of a police car?

As her fingers stroked the metal studs, something clicked in her mind. She realized where she'd heard the phrase about secrets being poison for the soul. It was from one of

Marianne's late-night sessions on World Connect. From a man calling himself Oliver who'd been holding forth on the literary bulletin board.

## Chapter Sixteen

A noise to her left made Jenny jump. Realizing she was still clutching the shirt, she dropped it quickly to the floor. She sat tensely, waiting for the man who said his name was Kane to slide behind the wheel. But who was he—really?

Her mind raced, trying to make sense of what was happening. She'd been kidnapped and almost murdered—by the man who had killed Marianne. Then Kane had shot him, and she'd thought she was finally safe. But now... Now she could toss every supposition she'd made out the car window.

Her brain felt as if it would explode. What she was thinking was too insane to put into words. Yet her life depended on making the leap from one set of assumptions to another. With an involuntary mental shift, she felt the pieces of the puzzle slide into a different shape. The new pattern was like a huge electric sign lighting up in her mind. There were *two* of them. *Two* different men. *Two* killers. Maybe they'd been working together and had had a fight. If so, one of them could have come after her, and the other had killed him. But that wasn't the important part. The important part was that the dead man wasn't the one who had killed Marianne. That was—Kane. Or the cowboy from the bar. Or Oliver from World Connect. Or whatever he wanted to call himself.

Kane—the man thumping around outside the car. And if he was the killer, he'd lied about talking to Ben or the police just now.

Frantically, she tried to dismiss the frightening new hypothesis. She was wildly off balance. Perhaps she'd made a terrible mistake. But the shirt was no mistake. The oddly worded phrase about secrets was no mistake. Neither was the way he'd shot her kidnapper when he could have hit her, too. She'd known that even without being able to see the action. But she hadn't wanted to believe it—even though she'd been uncomfortable with him from the very beginning.

The car door opened and every muscle in her body tensed. But he didn't reach for her; he only slipped behind the wheel. "Sorry, I was checking the left rear tire," he said.

"That's all right." *Steady,* she told herself silently. *Don't panic. If you run, he'll shoot you.*

Still, she had to escape. Because if they drove away from the house together, she was almost certain he was the last person who would see her alive.

BEN PULLED into the parking garage at police headquarters and cut the engine. He was still thinking about the man who was the master of disguises and what Sheryl Dyson had said about him. When he'd dumped the body, he'd been dressed like a meter reader. Only she'd known he wasn't the real McCoy because he was wearing running shoes. And they weren't part of the uniform.

They weren't part of a cop's uniform either, he thought with a sudden sick dread that started in his throat and spread through his body. As he pictured Officer Kane, he realized that the man had not been wearing standard uniform shoes. He'd been wearing running shoes.

Fighting down the apprehension, he reached for the portable phone and dialed the Howard County police. He'd been so upset, he'd hardly been paying attention to the officer. But now...

Praying, hoping against hope that he was wrong, he clutched the phone in a death grip.

"This is Detective Ben Brisco," he told the officer who answered. "I was guarding a witness in Howard County and was told your department had come in on the case. I was relieved by one of your uniformed officers. Denton Kane. I'd like to verify that."

"Just a moment, please."

Ben's pulse pounded in his temples as he waited for the man to check his computer files. Lord, he should have done this before he left Jenny's house. But she had been so anxious to have him leave and he'd been so upset that he hadn't been thinking clearly.

He drummed his fist against the steering wheel. He had no business blaming Jenny for his lapse in judgment. He should damn well have been on the ball. There was no excuse for his leaving her alone with the man.

An eternity passed before the personnel officer came back on the line.

"We have no officer named Denton Kane."

He cursed sharply. "Then get me an operational unit," he demanded even as he peeled out of the garage, siren blaring.

Quickly, he filled in the sergeant who came on the line. "Get as many units as you can over there now. But turn off the sirens when you reach the vicinity. He may kill her if he hears you coming."

KANE JINGLED the keys in his hand, and Jenny fought to keep from screaming as the metallic sound rattled in her head.

"We'll have you downtown at police headquarters in no time," he said in his maddening voice, which she now knew was as fake as his name. He was still playing the game he'd selected, still pretending to be the noble police officer who'd just rescued the blind woman in distress. Probably there was a smirk on his face that she couldn't see.

He could be taking her anywhere—to a ramshackle cabin in the woods, to an abandoned warehouse, anywhere he wanted. And she wouldn't know the difference until it was too late. She guessed that was why he hadn't grabbed her yet. He was having too much fun performing this particular role.

She made herself sit calmly as she heard him slip the key in the ignition. Before he could start the car, she made a show of running her fingers over the dial of her watch.

Then she cleared her throat. "Officer Kane."

"Yes."

"I—I was so upset by—by what just happened that I've made a terrible mistake," she stammered as if she were embarrassed to speak. "But—it—it's past time for me to take my anti-seizure medication. If I don't have it, I could go into convulsions." The last part came out as a breathy whisper.

"Convulsions?" he said.

She was pleased by his note of alarm. Maybe she was as good an actress as he was an actor. "Yes," she quavered. "They come on when I—when I get upset. I have to take my medication every twelve hours and I'm forty-five minutes late. So it could happen soon. Please, I left the pills upstairs in the bathroom. Inside the medicine cabinet, on the left side. Do you think you could get them for me? And some more water."

He let out an exasperated sigh. "Don't you have any in your purse?"

"No. I always keep the bottle in the bathroom. I always stick to my routine."

"All right." He heaved himself out of the car.

Daring to hope she had a chance, she listened to his footsteps cross the gravel and climb the porch steps. Her pulse was pounding as he stopped at the top. There was no way to know if he had turned to look at her, so she sat very still, hands clenched, cold sweat beading her brow until she heard the front door open. After counting to three to allow him to disappear inside, she moved. First she felt along the side of the door until she found the mechanism that locked the car.

As the locks snapped closed, she breathed out a tremendous sigh. Now Kane or whatever his real name was couldn't get in.

And she could drive his car away from here. Hysterical laughter shook her as she considered the insanity of her plan— even as she began to slide into the driver's seat. A blind woman was going to drive a car. The last time she'd driven, she'd killed somebody and wiped out her vision. No. Ben had set her straight on the homicide part. It wasn't her fault.

A frisson went through her as she thought of Ben. God, she loved him so much. She'd been such a fool to send him away. And if she didn't save herself, she suddenly realized, she'd be condemning him to living hell. The same hell that had trapped her since the accident. He'd blame himself for her death—for leaving her with the bogus Officer Kane—just the way she'd blamed herself for driving Craig Coopersmith's car that night. He'd be as wrong as she had been. And the real tragedy would be that she'd never get a chance to tell him.

She was still on the edge of terror. Yet, from some reserve of fortitude, she brought herself under better control. Teeth clamped together, she focused her concentration on the task at hand. While she fumbled with the seat belt and clicked it into place, she tried to think through the steps she was about to take. Executing them would take every skill she'd developed, every trick she'd learned over the past twelve years. But she had no choice. It was either escape or die.

It would be easier if she had more time. But time was a luxury she couldn't afford. Eventually Kane would stop fumbling through her medicine cabinet looking for nonexistent pills.

As quickly and efficiently as she could, she slid her hands around the driver's area, trying to familiarize herself with the car. First she found the lever to move the seat forward until she could reach the gas pedal. When she located the ignition, she turned the key. Then she stepped cautiously on the gas. When the engine caught, she moved the gear lever a notch and gave the car more fuel. It swung in an arc to the right.

There was no way to be sure she was aiming in the correct direction, but she'd been across the parking area thousands of times and was familiar with its geography. The surface sloped down toward the driveway. There was more gravel on the right side than the left because of the way rain water drained. She'd been meaning to have the problem corrected. Now she was glad that she'd let it go as she listened carefully to the sound of the tires on the gravel and judged the downward tilt of the car as she pointed herself toward escape.

Gingerly she pressed the accelerator and tried to estimate the distance she was traveling. Gravel gave way to dirt on her left. But her right bumper struck a low stone barrier. The car bounced, and her teeth slammed together. But at least she was pretty sure what she'd hit—one of the concrete posts that marked the road.

A scraping of metal accompanied her course correction as she swung to the left. Then, with a satisfying dip, the vehicle settled into the twin ruts that ran along the narrow drive. She let herself enjoy a moment of elation. If she followed the ruts downhill, she should be able to make it to the road. Of course, she wasn't sure what she'd do when she got there. Maybe listen to the traffic, pull out, and force someone to stop.

Concentrating on keeping the tires in the ruts, she gave the car a little more gas. She'd been lucky so far. Maybe she'd be out of sight before Kane came out of the house again.

But her luck didn't hold.

"Hey!" The angry shout from fifty yards behind her was as jarring as the collision with the stone pillar. Reflexively, she stepped harder on the gas, and the vehicle shot forward, the right front fender glancing off what she thought to be the trunk of a tree.

"What the hell do you think you're doing?" he called out. Then she heard feet pounding behind her, closing the distance between the car and the house.

Ignoring him, she kept going.

"Stop, or I'll shoot," he screamed.

No way was she going to stop, Jenny thought as she scrunched down in her seat to make a smaller target. Behind her the gun spat out a bullet, then another.

Instead of stopping, she pressed harder on the accelerator. Better a quick death than what he'd done to Marianne. For a panicked moment, she lost the tire tracks and yanked the wheel to the left. Then she found them again and lurched forward.

She was so focused on trying to aim in the right direction that it took several moments before she realized she hadn't been wounded. Nor had she felt the bullets tear into the car.

Above the sound of the engine she could hear his pounding footsteps drawing closer.

"Damn, you! Stop!" he screamed. "You haven't told me your secret yet."

Heart in her throat, she kept driving. When the car bounced, she realized with a sickening start that she was off course again. If she plowed into the woods, she'd had it. First she turned to the right, but the tires didn't settle into the ruts. Then she bucked left and thought she'd found the track, although now she wasn't sure.

A thump at her window made her cry out. He was there—cursing at her and banging on the glass with his fist. Her only option was to step on the gas and try to steer as the tires wove in and out of the depressions. Finally, the thumping stopped, and she breathed a sigh of relief.

The relief lasted for perhaps half a minute longer. Then she heard him again, running behind her. Moments later, he was back at the window—shouting a stream of obscenities that made her cringe.

Something made a terrible smashing sound against the window, and she jerked bolt upright. The crack came again, and the glass groaned but seemed to hold. With a clogged feeling in her throat, she realized that he was using a rock to batter his way inside.

Another crash and the glass cracked. She heard his shout of elation.

Sobbing, she imagined his hands reaching through and pulling her out past jagged shards of glass. Her only hope was to block his path with some obstacle. Recklessly, she jerked the wheel sharply to the left.

He shouted something that sounded like a warning—or a curse. In the next moment, a bloodcurdling scream split the air, followed by the sound of a body hitting the ground. She'd knocked him off. And she'd hurt him, she thought with a strange mixture of fear and triumph.

The elation was short-lived. The fear multiplied a thousand times as the car plowed into a series of obstructions that her brain told her must be saplings.

Pulling sharply on the wheel, she pitched to the right. But she was so disoriented and off course that she had no idea where she was heading. Too fast for her to react, the vehicle crossed the line of tire ruts and kept going. Easing up on the accelerator, she tried to find the middle of the road again. But before she could get back onto the track, she slammed into something so solid that the car came to rest with a sickening jolt. For a moment she could only gasp as she slammed forward. Then the seat belt caught and snapped her back against the headrest. She sat there struggling for breath and trying to figure out what to do now. It took several moments before she could act, but when she tried to put the car into reverse, the lever wouldn't move, and her frantic yanking only produced a grinding noise.

From somewhere behind her, she heard a strangled growl—a human voice twisted by fury and pain into something almost unrecognizable. He was hurt, and angry beyond all reason. When she realized he was drawing slowly closer, she bit her lip to keep from screaming in terror.

He was out there, wounded. And he was coming to get her. She wanted to huddle in the car but with the broken window there was no safety.

It was hard to make herself pull on the door handle. When she did, she found that the door would only open a couple of inches. Scrambling across the seat, she yanked at the handle on the passenger door and gave a little sob as it swung free. Then she was out of the car, standing on shaky legs in the tall grass. Reaching out, she steadied herself against the side of the car.

"You won't get away." Kane's voice lashed the words toward her.

He was close…and getting closer. She could hear him, smell him.

Desperately she knelt and felt along the ground for a rock or stick she could use as a weapon. There was nothing, and she wanted to scream as she crawled farther, bits of gravel digging into her palms and knees.

He was gaining on her, his wheezing breath making her skin crawl. She could hear one of his feet dragging and knew he must have hurt his leg when she'd smashed him against the tree.

She was about to scramble up and take her chances running blind when her fingers scraped against a fallen branch. With a strangled exclamation, she wrapped her hand around one end and pushed herself to her feet. Then she began to swing it in front of her like a cane. It was too short, so that she had to bend over. But it was better than nothing, and she started to pick up speed.

The end of the stick hit against a tangle of vines. Moving farther, she encountered a long mound of vegetation, punctuated with sagging wooden posts. When she realized what it was, she couldn't believe her good fortune. It was the old fence that marked the path to the quarry.

The air felt cold and damp on her face, almost like a fine curtain of mist. It was probably fully dark by now, and even foggy. She hoped that gave her an advantage over a man who needed to rely on his eyes.

The surface under her feet changed, and she knew she'd reached the mouth of the horseshoe-shaped quarry. Rock walls rose steeply on three sides. She remembered playing here as a child with the other kids in the area—although the place had been strictly forbidden to all of them. Now Jenny was thankful that she had strong memories of the place, because they might be her only means of thwarting Kane. Still using the branch as a makeshift cane, she headed for the rock wall on her right. When she reached it, she tossed the stick behind her. It would just be in the way when she started climbing.

BEN SWUNG HIS CAR into Jenny's driveway and careened up the track. Rounding a curve, he slammed on the brakes when his headlights bounced off a police cruiser blocking the way.

Jumping out, he saw a uniformed officer moving toward him. In the darkness, he thought it might be the impostor who'd called himself Kane, and his hand went to his gun. Then the man spoke, and he realized it was somebody else.

This time a legitimate member of the Howard County police force.

His tension level lowered a notch, but he couldn't shake the growing fear that had dogged him all the way back from the city. "Ben Brisco, Baltimore P. D.," he called out.

"Wayne Kopeck, Howard County," the other man replied. "You called in the report?"

"Yeah. You the only one they sent?"

"There's a breakout at the State Penitentiary. I was the only unit they could spare."

Ben nodded tightly.

Kopeck switched on a flashlight and pointed toward the woods, where the end of another cruiser was sticking out of the trees.

"What happened?"

"I found that disabled vehicle. It's got our insignia, but it's not one of ours."

"How do you know?" Ben asked.

"The crest is the wrong color. I was just going to have a look inside."

"I'll be with you in a minute." Ben trotted back to his own car and pulled out a flashlight. With a gun in one hand and a light in the other, he and the officer tramped through the long grass to the edge of the woods, where the car was hung up against the trunk of an oak tree.

The driver's door was wedged shut against a boulder, but the passenger door was open. Ben shone his light inside and noticed at once that there was another aberrant detail. "No radio," he informed Kopeck. On the floor was a crumpled man's shirt, a shirt with western studs in a pattern across the front. Like the cowboy's from the bar.

Perspiration beaded his brow as he looked for some sign of Jenny, hoping against hope that he wasn't going to find a body. God, where was she?

He tried to operate with his usual objectivity—as if this was simply a routine case. But there was no use kidding himself. He'd go crazy if he didn't find her alive and well. When he pulled her purse from under the passenger seat, he made a low sound that was more growl than anything else.

"Find something?" Kopeck asked.

He cleared his throat and tried to speak normally. "Jenny Larkin's pocketbook. He had her in the car, but he must have crashed."

"So where did they go?"

"I'd like to know." Ben looked around at the silent, misty woods. The darkness under the trees was as thick as an underground vault. He shook his head in anger and frustration. They could be a mile from here by now. Or the bastard could be holding a gun to her head and waiting for them to leave so he could finish what he'd started. He shuddered as he remembered the photos of Marianne Blaisdell after this man had gotten through with her.

*Please, God,* he silently prayed, *don't let that happen to Jenny. Please, God, I'll do anything you want. I'll give her up if that's what it takes. Only let her be all right. Let her get away from him.*

Kopeck slid into the car and checked the driver's side.

"Odd," he muttered as the headlights flashed on and then off again.

"What?" Ben struggled to bring his mind back to the car and the uniformed officer.

"No wonder he crashed. It looks like he was driving in the dark with the lights off."

Ben felt a shiver travel over his skin as he stood there in the blackened woods. The guy could have been driving with the lights off if he didn't want anyone to see him. Or there could be another explanation. Like someone had been behind the wheel who didn't need lights. The idea was insane. A blind woman driving away from a serial killer. He would have dismissed it out of hand, but he knew Jenny. If anyone would try a stunt like that, it would be her. "Is the seat too close to the wheel for you?" he asked, waiting tensely for the answer.

"Yeah. I was just wondering about that. Was the guy pretty short?"

"No, he was tall," Ben informed him. "Around six foot. With long legs and broad shoulders. So I think we have to assume the blind lady was driving."

"What? That's crazy."

Ben put his hand on the hood. It was still warm in the cooling night air. The accident couldn't have been all that long ago.

Feeling almost light-headed, he turned and trotted back along the route the car had taken, shining his flashlight alternately on the trees and the ground. When he came to a tree with a ragged piece of blue fabric sticking to the bark, he nodded in satisfaction. She'd been driving, all right. And the bogus officer Kane had been on foot. Jenny had bashed him against a tree hard enough to rip his clothes. He hoped she'd hurt the guy good. Good enough for her to put a lot of distance between the two of them when she had to get out of the car.

Cupping his hands around his mouth, he called Jenny's name into the night. He waited tensely, but no one answered.

# Chapter Seventeen

Jenny guessed she was six feet up the rock wall when she heard Ben shout her name. It was far away, but she would have known his voice anywhere.

Her heart lurched inside her chest. Ben was here! He'd come back. She longed to answer him but she knew if she did, she'd give away her location to the man who had dragged himself into the quarry.

"So your boyfriend came back. Well, I'll get you before he does," Kane promised in a voice that was laced with pain, "if it's the last damn thing I do."

For several seconds Jenny was paralyzed. Then, with every ounce of concentration she could muster, she started to climb again. She and her friends had discovered years ago that there was a series of handholds and a sheltered rock ledge halfway up the side of the quarry. It wasn't really a hard climb. But only the bravest kids had done it—she and a few of the others. She remembered the exhilaration of scrambling onto the ledge and looking out over the countryside. They'd pretended that they were Pueblo Indians living far above the floor of a desert valley, with the cowboys below. The cowboys were the ones who were afraid to make the climb. Now she was playing the game again. Only the cowboy might have a gun, she thought, repressing another hysterical laugh.

And she had to climb by feel, because she couldn't see. But neither could Jesse James, because it was dark. And even if by some chance he'd brought a flashlight, he couldn't hang on to it and come after her at the same time.

Buoyed by a sense of hope, she reached up, located another niche, and pulled herself upward. As she moved from handhold to foothold up the side of the cliff, she found the rhythm coming back to her. Then her foot dislodged some loose stones, and she cried out as she scrabbled for purchase. The stones tumbled down the rock face and thumped to the ground.

Jenny pressed herself against the rock wall, trying to be absolutely silent, but it was too late.

"Gotcha," the man below her snarled.

She couldn't suppress a low moan as she heard him coming up, his route marked by little falls of stones that told her he wasn't having an easy time climbing. But she knew from his steady progress that he wasn't going to turn back.

BEN HAD ALMOST given up hope of finding anything when the light hit a spot of red on the rocky ground. It was wet and shiny.

Kneeling, he examined it more closely, then shouted to Kopeck. "Over here."

The officer hurried to his side and squatted down. "What have you got?"

"Blood." He pointed to the small puddle staining a cluster of pebbles.

"From the woman?"

"No. She was in the car. She rammed Kane against a tree and tore his uniform. Let's see which way he went."

They both shone their lights in an arc around the area. Ben was the first to spot the trail of blood leading off to the right. First it zigzagged, then followed an old trail bordered by a vine-covered fence. Had Jenny gone that way—with the injured killer following? He had no way of knowing for sure, but it was the best bet.

Quickly the two men took the same path, checking the blood spots on the ground as they went.

JENNY CLIMBED higher, her mind on nothing except scaling the wall. If she thought about the man coming relentlessly after her, she'd fall. Finally, with a sense of triumph, she reached the ledge. Scrambling onto the horizontal surface, she rested, panting from the exertion. She knew she was about seventy feet above the floor of the quarry. She'd never been higher than this, and she wasn't sure if there were more hand and footholds above the ledge. Cautiously, she moved along the narrow space, exploring the area and trying to find another escape route. Without vision, she could discover no exit save the way she'd come—and that way was blocked by Kane.

Like a robot programmed to kill, he came after her, his advance marked by little showers of rock—and by his heavy breathing. She listened hard. He sounded winded, maybe even in pain, each breath ending in a kind of rattle.

"So you can't get any farther," he jibed. "I've got you trapped."

Could he see her? Or was he guessing?

The only thing she knew for sure was that he'd already marked her position, and she wouldn't give anything away by crying out.

"Ben!" she shouted. "Ben. I'm in the quarry. Near the top on the right. He's climbing after me."

Her words were greeted by a cascade of obscenities from the man pulling himself toward her.

"BEN!"

He heard Jenny's shout ring out in the darkness. The sound of his name came to him as an almost physical force.

She was alive.

He longed to shout back, to tell her that he was on his way, that he would rescue her. But anything he said to Jenny would warn the killer.

"The quarry," Kopeck repeated. "I've been there. I've chased out kids."

"Are we on the right path?"

"I think so. It's hard to tell in the dark."

They kept moving along the fence, following the trail of blood.

"Jeez. You say she's blind—and she's climbing the cliff?" Kopeck asked.

Ben made a strangled sound in his throat. "If she can drive a car, I guess she can climb a cliff," he muttered as he quickened his pace.

JENNY WAITED with her heart pounding, hoping against hope that she'd hear Ben answer. But there was only silence—except for the angry curse from the man below her. She was on her own, with nowhere else to go. But she wasn't simply going to wait for Kane to grab her.

A last-ditch idea began to form in her mind. She couldn't climb any farther, but perhaps there was a way to stop him from getting to the ledge. Cautiously, she began to crawl along the shelf of rock, collecting stones that had fallen from above. They were too small to do much damage but maybe they'd throw him off balance.

He was getting closer, she knew. She listened to his strained breathing interspersed with angry curses that raised goose bumps on her flesh. He couldn't be more than a few feet below her. The next handhold might be enough to pull him up.

God, what would he do when he got to her? Probably hurl her off the side of the cliff. And this time there wouldn't be any water to break her fall.

She concentrated on collecting more stones. A few were bigger. Maybe that would make a difference, she told herself as she raised the hem of her knit shirt to make a kind of sack. Holding it up with one hand, she stuffed in as many stones as she could find.

The killer's labored breathing was right below her. Before it was too late, she flung one of the stones in his direction and heard it strike rock.

Damn. Her cry of dismay was muffled by his loud exclamation. Correcting her aim, she flung another stone. This time it must have struck him because he yelped. Encouraged, she threw another missile. And another. The last one missed, because he had moved. He had pulled himself up. He was on the ledge. She could mark his progress as he limped toward her, his footsteps shaky, his breath ragged, but his pace unslacking. From the time it took the rocks to hit him, she judged he was only about five or six feet away.

She kept moving backward and throwing the stones. Twice she tripped over a boulder that must have fallen from above. Somehow she stayed on her feet—and kept throwing rocks. Some hit Kane. Some bounced off the quarry wall. Maybe they slowed him down. Maybe not. She knew only that she'd come to the end of the narrow shelf.

She had only two more rocks, and she had to make them count. It was hard to stop throwing and listen. But she did, holding very still, focusing on the hissing of his breath coming in and out of his mouth. Picturing his face, she threw one of her last stones as hard as she could and heard it score a direct hit on soft tissue.

This time he screamed and stopped advancing. For seconds there was nothing but silence, then he shouted something. It was difficult for her to believe what he was saying.

"Get that damn light out of my eyes," he screamed.

Light? Someone had a light. Was it Ben? Was he here?

The killer was close enough for her to feel his breath. Or perhaps it only was the misty air.

Then, to her horror, he began to move toward her again. Cautiously, inching her way, she crept to the very end of the ledge, where it was so narrow that she had to press backward and turn her feet sideways. Finally, there was nowhere else to go without tumbling off into space. All she could do was wait with her heart pounding.

"I'll take you with me, bitch," he growled.

When he lunged forward, she tried to merge her body with the rock. In the next moment, she heard flesh and bone collide with something solid. The collision was followed by a scrabbling sound.

Seconds later a scream reverberated off the quarry walls as she heard him go over the side. A sickening thud followed as he hit the ground.

Then everything was still except for the sound of running feet below her.

"JENNY? Are you all right, Jenny?" Ben called. In the light from the flash, he could see her at a dizzying height above the floor of the quarry. She was pressed against the cliff wall. There was so little ledge below her that he didn't know where she'd managed to put her feet.

"Yes," she answered, her voice shaking.

"Slowly—carefully, move to your left," he called, a silent prayer on his lips. *Please God, let her make it. Don't let her fall after she's been so brave. After she's been through so much. Please don't let her fall now.*

"Kane…" she whispered.

"He's dead."

He kept the light trained on her, not because it would do her any good, but because he needed to see what was happening. "Jenny, move to your left where the ledge is wider."

Her face was pale, but her steps were steady as she began to inch along the sheer rock. He couldn't stand watching. He wanted to look away, but he kept the light and his anxious gaze glued to her. Finally she reached the wider part of the ledge, and he let out the breath he'd been holding. "Thank the Lord," he muttered swiping his hand across his damp forehead.

"You shined a light in his eyes."

"I'm sorry. It was all I could do. He was too close to you to take a chance on shooting."

"It was enough," she murmured.

"There's a real officer with me," he informed her, remembering for the first time in minutes that he wasn't alone. "He's going to call for help. I'm coming up to get you."

"Don't, Ben." Her voice rose in alarm. "It's dark. I don't want you to fall."

"Me? What about you?" he choked out.

"I don't need to see to get down. I used to play up here when I was a kid."

"Jenny, don't—"

"I can't stay here." She kept moving, feeling along the wall with her hands. He wanted to scramble up and grab her and stay there until somebody came with ropes to make sure she was safe. But he didn't have a clue about what route to take. All he could do was stand helplessly on the ground and watch as she reached a spot about halfway along the overhang. Sitting down, she ran her hand along the edge until she seemed to find something that she was looking for.

"Jenny, for God's sake—"

"I'm fine." She turned and slid over the side. It took every ounce of willpower he had to keep from shouting for her to stop. But he was afraid to startle her.

So he looked on, with his heart blocking his windpipe, and angled into a position where he could catch her if she fell.

Slowly she climbed down, moving from one handhold and foothold to the next with amazing dexterity. Fear choked him as he marked her slow progress down the side of the sheer, dark cliff. Yet he knew she was moving carefully—and confidently. When she was five feet from the ground, he surged forward and reached for her. The moon, which had come out from behind a cloud, glimmered on her hair.

"I've got you, sweetheart. I've got you." He circled her hips, then her waist with his hands. She eased into his grasp, and he lowered her the final few feet. Then he was turning her, crushing her to him, holding on to her for dear life.

There were so many things bursting to be said, but he cut to the essentials. "I love you, Jenny. Don't send me away. Please."

To his relief and joy, she clasped him tightly. "Sending you away was...was witless."

"No," he answered quickly. "You were hurting."

"I was confused," she said in a low voice. Then more strongly as if making a declaration to the silent quarry, "I'm not confused now. I love you, Ben. I want to marry you. If you still want that."

"Don't ever doubt it." Bending, he touched his lips to the tears sparkling on her lashes in the moonlight.

"Oh, God, do I want you," he managed, gathering her close. He could feel his heart pounding—and hers, and for several moments he couldn't conquer the storm of emotions sweeping over him. He had her safe in his arms and she wanted him.

She finally choked out some words, but he brought his mouth down on her, cutting them off. He feasted on her sweetness, angling his head first one way and then the other, unable to get enough of her. It was long moments before the kiss ended. Joy swelled inside him as he came to realize this was real.

"The area's going to be swarming with Howard County cops," he muttered, conceding there was another reality they had to face. "Then Erin and your friends are going to descend—to make sure you're all right."

"Yes."

"But I want to be alone with you first." Swinging Jenny into his arms, he carried her away from the towering walls of stone to a little stand of trees, where he set her down. But it was impossible to turn her loose. He would never turn her loose.

"Are you all right?" he asked gruffly. "He didn't…do anything…"

"I'm fine." She nestled against him, breathing deeply and evenly, and he sensed she was striving for calm. "I have to tell you…there were two of them," she said.

"What?"

"Two different men. The one you call Jesse James—that was the one who called himself Kane—killed Marianne. Someone else was after her computer. Jesse said his name was Jack Colmars. When Randolph took her computer back, he switched his attentions to mine—and to me. But they're not the same person."

"How do you know?" he asked quickly. Did he still have to worry about her safety?

She must have felt him stiffen and realized what he was thinking. "It's all right. They're both dead."

"Are you sure? What happened?"

"Colmars was in the woods, watching the house. He was the one who threw me off the bridge. He grabbed me and started dragging me away. Jesse shot him—while he was carrying me." She gulped. "Jesse said he was phoning for a crime-scene team. And I asked him to call you. I'm sure he didn't do either."

Ben swore. "The bastard could have shot you. I should never have left you with him."

She reached to press her fingers against his mouth, to stroke her lips. At the gentle touch, he kissed her fingertips.

"No, Ben. Don't blame yourself," she said softly. "It wasn't your fault. I sent you away. And I didn't start to figure out who he was until he repeated something strange he'd said on World Connect. Then I got in the car and found the shirt and put it all together."

"I should—"

She pressed his lips more firmly with her fingers. "Don't. You were upset. We were both upset. Don't second-guess. Don't make the same mistake I did."

He swallowed hard, trying to grasp what she was saying.

"I know you thought I wasn't listening when you were talking about Craig and the accident. But I heard you. You convinced me to let the past go, not to let it poison our future. Now you have to do the same thing."

"But I—"

She took him firmly by the shoulders and raised her head so that she seemed to be staring into his eyes—into his soul. "It's over. Finished. Don't beat up on yourself because a clever actor fooled both of us."

"*You* tricked him into leaving," he breathed. "Then you drove away."

She laughed. "Yes. But I didn't get too far."

"God, you're amazing."

"Don't change the subject," she said with mock seriousness. "We were talking about you. Promise me that you'll never blame yourself for any of this. You're only human, and you couldn't have pegged him without more information."

"He had on the wrong shoes," he protested. "I—"

Her fingers dug into his shoulders. "Drop it—and we're even."

As he gazed down at her, he gave in. She was right. It would only make him crazy to keep thinking about what might have happened. She was safe. That was the important thing. "All right."

She sighed deeply and relaxed against him.

"I'm smiling, in case you can't tell," he whispered.

"Same here."

She folded him into her embrace and kissed him. He was thinking about dragging her farther into the woods when he heard a police siren in the distance. "Damn. Company."

"They'll leave eventually," she murmured.

"We'd better get back to the house. The trouble is, I've dropped my flashlight, and the moon has gone behind a cloud again, so I'll be stumbling around in the dark."

"Looks like I'll have to lead you back. If you'll cut me a stick to use."

He pulled out his pen knife and sliced off one of the small branches overhead. After stripping away the leaves, he handed it to her. "Lead the way."

She took his arm in one hand and the stick in the other swinging it in front of her. "I guess you never know when a blind lady will come in handy."

His throat tightened. "You're wrong. I know. I definitely know."

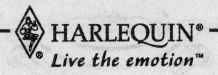

**Harlequin® Historical**
Historical Romantic Adventure!

*Imagine a time of chivalrous knights and unconventional ladies, roguish rakes and impetuous heiresses, rugged cowboys and spirited frontierswomen— these rich and vivid tales will capture your imagination!*

*Harlequin Historical . . . they're too good to miss!*

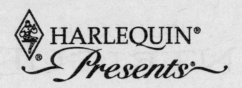

# HARLEQUIN®
## *Presents*

**The world's bestselling romance series...**
**The series that brings you your favorite authors,**
**month after month:**

Helen Bianchin...Emma Darcy
Lynne Graham...Penny Jordan
Miranda Lee...Sandra Marton
Anne Mather...Carole Mortimer
Susan Napier...Michelle Reid

**and many more uniquely talented authors!**

Wealthy, powerful, gorgeous men...
Women who have feelings just like your own...
The stories you love, set in exotic, glamorous locations...

# HARLEQUIN®
## *Presents*

**Seduction and Passion Guaranteed!**

HPDIR104

# HARLEQUIN®
# INTRIGUE®

## BREATHTAKING ROMANTIC SUSPENSE

Shared dangers and passions lead to electrifying
romance and heart-stopping suspense!

Every month, you'll meet six new heroes
who are guaranteed to make your spine tingle
and your pulse pound. With them you'll enter
into the exciting world of Harlequin Intrigue—
where your life is on the line
and so is your heart!

### THAT'S INTRIGUE—
### ROMANTIC SUSPENSE
### AT ITS BEST!

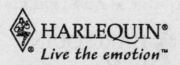

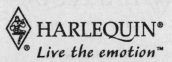

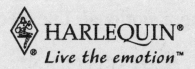